Fredrica Alleyn is the pseudonym of an author who also writes crime and horror fiction. She lives in Lincoln.

Fredrica is the author of *Cassandra's Chateau*, *Cassandra's Conflict*, *Dark Obsession*, *Deborah's Discovery*, *Dramatic Affairs*, *Fiona's Fate* and *The Gallery*, also available from *Black Lace*.

She also writes as Marina Anderson – the bestselling author of *Haven of Obedience*.

The
Bracelet

FREDRICA ALLEYN

BLACK
LACE

1 3 5 7 9 10 8 6 4 2

First published in 1996 by Black Lace, an imprint of Virgin Books
This edition published in 2013 by Black Lace, an imprint of Ebury Publishing
A Random House Group Company

Copyright © Fredrica Alleyn, 1996

Fredrica Alleyn has asserted her right to be identified as the author of this
Work in accordance with the Copyright, Designs and Patents Act 1988

The Random House Group Limited Reg. No. 954009

Addresses for companies within the Random House Group can be found at:
www.randomhouse.co.uk

A CIP catalogue record for this book is available from the British Library

The Random House Group Limited supports The Forest Stewardship
Council® (FSC®), the leading international forest certification organisation.
Our books carrying the FSC label are printed on FSC® certified paper.
FSC is the only forest certification scheme endorsed by the
leading environmental organisations, including Greenpeace.
Our paper procurement policy can be found at:
www.randomhouse.co.uk/environment

Printed and bound by CPI Group (UK) Ltd, Croydon, CR0 4YY

ISBN 9780753541593

To buy books by your favourite authors and register for offers visit:
www.blacklace.co.uk

Chapter One

Kristina Masterton picked up her copy of *The Publishing News* and studied the front page article carefully. 'Kristina Goes for the Kill' screamed the headline and beneath it was an accurate, if unflattering, description of the way she'd handled the auction for Martin Templar's new thriller. 'Attractive Kristina said afterwards that she was "very pleased" with the way things had gone,' concluded the article. 'This can only make one wonder what it would take to make her delighted.'

With a sigh, Kristina put the glossy paper down on her desk and leaned back in her chair. It was a fair article, there was a very flattering picture of her to accompany it, and if the comments were slightly barbed she knew they held the ring of truth.

She tried in vain to remember when she had last felt 'delighted' about anything. According to magazines and newspapers she was the young businesswoman who, at the early age of twenty-six, had it all. In her book deals she pushed hard to get the best for her clients, but that was a literary agent's job and to do less would be unforgivable. Exactly why she'd been so successful so early she had no idea. A combination of luck and hard work, probably.

The trouble was that she knew she was lucky, she knew she was successful and she also knew, with painful clarity, that she did not 'have it all'. Something was missing from her life, yet try as she might she couldn't think what it was.

She'd been going out with Ben, an advertising copy-writer, for four years and they lived in a pretty little mews house in Chelsea which she'd had decorated exactly as she had wanted. Ben was very easy-going and since her taste was for clean uncluttered lines and neutral calm colours she assumed that he didn't feel he had any reason to complain. He had a nice home to come back to at the end of the day, and during the course of the four years they'd settled into a comfortable and mutually satisfying sex life. Not that it played quite such a large part in their lives as it used to, she thought to herself, but then after four years that was probably the same for all couples.

Her phone rang and she picked it up, grateful for the interruption. It was surprising, but thinking about her sex life with Ben was slightly depressing and this realisation was something she didn't particularly want to face right now.

'Kristina? Hi, it's Lucretia here. Have you got a few minutes to spare, only I'm stuck.'

Kristina's fingers tightened round the telephone receiver. Lucretia was one of her biggest earners. She produced steamy pot-boilers at the rate of two a year and they sold in massive quantities all over the world, but she was also difficult. The moment her fingers ground to a halt over her keyboard she'd be on the phone to Kristina, wailing about writer's block and certain that she'd never be on the best-seller list again. After half an hour or so of chat she'd go back to her computer, ego soothed, self-confidence boosted, and churn out another chapter for her adoring public, leaving Kristina drained and exhausted in her place.

'Sure, Lucretia, you know I'm always here for you,' said Kristina in her most reassuring voice, then she stared out of her office window as the usual stream of complaints came down the line. Murmuring, 'Of course you can,' and 'But you know how they all adore you,' at regular intervals she allowed her thoughts to wander.

If she really 'had it all', she thought, then she'd be happy. Why did she wake up each morning feeling slightly irritated and then have to force herself to go into the office? Once, she'd greeted every new morning with enthusiasm, eager for the kill, as *The Pubishing News* would put it. But she still loved her work, and thrived on the rush of adrenalin that a fiercely contested book auction could give her. So what was the problem?

'Do you think that would work, Kristina?' asked Lucretia plaintively.

Guiltily Kristina realised that she had no idea what

her client was talking about. 'Of course it will, Cretia,' she said warmly. 'You must trust your instincts. In the end you know you're always right. Your sales should tell you that!'

'You're an absolute angel,' gushed Lucretia. 'I don't know what I'd do without you. I'll get straight back to work, and you'll get first mention in my list of acknowledgements, I promise you.'

'There's no need for that!' laughed Kristina, knowing full well that she wouldn't because this was a promise regularly delivered and never kept. 'It's my job to give you advice.'

'Not just a job I hope,' retorted Lucretia. 'I think of you as my better half, my fountain of wisdom.'

'Well, that's very kind but quite untrue. You do it all yourself and you know it, but if I do help in any way then I'm very pleased. I must go now, my other phone's ringing. Talk to you soon.'

With great relief she replaced the receiver. Sometimes when she was talking to Lucretia she wondered how on earth the woman managed to sell so well. She certainly used better words in her novels than in her speech, when ghastly clichés fell from her lips like rain from a cloud.

'Stop it!' said Kristina out loud. 'You're being rude and unkind for no reason at all. It isn't her fault you're in a bad mood. She's a nice woman who works hard and deserves the money she earns.'

'Who is?' asked Kristina's assistant, walking into the room with coffee for her boss.

'Lucretia Forrest.'

Sue laughed. 'No one deserves that much money! Are you all right?' she added. 'You look a bit tired.'

'I'm fine, well, health-wise I'm fine. I don't know, Sue, sometimes I wonder what it's all about. Do you get days like that?'

Sue, who was nineteen and had been with Kristina for two years, shook her head. 'Not really; life's fun. I love my job and I love David. Right now there isn't much more I could ask for. Don't forget to ring Claire Webster's publisher about that jacket for her new book. She's rung me twice already today to see if you've managed to persuade them it's tacky rather than eye-catching.'

'Sure, I'd forgotten but I'll get on to it now. And thanks, Sue.'

'For what?'

Kristina smiled. 'For pointing me in the right direction.

Sue looked surprised. 'It's what I'm here for, and I know that book jackets aren't high on your list of priorities.'

After her assistant had gone, Kristina swivelled her chair round and stared out over London. She hadn't been talking about the book jackets, but there was no way she'd ever let Sue know that. No, what she'd been talking about was that Sue had made her face up to one rather unpleasant fact. She was used to Ben; they had a comfortable life together and were at ease with each other but there was no way she could put her hand on her heart and say, as Sue had just done, that she loved him. 'Did I ever?' she wondered aloud, reaching for the phone.

After that, as she began to crisply point out to the publisher of Claire's latest book that the jacket would probably decrease sales by about 25 per cent, and then moved on through a typically hectic day, she had no more time to consider her moment of truth, but it was temporarily shelved rather than permanently discarded. After all, it explained why she hadn't, as the articles claimed, got it all.

When she got back to the mews house at seven that evening Ben was already home. He'd changed into jeans and a polo-neck top and was cooking a stir-fry in the wok. Normally she'd have been relieved that she didn't have to cook, but this evening she felt a surge of irritation at the sight of him happily engaged in such a domestic chore.

'It was my turn to cook tonight,' she pointed out as she hung up her beige cashmere coat.

Ben nodded. 'I know, but as I got in early and you were late there didn't seem any point in waiting.'

'I bought some fresh pasta on my way back. I also spent ages choosing ingredients for the sauce and . . .'

'We'll have that tomorrow,' retorted Ben. 'What's the matter? Bad day at work?'

'We can't have it tomorrow: we're going out to

dinner with Jacqueline and William, remember?' said Kristina crossly.

'Okay then, chuck the pasta away. It's no big deal is it? Why are we going out with them? Is it a birthday or a promotion?'

'Neither as far as I know,' confessed Kristina, wishing she hadn't snapped at Ben when he was only trying to be helpful. After all, women across the country were screaming for a New Man to split the domestic chores fifty–fifty and pull their weight as equal partners, so why should she complain when she'd got one? Because it isn't what I want, said a small voice in her ear.

'What's it for?' persisted Ben, taking out pre-heated plates from the oven and serving the food quickly and efficiently.

'I've got a feeling they may be going to announce their engagement,' said Kristina. 'Not that Jackie said anything to me, but she sounded pretty pleased with herself over the phone and they have been living together for five years now. Marriage seems the logical step.'

'It certainly does,' said Ben, giving her a meaningful look.

'I'm surprised though,' said Kristina quickly. 'I wouldn't have expected it because Jackie's always been like me, very against marriage. Like we always say, why mess with something that works?'

'I'm not so sure about that any more,' said Ben.

'Open the wine,' said Kristina quickly. 'This is a

delicious meal, Ben. That's probably why I snapped at you when I got in. I know you're a better cook than I am!' Ben smiled complacently and didn't deny it. Illogically, this annoyed Kristina. He *was* a better cook than her, but he didn't have to agree quite so readily.

Later that evening, as Kristina sat reading an unsolicited manuscript that one of her outside readers had said showed flair and originality, Ben came and sat down next to her on the sofa.

'Tiring day?' he asked.

She knew what that meant. 'No, not particularly,' she replied.

'Well, how about an early night anyway?' he suggested, kissing her on the side of her neck. He always kissed the side of her neck when he wanted to make love to her.

She put the manuscript to one side. 'Sounds like a good idea.'

Ben immediately put out his hands to help her to her feet. Kristina looked up at him. 'Why don't we do it here?'

'The sofa's not very comfortable; I prefer the bed,' he protested. 'It's different for you, you're not six feet tall.'

She'd known he wouldn't agree, but just for once she wanted something different, something more exciting than their routine couplings that had recently begun to leave her feeling dissatisfied. 'In the bathroom then? On the new carpet! There's plenty of room there.'

'We've got a perfectly good bed,' protested Ben.

'I want to do it in the bathroom,' insisted Kristina.

'Okay then,' agreed Ben reluctantly. Kristina had known that he'd give in this time.

Once in the warm bathroom she quickly began to undress him, pulling down the zip on his jeans then easing them over his hips and down to his ankles. Carefully she eased his erection free of his Y-fronts and taking it in her mouth sucked gently on it as her hands ran up and down his legs. He sighed with pleasure and his hands rested on her shoulders, the fingers straying up her neck and into her hair in soft, caressing movements.

When he was fully erect and rock-hard Kristina slowly began to peel off her own clothes, and when she was naked she pressed her breasts against his chest and rotated her upper body so that her nipples grew hard against the hairs on his chest.

Ben reached for her, his hands going round her bottom as he pulled her hips against him and they sank slowly to the floor. Ben lay beneath Kristina, which was the way she preferred it, and as she knelt above him, letting the tip of his penis brush against her pubic hair, his eyes widened with excitement and he tried to pull her down quickly on to him.

'Not yet,' she said sharply, and to her disappointment Ben, as usual, obeyed her. She didn't know why she was disappointed. They both knew that she liked to be in control, and were equally turned on by this, but suddenly she wanted him to break out of the roles they'd adopted. She wanted him to grab her and force her down on to his erection, then grip her hips and move her swiftly and urgently up and down until they both came together in a shattering explosion.

It didn't happen. As usual she teased and tantalised him, lowering herself sufficiently for the tip of his straining erection to enter her warm, moist vagina and then lifting herself up again. She changed position and spread herself along the length of him, rubbing up and down against his naked body so that her clitoris was stimulated by the underside of his glans and in the process she nearly made him come too soon, but still he didn't try and stop her or take the initiative.

'Do you want me to suck your nipples?' he murmured, and once more Kristina felt an illogical surge of irritation. Surely he didn't have to ask after all this time, she thought. He knew her body inside out, knew exactly what she did and didn't like, so why ask?

'Yes,' she muttered through gritted teeth, and when his mouth closed greedily about the small pale pink peaks the familiar surge of pleasure washed over her as her climax began to build.

Ben's hands were playing with the cheeks of her bottom, squeezing and stroking them before he managed to slip one hand upwards beneath her and now it was his fingers that were stimulating her clitoris and she gave a tiny cry of excitement as the tight hot feeling grew deep within her.

When she knew she was on the brink of her orgasm

she lifted herself up and then lowered herself down on to his by now painfully hard penis, and as the pleasure mounted she threw her head back and rode him without any thought at all for his needs and desires. All she was concentrating on was the steady build-up of pressure that was tightening her belly and drawing her insides into a hard little knot that she knew would only be released at the moment of climax.

'I can't keep going much longer,' groaned Ben, his face contorted with effort.

'Wait just a moment,' Kristina implored him, and then at last she was there and the wonderful rushing heat suffused her whole body. She cried out with satisfaction and within seconds Ben was crying out too as he writhed beneath her, his orgasm all the more intense because of the amount of self-control he'd had to exercise.

'There,' he said with a smile. 'That was good wasn't it?'

Kristina rolled off him and on to the soft carpet, feeling its deep wool pile caress her still tingling flesh. 'Yes,' she agreed. 'It was great.' But it hadn't been. Unlike the manuscript it had all lacked flair and originality. The trouble was, Kristina had the feeling that she had only herself to blame.

The following evening it was Ben's turn to get back late. By the time he arrived, Kristina had already tried on and discarded three outfits for the evening and was frantically going through her wardrobe for something that fitted her mood. Black with a veil might be appro-priate, she thought to herself with a wry smile.

'Have I time for a shower?' asked Ben, coming up behind her and resting his hands on each side of her bare waist.

'As long as you're quick. Don't do that, Ben, I'm trying to think.'

'Let me distract you,' he murmured, nuzzling the nape of her neck.

Kristina felt like screaming at him. 'Please, Ben, hurry up and shower. If this is an engagement announcement we mustn't be late.'

'It's your fault,' retorted Ben, sounding quite put out for him. 'You stand around half-naked and then expect me to ignore the fact. I'm only human, you know.'

'I didn't realise I was that irresistible,' she quipped, once again regretting the way she'd been snapping at him over the last few days.

'You are to me,' he assured her as he stripped off his clothes and made his way to the shower. Kristina wondered what other men would think.

Standing in front of the full-length mirror she studied herself critically. She was definitely striking, she knew that, but more by virtue of the fact that she had such an unusual combination of hair and skin colouring than because of any outstanding individual features. Her hair was very dark and naturally curly. Without any effort on her part it looked sexily tousled and casual, but her eyes beneath equally dark brows were a startling deep blue and her skin was incredibly pale, like the finest porcelain.

She was quite tall, five foot seven, and slim but she thought that her breasts were too small and her bottom too large. The fact that men always found her sexy and she'd never had any shortage of admirers still hadn't given her the kind of confidence in her looks that she felt she should have. The trouble was, she longed to be a cool blonde with a hint of colour along high cheekbones and a wonderful figure with a cleavage she could show off in low-cut dresses. Someone more like Jacqueline she supposed.

Finally she settled for a pine-green fit-and-flare dress overlaid with an asymmetrically cut tunic of see-through lace. The outfit clung to her body like a second skin and the slightly scooped neckline and long sleeves of the lace over-tunic disguised her slenderness a little, making her look more interesting, she thought. Not that there was a lot of point in looking interesting. She'd known William for five years and Jacqueline for twelve. Neither of them were likely to take more than a cursory glance at her, but for some reason she felt that she had to start changing things, making more of an effort to get out of the rut that she was in. It might be a high-powered rut, but it was still a rut.

'Hey, that's a bit over the top isn't it?' asked Ben as he started dressing. 'We're only going to a bistro.'

'I felt like dressing up.'

'You look incredibly sexy,' he admitted. 'Are you sure we haven't got time for a quickie?'

'Quite sure,' she said firmly. She never enjoyed Ben's quickies. It was rather like being really hungry and then having someone give you a bowl of thin soup and expecting you to be grateful. 'I wonder when they'll be getting married,' she asked as they climbed into Ben's car. 'The summer I suppose. Summer weddings are nice.'

'Do I detect a brooding note?' asked Ben with a grin.

'Certainly not,' said Kristina sharply, and Ben retreated into hurt silence for the rest of the journey.

The restaurant was crowded and it took them a few moments to find Jacqueline, but then Kristina noticed her very blonde hair at the far side of the room and she waved. Jacqueline waved back, and Kristina thought she'd never seen her friend look so happy. 'There they are,' she said to Ben.

'Where?'

'Over there, by the window. Jackie's had her hair cut short. Doesn't it look great?'

'Yes, great. William appears to have had a head transplant,' he added in a low voice.

'A what?' asked Kristina as they approached the table, but before he could answer her they were there and then she realised what he'd meant because the man sitting next to Jacqueline wasn't William at all, it was a complete stranger.

Jacqueline smiled broadly at Kristina. 'I thought

you'd forgotten, you're not usually late. Laurence, I'd like you to meet my oldest friend Kristina and her partner Ben. Kristina, Ben, this is Laurence van Kitson.'

Laurence rose to his feet, and by the way he towered over Ben, Kristina realised that he must be at least six foot three and very well built. His hair was as blond as Jacqueline's and his rather angular face was tanned. His light blue eyes seemed to look straight through Kristina and she felt a faint shiver of something strangely like fear run through her.

He held out a large hand but when she took it his grip was surprisingly gentle, almost a caress. 'Pleased to meet you,' he said in a clipped voice, and she realised then that he was a South African, which explained both the name and the colouring.

'Who is he?' whispered Ben as the pair of them sat down.

'No idea,' Kristina whispered back.

'No engagement announcement by the look of it,' he muttered, and looking at the glow on Jackie's face and the way she was smiling at Laurence, Kristina had to agree. William, it seemed, had vanished from the scene.

'Love the outfit,' she remarked to Jacqueline, who was wearing a soft purple-heather coloured trouser suit that looked to be made of some kind of damask material. The long tunic with side vents and pointed sleeves was extremely soft and flattering, totally unlike her friend's usual fitted dresses or sharp suits. In fact, now she came to look at her more closely, Jackie looked altogether softer and more relaxed tonight than Kristina had ever seen her.

'Shall we order?' asked Laurence.

Before anyone could reply he'd clicked his fingers and immediately, despite the fact that the restaurant was full and the waiters rushed off their feet, one appeared at their table, pencil poised over his pad.

Kristina felt totally thrown off balance. Not only was William missing, Jacqueline didn't seem the same and this man Laurence clearly thought himself in charge, despite the fact that neither she nor Ben had ever met him before.

'I think the melon for the first course, and then the salmon,' he said decisively.

'And the young lady?' asked the waiter, his eyes lingering appreciatively on Jacqueline.

'She'll have the same,' said Laurence smoothly.

Kristina glanced at him in open astonishment. William would never have ordered for Jackie without consulting her first, but amazingly Jackie was still smiling happily and didn't seem to think Laurence had done anything unusual.

'I'd like vegetable soup and then the beef stroganoff,' said Kristina after a short pause. 'What about you, Ben?' Ben also chose soup followed by trout in almonds and the waiter left them to study the wine list.

'Any preferences?' Laurence asked Ben. Ben shrugged. 'Not really. Nothing too sweet.'

'I'd like a Chardonnay,' said Kristina crisply.

Laurence's light blue eyes flicked to her face. 'Then a Chardonnay you must have, Kristina! Jackie and I will share a Sauvignon.'

Kristina felt like laughing aloud. Now he'd really put his foot in it. Jacqueline loved Chardonnay, in fact she could put away an entire bottle without any trouble at all. She always claimed it was her favourite food as well as her favourite drink.

'Do you hear that, Jackie?' asked Kristina. 'Laurence thinks you'd like a Sauvignon.'

'That sounds perfect,' agreed Jacqueline, and Laurence put a hand over hers on the table top, his fingers closing around her hand in a grip that seemed both restraining and possessive. Kristina's stomach lurched and she wondered what on earth was going on between the couple opposite her. Clearly they were lovers, but how had they met and what kind of a relationship did they have?

With William, Jackie had been very much the dominant partner, and like Kristina this was the way she'd always run her romantic life. Could she really have changed so radically, or was this just some wild aberration on her part, or even a joke? Perhaps she was going out with Laurence to amuse herself, as a contrast to the reliable, dependable William. Yet somehow, watching the way Laurence kept touching her friend and resting his arm along the back of her chair she didn't feel that this was the answer.

'He won't last long,' muttered Ben as their first

courses were brought to the table. 'Far too much of a chauvinist for Jackie. Is he something to do with her paper do you think?' Kristina shrugged. She had no more idea than he did, but she intended to find out as soon as possible.

'Are you in journalism too, Laurence?' she asked him.

He glanced across the table at her, his expression surprised. 'Of course not. Whatever gave you that idea?'

Kristina shrugged. 'I suppose that since Jackie's a journalist it seemed a reasonable assumption.'

'Not to me. After all, what is it that you do? Something connected with books I seem to remember Jacqueline saying. Is that right?'

'Yes,' replied Kristina shortly. 'I'm a literary agent.'

'And is Ben a novelist? Or a publisher perhaps?'

'No, he's in advertising.'

'There you are then,' said Laurence with a smile that didn't reach his eyes. 'You don't go out exclusively with people in your line of work, and neither does Jacqueline.'

Kristina looked at her friend to see how she was taking all this, but to her surprise Jacqueline didn't appear to be listening. She was gazing at Laurence with an expression of pure physical lust. She had an extraordinary look of yearning in her eyes that made Kristina's mouth go unexpectedly dry.

'Then what do you do?' she persisted, suddenly determined to make this handsome but distinctly impolite man answer her question.

'I deal in diamonds,' he said curtly.

'Lucky you, Jackie!' laughed Ben. 'Wearing any tonight?'

Jackie shook her head. 'I don't like diamonds, sapphires are my favourite stone.'

'I think diamonds are very useful,' said Kristina. 'They can always be sold for a good price after you've changed the man in your life!'

'Or the man in your life's moved on!' said Laurence with a laugh.

Kristina was beginning to dislike him intensely. 'I suppose it does sometimes happen that way round,' she conceded, looking to Jackie for support. Jackie though was clearly useless tonight. She refused to back up Kristina's remark and simply smiled apologetically at Laurence, who didn't smile back but instead lifted a hand and with one finger carefully traced the outline of her mouth. Jacqueline's lips parted and her breathing grew visibly more rapid, but then he removed his hand and the brief, sensual moment passed.

Kristina was beginning to feel very uncomfortable. This wasn't the Jackie she'd known for years, the control freak who ran her life like a military operation, and used to schedule sex with William around her assignments, days in advance.

'Are diamonds doing well at the moment?' asked Ben cheerfully.

'Yes,' replied Laurence shortly, stopping that line of conversation dead in its tracks.

Ben blinked in surprise. 'Oh, well good for you. Of course it isn't the same in advertising. I mean, you're not relying on how much people want a particular product at a given moment. You're the one trying to persuade them that they can't do without it!'

'Quite,' agreed Laurence, finishing his main course and putting his knife and fork together tidily on the side of his plate. 'Jacqueline, your mascara's smudged. Perhaps you'd like to repair the damage before we have dessert?'

Kristina's mouth opened in shock. She couldn't believe that she was hearing right, that anyone would be so rude as to talk to their date as if she were a child of six who had to be told when to wash and tidy up. She waited for Jackie's explosion, but she waited in vain.

Jackie stared at Laurence in amazement, but then after opening her mouth to reply she seemed to think better of it and checked herself. She took a few deep breaths and smiled at him. 'What a good idea. Excuse me a moment everyone, please.' With that she rose from her chair and walked across the restaurant to the ladies' room.

'I think I'll join her,' said Kristina quickly, and without even looking at Laurence she hurried after her friend.

She found her sitting on a stool gazing into the tiled mirror, carefully examining her make-up for flaws.

'There's nothing wrong with your mascara,' said Kristina. 'I think he's mad! Where did you find him? And what's happened to William?'

'William? Oh, William's gone. I decided he wasn't right for me.'

'But you made the perfect couple. I remember you saying that you'd never find anyone who suited you better. He never minded when your job took you away, he was romantic and . . .'

'I got bored,' said Jackie shortly.

'Bored?'

'You know how it is, or perhaps you don't, but I realised that I always knew exactly what he was going to do, or say. And as for sex . . . Well, he might as well have made love to me by numbers. Nothing was ever changed; he knew what I liked so that's what he did.'

'Well, you wouldn't have wanted him doing things you didn't like!' retorted Kristina.

Jackie laughed. 'No, of course I wouldn't, but there are other things you can do, new things to try and William wasn't the kind of man to want to experiment.'

'Laurence seems the kind of man who wants nothing but an obedient doll,' said Kristina sharply. 'I mean, what are you thinking of? He's everything you hate in men. He even chose what you ate and drank tonight! As for this business of make-up, it's pure rubbish.'

Jacqueline shook her head. 'No, he was right. I did have a smudge. I've put it right now. And as for the meal, it makes a change to have someone make a decision for me, especially after the day I've had.'

'You look well,' conceded Kristina. 'There must be something good about him. You're definitely glowing!'

'That's thanks to Laurence. You must agree that he's good looking, Kristina.'

'I suppose he is, in a rather hard way though. He's got the strangest eyes, they seem to see right through you.'

Jacqueline didn't answer. Instead she sprayed herself with some perfume and then slid from the stool. 'Time to rejoin the men I think. Laurence will wonder what we've been up to!'

'Let him wonder. Since when did what a man thought worry you?'

'Perhaps I just don't want to be away from him for too long,' laughed Jackie.

'Are you living together?' enquired Kristina with interest.

Her friend shook her head. 'No, nothing like that. We meet up once or twice a week I suppose. He's a very private person, and now that William's gone I'm rather relishing my own privacy too.'

'What's he like in bed?' asked Kristina.

To her surprise Jacqueline bent her head and began to rummage in her handbag, clearly determined not to let Kristina see the expression on her face. 'Fantastic,' she muttered. 'Where did I put my lipstick? I can't seem to find it anywhere.'

'Just fantastic? No details?' persisted Kristina.

At last Jackie lifted her head again. 'That's right, no details. Come on, we must get back.'

As she stood up she brushed her blonde hair back off

her forehead and dangling from her left wrist Kristina saw a fine gold chain with a tiny letter 'B' suspended from it.

'That's rather beautiful,' she commented.

'What?' asked Jacqueline.

'Your bracelet. Let me look closer. Yes, I thought it was a letter 'B'. Why 'B'? Your name's Jacqueline.'

'It's a shape, not a letter,' said Jacqueline, blushing furiously. 'And it was a present from Laurence. Come on, he and Ben will think we've run off and left them.'

Intrigued, Kristina followed her friend back to their table. She knew Jackie wasn't telling the truth. It was a letter 'B' and clearly the bracelet was of some significance. It was unusual for Jackie to blush about anything, let alone a piece of jewellery.

During the remainder of the meal Kristina studied Laurence and Jacqueline carefully. Once or twice she thought that Laurence was aware of her scrutiny, but Jacqueline remained oblivious mainly because all of her attention was centred on her new, blond-haired boyfriend.

Laurence was surprisingly tactile. He touched Jacqueline a lot, brushing his hand down her arm, stroking the nape of her neck and once or twice Kristina was convinced he was touching her more intimately beneath the table but never once did Jacqueline touch him. She merely responded to each touch by blossoming in front of Kristina's eyes as the evening progressed.

When they all parted company, Jacqueline's eyes were glowing and her face was alight with happiness. As Laurence slipped her coat over her shoulders she smiled up at him with a look of such adoration that Kristina wondered if the man was a hypnotist of some kind. He'd certainly changed her friend.

'I'll ring you,' Kristina said to Jackie as they parted company, but Laurence was already leading her away towards where his car was parked and Jackie either didn't hear or didn't choose to reply.

'What did you make of that?' Kristina asked Ben as they drove home.

'A bit of a boring evening really. He doesn't say much does he? Not the life and soul of the party. Did you find out where William was?'

'He's been given the elbow,' said Kristina. 'It seems . . .' She stopped. She'd been about to say that it seemed he'd bored Jackie, but then she decided not to. It might lead the conversation into tricky waters, because she knew that the same thing was happening to her with Ben, and now was definitely not the moment to bring that up. 'They decided to split,' she said quickly. 'Grown too used to each other or something.'

'Pity, he was a good chap,' said Ben.

That night, after they'd made love and Ben was sleeping, Kristina re-ran the evening in her mind and was surprised at how much impact Laurence had made on her. Not only that, it was clear that there was some-thing very special going on between him and Jacqueline, something that Jacqueline wasn't prepared to discuss even with her best friend.

Before she too fell asleep, Kristina vowed to find out as soon as possible what exactly it was that had both totally changed her friend's attitude and at the same time given her the glow of a woman who was having the time of her life in bed.

Chapter Two

Kristina put down the telephone in her office and buzzed for Sue to come through. 'We'll have to write a suitably grovelling email to Peter Hitchens' publishers,' she said ruefully. 'The wretched man still hasn't finished the first draft of his manuscript and we'd promised delivery two months ago.'

'What shall we plead? Illness? Family problems?' asked Sue.

'I feel like telling them the truth; that he's got far too big for his boots since he won that literary prize! No, I'm joking. We'll say he isn't satisfied and doesn't want to send them anything that's not up to standard. It's true up to a point; he can hardly be satisfied with a book he hasn't written yet!'

'At least Lucretia's still writing happily. You haven't heard from her for at least two weeks,' commented Sue as she jotted down what Kristina was telling her.

'Is it two weeks?' asked Kristina in surprise.

'Definitely. I know because I made a note in my

diary. I always do that with her, just to amuse myself! Anything else?'

'Not as far as I know. I'm meeting that new editor this afternoon and then I'll probably take a manuscript from the slush pile home. That last one Paul recommended I've decided to take on, and he thinks this is almost as good. The only problem these days is selling new authors to publishing houses.'

'If anyone can do it you can,' Sue assured her.

After she'd gone, Kristina sat thinking about what Sue had said. If it was two weeks since Lucretia had last rung then it was two weeks since she'd seen Jacqueline. After their dinner she'd tried phoning her almost every night, but Jackie wasn't just out, she'd also turned off her voicemail. All in all she was proving highly elusive to contact, and Kristina was desperate to find out more about the handsome but strange Laurence van Kitson.

On a sudden impulse she picked up her phone and dialled the paper where Jackie worked. She had started there as a junior reporter but was now rapidly becoming one of the leading women journalists of the day with her own weekly column and a growing army of fans who enjoyed her sardonic wit and occasional in-depth interview.

Usually she was out of the office, but this time Kristina was lucky and within minutes Jacqueline was on the other end of the line. Kristina could tell from her muted response that Jackie didn't really want to talk to her, so she rushed on quickly before her friend could terminate the call.

'Look, Jackie, I've got a few problems with Ben,' she said, which was at least partly true. 'I thought perhaps we could meet up and have a chat. I'd really value your opinion, especially as you've recently split from William.'

There was a short pause. 'I'm rather busy at the moment,' replied Jacqueline cautiously.

'Aren't we all! The truth is, I desperately need to hear someone else's point of view, and you're the person I trust most,' said Kristina, despising herself for lacking the courage to come out with the real reason she wanted the meeting but knowing that her instinct was right, and that anyway if she did Jackie would refuse to see her.

'Okay then,' conceded her friend. 'I can't make it tonight, and Friday's out too but I suppose tomorrow would be all right.'

'Great. Shall I come round to your place? We can hardly talk about Ben at mine!'

'Why not meet for a meal?' suggested Jacqueline.

'It's a bit personal for that,' protested Kristina. 'Besides, now that you're getting so well known we'd never have a moment's peace.'

'I'm hardly Kate Middleton!' Jackie laughed, finally relaxing. 'Still, you've got a point. See you tomorrow then. Let's say about eight. Must dash now.'

That evening, as Kristina went through a contract

with a new publisher with a fine-tooth comb, checking for any hidden clauses that were to the author's disadvantage, Ben got out the ironing board and started pressing some of his shirts.

'Can't that wait?' asked Kristina abruptly.

He looked at her in surprise. 'Actually, no it can't. I'm out of shirts. Why? Did you want to do them yourself?'

'No, of course not! It's only that . . .'

'Only that what?' he demanded.

Kristina bit on her bottom lip. She didn't know how to answer him. There really wasn't any reason for her to say a word. She'd never been the kind of partner who ironed his shirts or did all his laundry, and normally she wouldn't have taken any notice of what he was doing. It was simply that without any warning, she'd had a vision of Laurence van Kitson doing his own ironing, and the idea had been so preposterous that it had made her want to laugh. Realising that the idea of him ironing was amusing had made her feel annoyed with Ben for doing it, because Ben ironing wasn't remotely amusing, and that worried her.

'I'm sorry,' she said softly. 'I don't know what's wrong with me these days. I feel on edge all the time, as though there's something wrong but I don't know what.'

'Did you want to go to bed?' asked Ben, his eyes eager.

Kristina knew that the very last thing she wanted to do right then was to go to bed with Ben and have him, as Jackie had said about William, make love to her by numbers. She forced herself to smile. 'No, honestly I'm fine and I have to get this contract checked. Sorry, Ben; you carry on.'

In the early hours of the morning Kristina awoke from a strange, sensual dream in which someone unknown and faceless had been touching her softly and intimately. She awoke desperate for sexual satisfaction, her lower belly and the soft flesh between her thighs aching with sexual tension and without a second thought she climbed on top of the naked Ben and began to arouse him with her body.

He responded automatically, but it was only when she actually started to lower herself on to his erection that he awoke properly. He groaned with sleepy pleasure and then idly ran his hands down the sides of her body as she rode him until her climax swept over her and she was released from the terrible tension caused by the dream.

'That was nice,' he muttered, turning over on his side again. 'You can do that again any time you like!'

Kristina lay next to him and knew that she wouldn't do it again, not ever. The physical ache had gone, but she felt empty and hollow instead. She wished that when Ben had woken he'd taken the initiative, thrown her on to her back and plunged into her himself, his hands pinioning her shoulders to the pillow. But that would never happen. Their love-making had never been like that. She'd never before wanted it to be, so how could Ben be expected to know that suddenly she longed for things to change?

The following evening she arrived at Jacqueline's Kensington town house with two bottles of Chardonnay. Jackie opened the door to her wearing her usual leisure outfit of jogging pants and top, while on her feet she had a pair of huge pig slippers with ears that waved as she walked.

'Very elegant!' laughed Kristina. 'Do you let Laurence see you like this?'

Jackie's smile faded. 'No, I don't. He wouldn't be at all amused. Come on through. Excuse the mess but my cleaning lady's deserted me and I can't find a replacement.'

'You mean now that William's gone you haven't got anyone to tidy up after you!' laughed Kristina.

Jacqueline gave a wry grin. 'I guess that is the truth! Here, let me chill that wine for a few minutes, then we can have a good gossip.'

'You're leading a busy social life at the moment,' Kristina remarked. 'I've tried to get you loads of times, but you haven't even been leaving your voicemail on.'

'God, haven't I? I must try and remember that. I can't afford to screw up my job just because . . .'

'Just because what?' asked Kristina curiously.

'Nothing,' said Jackie quickly. 'Let's start drinking shall we and you can tell me all your woes.'

As they talked Kristina realised that she was being totally honest with herself as well as with Jacqueline, and for the first time she admitted that Ben was getting on her nerves. 'He hasn't changed,' she concluded after over an hour. 'I know that, just as I know I'm being totally unreasonable. The fact of the matter is, I've changed and I don't know how to tell him.'

'Tell him what?' asked Jackie.

'That I'd like him to change too I suppose.'

Jackie smiled. 'But he won't be able to. That's like buying a Cavalier King Charles Spaniel and asking it to behave like a Rotweiller! Ben's Ben, he can't become someone else because your needs have changed. He likes the life he's got, and he loves you the way you are, or were. He wouldn't like the changes you want to take place. If Ben were the kind of man who wanted to be in charge he wouldn't have moved in with you in the first place.'

'I don't want a selfish chauvinist,' said Kristina crossly. 'I only want him to take control sometimes. I'd like him to take me by surprise, do things differently now and again. Is that too much to ask?'

'Yes, of Ben it is,' replied Jacqueline. 'William was the same; that's why he had to go.'

'Well, I don't want someone like Laurence,' said Kristina firmly. 'He may be your idea of a fun date but he wouldn't be mine. There must be a happy medium! I mean, does Laurence do anything for you?'

Jacqueline smiled a strange, secret smile. 'Yes, lots of things.'

'Like what?' demanded Kristina.

'If I tell you,' said Jacqueline softly, 'you must promise not to tell anyone else, ever. Do you promise?'

Kristina frowned. 'Sure, but I can't imagine why you're being so secretive. What you do isn't illegal is it?'

'Of course not! But it is meant to be secret. The whole affair is, well, strange. It isn't like you'd think, you see. It's a kind of arrangement. A sexual arrangement.'

'He isn't a gigolo? You don't pay him for sex?' exclaimed Kristina in horror.

Jacqueline refilled their wine glasses and smiled at her friend. 'Hardly! No, it's much more difficult to explain than that. I suppose I ought to begin with the bracelet, the one you admired when we had that meal out. You remember?'

'Yes,' said Kristina. 'I thought it had the letter "B" on it, but you said it wasn't, it was simply a shape.'

'Yes, but you were right, Kristina, it is a "B". You see, it's a bracelet of bondage.'

'Bondage?' queried Kristina stupidly. 'You mean, you're into being tied up? Is that what Laurence does to you?'

'You're shocked aren't you?' said Jacqueline, and she smiled. 'Actually, no, that isn't what it means, but since you ask Laurence does sometimes tie me up, when he wants to that is. But mostly we do other things.'

'I don't understand a word you're saying,' said Kristina, annoyed by the look of amused superiority on her friend's face. 'Okay, so you're into bondage, what's that got to do with the bracelet, or even Laurence? Surely William would have tied you up if that's what you wanted?'

Jacqueline nodded. 'Of course he would. William would have done anything I wanted, but Laurence does what *he* wants. There's a big difference. Until I joined the society I didn't even know myself what I really liked, and William would certainly never have been able to assess my needs in the way Laurence does.'

'But you're a modern, liberated woman,' protested Kristina. 'What's the point of women's new-found freedom if you end up getting some blond-haired South African hunk to tie you up and use you for his own pleasure? Don't you think you're rather letting the side down?'

'Listen,' said Jacqueline, refilling her wine glass. 'You came here tonight because you wanted someone to hear how you were feeling about Ben, about your sex life really, isn't that true?'

'Yes,' conceded Kristina.

'Haven't you ever stopped to think that perhaps because we're successful career women we've trapped ourselves in a life where we're always in control. Don't you sometimes long for someone else to make a decision for you?'

'Of course I do!'

'Right, and so do a lot of other highly qualified, intelligent, high-profile women. This society, the society that I've joined, is intended for people like us. The "have-it-all" women who find they haven't got it all.'

Kristina remembered the article about her in *The Publishing News*, and the strange unexplained emptiness that often filled her after she and Ben had made love, and kept silent. She suddenly wanted to hear more.

'When I put on the bracelet,' continued Jacqueline, 'I know that for the time I wear it I'm totally subservient to Laurence. He controls everything. That's why he chose my meal for me when we were out, and why he sent me off to the ladies room. He knew I didn't need to go, and so did I, but because I'd chosen to wear the bracelet that night I had no choice. And do you know what? It was an incredibly exciting sensation. When I walk into his house and put that bracelet on I feel so aroused, so sensual, that sometimes I think I'll explode the moment he touches me. Only of course I'm never allowed to.'

'Not allowed to?' asked Kristina.

'No. He controls my pleasure, how much I have and when I'm allowed it. One evening the moment I arrived he told me that I couldn't have my first climax for another two hours. He played with me, aroused me, stimulated me in ways you could never begin to imagine, but he made sure that he never allowed me to topple over the edge into a climax for the whole of the two hours.'

Kristina felt her cheeks growing hot and her body began to feel tight at the extraordinary story she was hearing. The trouble was, she could imagine the scene only too well. Could almost feel the touch of the South African's hands on her own skin, and the incredible tension that must have been endured by her friend.

'What was it like, when you finally did come?' she whispered.

Jacqueline closed her eyes for a moment, remembering and savouring the moment again. 'It was like nothing I'd ever imagined possible. I felt as though I was shattering into hundreds of pieces, as though my body would be torn apart by the power of the orgasm. Believe me, Kristina. It was the most wonderful sexual experience of my life.'

'What if you don't like what he does to you?' asked Kristina, her voice trembling.

'Then I remove the bracelet. Once that's off the relationship is a normal one. We talk, or make love the way we both choose. Only it hardly ever happens. I mean, I do remove it sometimes but the whole point of these meetings is that I'm wearing the bracelet. Removing it is simply a safety precaution, in case your partner's choice of game isn't to your liking.'

'How do you join?' asked Kristina in a low voice.

'It isn't easy. A member has to put your name forward, and then you have to be approved by the committee. I don't know who makes up the committee but they turn down far more women than they accept. They have to be sure that they get the right kind of women because the men involved are all highly successful in their fields and they're very fussy.'

'You mean there are a lot of men doing this?'

Jacqueline laughed. 'You didn't imagine Laurence satisfied all the women did you? Of course there are lots of men. If you get accepted you're informed and then all your details are fed into a computer. After a time one of the men from the society chooses you and you get an invitation to go along and meet him. Sometimes it's a phone call or an email, sometimes a written invitation, but the initial meeting usually lasts about an hour. If that goes well you arrange another meeting, but if it doesn't work out for either of you then you just wait and try the next man who asks to see you.'

'Why can't a woman ask to meet a certain man?' asked Kristina.

Jacqueline sighed. 'That would ruin the whole thing, Kristina. The entire point of this is that the women who join want, for brief periods in their lives, to be controlled rather than to control. That's why the women wait to be chosen, it's a passive role, not an active one. If that doesn't appeal to you then you wouldn't be suitable for the society anyway.'

'How often do you see Laurence?' asked Kristina, her interest and desire growing the more Jacqueline talked.

Jacqueline looked slightly shamefaced. 'At first I only used to wear the bracelet for an hour or two a week. Laurence would ring and I'd go round for a couple of hours just one night. At other times when he called I'd say I wasn't in the mood. But now, when I'm not working, I hardly take it off. I can't wait for him to call. I crave our time together and when I'm not wearing it I feel lost, bereft.

'The awful truth is, Kristina, that for women like us, women who spend their working lives taking all the responsibility and making all the decisions, this bracelet is addictive. Just between ourselves, it's beginning to frighten me. I resent going to work. I hate entertaining men who bore me or going to parties where everyone's boring and I have to retain the facade of the famous journalist, witty, sexy and sparkling, for the benefit of everyone there.

'All I want is to be wearing the bracelet for Laurence. I think about it constantly, and that's why I'm never in when you call and why I don't leave my mobile or voicemail on when I'm with him. I want to shut the rest of the world out because the physical pleasure and the incredible sensuality of the whole situation has become my life instead of my safety valve.'

Kristina shivered, not from cold but from fear. Yet the fear was not of what she was hearing, but of the effect it was having on her. She was aroused by the idea of wearing the bracelet, and afraid of what the consequences might be if she took the step of asking Jacqueline to put her name forward as a prospective member of the society.

'Did you have to get rid of William before you could join?' she asked, thinking that she couldn't possibly split from Ben just because of what she'd heard tonight. The idea attracted her, drew her, but there was always the possibility that once involved she might not enjoy it as much as Jacqueline did. She might even realise that Ben was as perfect for her as she'd thought when they first met. She would never allow them to part at this stage, all because of the strange, darkly erotic story told to her by her friend.

'You never *have* to do anything, except when you're wearing the bracelet,' explained Jacqueline carefully. 'No one in the society cares about your life outside of the times you're enjoying the benefits of the bracelet. William and I had to split. Once I knew myself better, understood how I got my deepest sexual satisfaction, there was no point in us staying together, but the choice was mine.'

'Suppose I like the idea?' said Kristina slowly. 'Let's say I want to join, if only to find out whether it proves as satisfying to me as it does to you. Would you put my name forward?'

'Yes, of course I would. Mind you, that doesn't mean you'd be accepted. It probably depends on how far your fame as a literary agent has spread. I think most of the women are business directors, or run their own PR companies, that kind of thing.'

Kristina frowned. 'That's a pretty insulting thing to say, Jackie. I am considered to be one of the leading literary agents of the day.'

'I know that,' Jacqueline assured her. 'I'm only saying that I can't speak for the committee, and I can't influence them either. Once your name goes forward that's it as far as I'm concerned. They make their own enquiries.'

'What about safety?' continued Kristina. 'How can the women who join be sure they're safe?'

'I've no idea how the checks are done,' admitted Jackie. 'The only thing I can tell you is that the whole thing's been going for five years now and there's never once been any kind of trouble or scandal. I suppose, looking at it in the cold light of day, there's an element of danger, risk if you like, but that's probably what makes it so attractive. You know, rather like turning down a really good offer for a book because you're sure a better one will come along. You know in your bones you're right, but there's always the chance you're not. You get a thrill from that don't you?'

'I suppose I do, in a masochistic kind of way!'

'There you are then. Women like us have to be risk takers to a degree, but there's no fear of physical harm, blackmail or scandal. Probably the worst thing that could happen would be to fall in love with your partner. I heard it happened once and the couple left. This isn't about love; it's about desire and sexuality, freedom from responsibility and an escape from real life.'

'You're not falling in love with Laurence then?' queried Kristina.

Jacqueline sighed. 'Sometimes I think I am, but when I take the bracelet off it isn't the same. I feel quite differently about him when we're on equal terms, so I don't think it's really a worry.'

'Do you see other men in the society?' asked Kristina.

Jackie shook her head. 'No; I could, but I don't choose

to. Laurence sees other women though. He sometimes tells me about them when I'm wearing the bracelet and I have to listen to how they respond to what he's doing to me at that particular time.'

Kristina realised that her breathing had become rapid and shallow and that her lower belly was starting to ache with sexual desire. Suddenly she didn't want to hear any more about what Jacqueline and Laurence did; she wanted to have a chance to try the experience for herself. Then, at last, she might begin to feel content with her life once more.

'I'd definitely like you to put my name forward,' she said softly. 'You and I are very similar. When I saw you with Laurence the other night, saw the way you were together and that special look that you had about you, I envied you. If that's what this society can do for me, then I want to join now!'

'You must be sure,' cautioned Jacqueline. 'If you're not and you back out at the last minute, then as your proposer I'll lose my membership as well. We're not expected to make mistakes of judgement like that.'

Kristina looked at her friend and smiled. 'Don't worry, I won't let you down. I'm quite sure this is something I want to try.'

Jacqueline nodded. 'I think you've made the right decision, and I'll keep my fingers crossed that they accept you! Now, do you want the last of this wine before you go back to patient Ben?'

'I think I'll go now if you don't mind. Listening to all

this has made me pretty impatient to see him! How will I know if I've been accepted?'

'You'll just get an invitation and that will be it. If you're not accepted you won't get one. There's never any explanation given, and there's no right of appeal either.'

'How long does it take?' asked Kristina, shifting restlessly on her chair.

'In my case it took ten days, but I know some women who had to wait over a month. Remember, even if you're accepted and fed into the computer, some man has to choose you.'

'Yes, well hopefully at least one man will find me a reasonably exciting prospect,' retorted Kristina.

'If any of the men know you, or rather your reputa-tion, then they will! You of all people should present quite a challenge, and that's what these men want. They don't want women who spend their lives being subservient. They want someone who finds it hard to adapt. A mental virgin you might call it!' Jackie laughed, but Kristina didn't. She was excited, nervous and on edge, but she certainly wasn't amused.

'Had a good time?' asked Ben when she walked into the house.

'Yes thanks. We chatted and had some wine, it made a nice change,' said Kristina, winding her arms round his neck and kissing him deeply, her tongue flicking between his slightly parted lips.

Ben drew back in surprise. 'Hey, what's all this about?'

Still aroused by all she'd heard that evening, Kristina rubbed herself against him, her hands starting to unbutton his shirt. 'Aren't you pleased to see me back?'

'Sure, but you've only been away four hours and in case you've forgotten I've got a presentation to make at eight in the morning. It's my working breakfast, remember?'

Kristina released him, feeling slightly foolish. 'Sorry, time for bed and Horlicks is it?'

'That's not fair, Kristina. You've been out relaxing, but I've been working on this damned advert and I'm still not happy with it. Now I've got to try and sleep before convincing the board tomorrow that I've got it right and this is the exact slogan they've been waiting for for the past six months. Tonight, sex isn't high on my list of priorities.'

'Fine, sorry, forget it. Your presentation had completely slipped my mind. You go on up; I'll wait a few minutes, try and unscramble my thoughts. You know what it's like when you've been chattering for hours.'

'I know what it's like when you've been chattering and drinking,' commented Ben stiffly.

Kristina felt like hurling one of the sofa cushions after him. There were times, times like tonight, when he could be positively pompous, she thought furiously, and she waited a long time before joining him in bed. Even then her flesh was still tingling, and she longed for some kind of release from the sexual tension that Jacqueline's revelations had brought about. Ben, sleeping soundly beside her, was an added irritation.

'Damn and blast the man!' exclaimed Kristina irritably as Sue sat down in the chair opposite her.

'Not Michael Shaw, professional charmer and mildly eccentric publisher?' asked Sue with a laugh.

'The very same. He's sat on that manuscript for six months saying how original, witty and clever it is and now he's decided it doesn't fit his list. Think of the time we've wasted! I'll have to ring Peter and explain why his clever manuscript isn't, after all, clever enough and has to go off to someone else.'

'All in a day's work,' said Sue soothingly. 'What's wrong? It isn't like you to get so worked up over something like this.'

Kristina rubbed at her eyes. 'Sorry, bit tired I guess. You're right, it is an everyday occurrence. I just happened to have thought we'd definitely got that placed. Never mind, back to the drawing-board. Can you get the emails finished by five-thirty? Only I'd like them all to go off tonight.'

'Sure,' agreed Sue calmly.

When she'd left the office, Kristina gave herself a mental shake. It wasn't really Michael Shaw who'd annoyed her, it was the fact that three weeks had passed since she'd spoken to Jacqueline and she still hadn't heard a word from anyone. Every time the phone rang or she got a letter she didn't recognise through the post her pulse would quicken, and then her stomach would plunge with disappointment when it proved to be entirely unconnected with the society of the bracelet. Her phone rang again and she picked it up automatically.

'Yes?' she queried.

'Is that Kristina Masterton?' asked an unknown male voice.

'It is.'

'You don't know me,' continued the voice, 'but I selected you from our society's computer. I wondered if you could meet me at Luigi's bar in Bayswater tonight at eight forty-five?'

Her fingers tightened round the receiver and the palms of her hands felt damp. 'Tonight? I'm not sure that I . . .'

'It's the only night that's convenient for me,' the voice continued smoothly.

It was an unusual voice, soft and yet clipped at the same time, and very grave, as though the owner was used to taking life seriously. Kristina wasn't certain the man was English.

'In that case I'd better say yes,' she replied, realising that if she refused he would probably move on to someone else, and she was unwilling to pass up her first chance of a meeting.

'Excellent. I look forward to making your acquaintance this evening. There won't be a problem over recognition since I've seen your photograph in several magazines.'

Before she could respond to that the line went dead and for several seconds she sat holding the receiver as the dialling tone sounded in her ear. It had happened, she thought triumphantly. Her application had been accepted and now one of the members had sought her out, a man who had seen her photo and knew her line of work.

Reluctantly she replaced the phone and then sat staring into space. She'd been so on edge waiting for this call that now it had come she didn't know what to do. She wondered how she should dress, and what they would talk about. She wondered if the man was handsome, and what he did for a living. But above all, she hoped with every fibre of her being that when it came to making love to her he'd know exactly what her body craved, know more about her than even she knew about herself.

'Fool,' she said sharply. 'He's only an ordinary man, just like other men. Don't build your hopes up too high. Besides, you might never get as far as the bedroom. You might hate each other on sight.' She hoped not. She'd liked the sound of his voice.

That evening, when she was dressing to go out, Kristina found herself totally unable to decide what to wear. She was glad that Ben wasn't home – he'd had a late meeting and was going on to his squash club – otherwise he might have wondered at the amount of time she was spending choosing an outfit.

She couldn't work out whether she should look the way the unknown man would expect her to look from the photos he'd seen, or go for an entirely different approach that was more suited to the society and all it involved. In the end she decided to dress as she would for a drink with a client. This man had chosen her for all the qualities he thought he'd seen in her picture and her comprehensive CV. He wouldn't want her to look different or the reason for the attraction would be gone.

She settled on a striking bright fuchsia and grey two-piece. The skirt was plain grey, finishing an inch above her knees and with a front slit, while the jacket was fuchsia, nipped in at the waist and with a black and fuchsia collar that had a detachable bib inset. This disguised the depth of the collar. Without the bib most of her breasts would have been revealed. The overall effect was sharp and very striking.

Luigi's wine bar was off Queensway and because the traffic was heavier than she'd expected, Kristina arrived two minutes late instead of the five minutes early that she'd planned. She'd wanted to be seated at the bar so that she could see all the men as they arrived. Now she guessed that the stranger, the man who might introduce her to the incredible world that Jacqueline had described, was probably already there.

Feeling far more self-conscious than usual, she walked through the doors and towards the bar. A man rose from one of the tables set in semi-darkness at the side of the room and blocked her way. 'Kristina Masterton?' he asked quietly, holding out his right hand.

Kristina felt her heart jump into her throat but she kept her voice steady as she too held out her hand. 'That's right. I'm sorry I'm a few minutes late.'

'It doesn't matter. The traffic was particularly heavy tonight.'

Again Kristina noted the carefully correct way he spoke, as though English was not his first language, and after he'd asked her what she'd like to drink and gone over to the bar she was able to study him properly for the first time.

He was about six feet tall with smooth golden-brown skin and very black hair that had a few streaks of grey. The hair was thick and wavy, swept back off his high forehead. He was wearing an expensive grey silk suit, crisp white shirt and a silver and grey tie and as he returned to their table she saw that he was solidly built with broad shoulders and well-defined muscles.

Sitting down he poured them each a glass of the Australian Chardonnay. 'To our meeting,' he said quietly, his deep-set dark eyes unsmiling.

Kristina felt slightly intimidated, but she smiled brightly at him. 'To our meeting,' she agreed, and sipped at the cool liquid.

Now that he was close to her she realised that his nose was slightly hooked and his top lip thin, but his lower lip was full, hinting at a sensuality that wasn't obvious in the rest of his features, apart from his eyes.

His eyes were startling. They were the darkest eyes she'd ever seen, and so deep-set and shadowed that she couldn't help thinking of a panda that she'd once seen at London Zoo, while his eyebrows were heavy and winged and his eyelids so dark that they looked almost grey.

'Do I pass?' he murmured.

Kristina felt herself blush. 'I'm sorry, was I staring? I'm afraid my thoughts were miles away. It's a bad habit of mine, people often think I'm looking at them when really I'm working out what I need to buy for supper!'

'I would have thought your mind was more usually occupied with how many dollars you were likely to get for Lucretia Forrest's next book at the American auction,' he responded.

Kristina nodded approvingly. 'Very good, you know who one of my clients is.'

'I know all your clients,' he assured her. 'I know a great deal about your work, but very little about you yourself, which is why I thought we should have this meeting.'

'What more do you need to know?' asked Kristina with a smile. 'After all, you already have the advantage. I know nothing at all about you, not even your name.'

For the first time since they'd met he smiled, and the sudden lightening of his features, the almost mischievous look that crossed his face, startled her. That smile changed him totally, opening up a vision of an entirely different man with a lightness and humour that she would never have expected. The contrast excited her, suggesting as it did that this was a very complex man.

'I'm sorry,' he apologised. 'I quite forgot that you didn't know! I'm Tarquin Rashid, and I'm a psychologist.'

'A psychologist!'

'You're surprised?'

Kristina nodded. 'I thought psychologists were people who watched how others responded to members of the opposite sex, not people who ever got involved themselves!'

He shook his head slightly. 'We're the same as everyone else. We have the same desires, secrets and needs as anyone.'

His words changed the atmosphere. Kristina was suddenly acutely aware of her own needs and desires, and right now her most overwhelming desire was to be taken back to Tarquin's home, given a bracelet to slip on and then to let him show her exactly what he meant by desires and secrets. As his golden-brown hand lifted his glass to his lips she found herself studying the sprinkling of dark hairs on his wrist and felt such a fierce need for him that it startled her.

'I suppose you do,' she managed to say, moistening her suddenly dry lips. 'But it must make it difficult to lose yourself in emotions when you're used to analysing them.'

'Not at all. When I finish work I leave all that behind

me,' he assured her, but she didn't totally believe him. His eyes were assessing her even as he spoke, and she felt certain that he spent most of his time analysing other people if not himself.

'You're not English,' she commented.

'No, a rather strange mixture of cultures I'm afraid. My father is Egyptian, my mother half-Tamil and half-English. What does that make me do you think?'

'Interesting!' laughed Kristina.

He nodded. 'Yes.' The word was abrupt but his deep-set eyes were placid.

'Have you . . . belonged to the society very long?' asked Kristina, uncertain as to whether or not she could mention the society.

'No, not very long. You, I seem to remember, are a new member.'

Kristina nodded. 'That's right. A friend of mine told me about it.'

'Yes, I think most of us join through word of mouth recommendation. I don't suppose there's any other way. They can hardly advertise!' Once more he gave a sudden smile, and Kristina could imagine being willing to do almost anything in order to make him smile. Almost anything. She shivered at her own thoughts.

'Were you born in London?' he asked her as he refilled her glass.

'No, Hampshire,' she responded, and for the next twenty minutes he led her skilfully through a brief resume of her childhood, education and then her astonishingly quick rise to success as a literary agent. Only when she finally stopped talking did she realise quite how much she must have given away about herself, while Tarquin had said nothing at all about his life.

'Your turn now,' she said quickly.

He glanced at his watch. 'Regretfully I have another appointment in twenty minutes, otherwise I would have been delighted to oblige you.' He half-rose from his chair and extended his hand. 'It's been a very interesting meeting. Thank you for keeping the appointment.'

Kristina stared blankly at him, unable to believe what she was hearing. It seemed that the evening was over, and he'd given no indication at all that he found her in any way attractive or desirable, nor was he speaking as though they were going to meet again.

She wanted to ask him why. To beg him to see her again because she knew without any doubt that this was exactly the kind of man she'd hoped to meet through the society, but luckily her normal sense of self-worth took over and helped her control her emotions. She might be devastated, but she wasn't going to show it.

'It was interesting for me too, and if I hadn't come I'd only have worked so it made a pleasant change.'

'You work every evening?' he queried.

Kristina forced herself to laugh. 'Of course not! My boyfriend, Ben, is playing squash tonight. I usually work when he isn't around. It's a chance to catch up on my slush pile.'

'Slush pile?'

She let her hand rest in his as she prepared to leave. 'Don't tell me that your research didn't include slush piles! They're the stuff of publishing nightmares, but just occasionally publishing dreams! Goodnight, Tarquin.' It took a huge effort of will, but she managed to walk away from him and out of the wine bar without once looking back.

Once home, however, her composure snapped and she rushed to the phone to call Jacqueline. She was grateful that her friend was in for once.

'Jackie, I've just had my first meeting since I joined the society. He was the most incredible man, really deep and serious but you felt that underneath there was this other, totally different person. I couldn't believe my luck!'

'I told you the system works well,' laughed Jackie.

'But it doesn't!' Kristina could hear the childlike wail in her voice. 'I don't think he fancied me at all. When we parted he never mentioned anything about meeting up again.'

'Oh,' said Jackie, suddenly subdued.

'When you first met Laurence, did you arrange when you'd next meet?'

'Well, to be honest we went straight back to his place that first time. He said later that he couldn't wait to see me put the bracelet on, and I felt the same.'

'So did I!' exclaimed Kristina. 'I kept imagining what it would be like to have him dictating my every move, touching me when and where he wanted, arousing me in ways I'd never known before and . . .'

'Kristina, stop it!' said Jacqueline crisply. 'You can't force him to feel the same.'

'Can't I do anything about another meeting? Do I have to leave it to him?'

'Yes,' said Jacqueline sadly. 'That's the whole point, don't you see? The women are passive in this relationship. We can't go and ask the men out like we do in our everyday lives. This is the society, and the men are in total control right from the moment you first meet.'

'I wish I'd never heard of the society then!' shouted Kristina, and she slammed down the phone.

When Ben got in later she was already in bed and pretended to be asleep. If she couldn't feel Tarquin's hands on her body, or give reign to her sensuality under his tuition, then she certainly didn't want Ben anywhere near her tonight. But she could have cried from fury and frustration.

Chapter Three

For the next three days Kristina continued to feel frustrated and confused. She'd never had a problem in getting any man she wanted, in fact her problem had been getting rid of the ones she didn't. This turnaround had thrown her off balance, and she hated it. As a result she channelled all her rage and frustration into her work and drove an even harder bargain than usual with publishers and foreign agents.

'We've had a good three days!' remarked Sue as she went over the contracts she'd had to prepare. 'You've got the magic touch this week.'

'I wanted someone else's magic touch,' muttered Kristina.

'Sorry?'

'Nothing,' said Kristina quickly. 'Talking to myself I'm afraid. Oh no, not the phone again. I wanted to get these emails sorted out. Ask them to call back would you. Say I'm in a meeting.'

She watched Sue pick up the phone, and then saw

her frown. 'Could you repeat the name?' asked Sue. 'It just doesn't ring a bell right now. I'm sure I . . .'

Kristina didn't wait to hear any more; she snatched the receiver from her startled assistant. 'Kristina Masterton here. Can I help you?'

'Yes you can, Kristina Masterton,' replied a blessedly familiar voice. 'I'd like you to come to my house at nine tonight.' He gave her his address, then said, 'Please do not wear any perfume or jewellery. That will be supplied.'

He gave her no time to reply, no chance to say yes or no, he simply replaced his telephone and Kristina was left with her heart racing and her hands trembling at the realisation that it really was going to happen after all. Tonight she would have to put on the bracelet.

'Who was that?' asked Sue. 'He had a lovely voice. Very cultured and soothing.'

'My gynaecologist,' said Kristina wildly, unable to think up anything better on the spur of the moment.

'Really? Give me his name and address! Shall we do those emails then?'

Kristina gave herself a mental shake. There were hours to go still; hours that she needed to fill with urgent work. She had to push all thoughts of tonight to the back of her mind until later, but although she managed to, she resented doing it because what she really wanted was to enjoy the anticipation of the moment. For the first time in years work was not uppermost in her mind.

*

At exactly nine o'clock that night, Kristina stood on the top step outside the address she'd been given and after taking a deep breath, reached out and pressed the doorbell. She heard the faintest echo of chimes from deep inside the house and then the door was opened by a slim Indian girl who looked to be about nineteen. She smiled at Kristina, but didn't speak. Instead she stepped back and inclined her head in what Kristina assumed to be a gesture of welcome.

The hall was dark, the mahogany-stained floor highly polished with one large gold and green Persian rug covering the centre, while on the side tables stood expensive porcelain figures, mostly of eastern origin.

The girl who'd let Kristina in remained standing to one side, her eyes on the floor, and just as Kristina was about to ask if Tarquin was at home he walked out of one of the doors that led off the hallway.

She'd wondered earlier if he was really as darkly sensual looking as she'd remembered, but the moment he appeared she knew that she hadn't been wrong; in fact if anything he looked even better tonight.

Once again he was in a suit, but this time it was dark blue, and the pale blue shirt had an unusual cutaway collar that enabled him to tie a large knot in his blue and red tie. As he smiled and stretched out his hand she saw that he was wearing a large Patek Philippe watch with a bold but simple face to it. Expensive but very tasteful, she thought appreciatively.

She reached out to take his hand, and it was then that

she saw it. Lying in his palm was a tiny gold bracelet with the familiar letter 'B' suspended in the middle. 'For you,' he said softly. At that moment, for one fleeting second, Kristina hesitated. She wanted to put it on, had dreamt of nothing else since their first meeting, but to actually place herself in this man's hands was a huge step to take and she felt panic stir in her.

Tarquin Rashid watched her without expression. The choice had to be hers and hers alone, but he hoped that she wouldn't back out because he, like Kristina, had anticipated this moment with increasing excitement and desire.

At last she picked the bracelet up and thought that she heard a slow exhalation of breath from Tarquin, but then she was slipping it on and at the touch of the cool gold on her skin she began to tremble.

'Excellent,' remarked Tarquin, gesturing for the Indian girl to go up the stairs ahead of them. 'Now we can begin.'

Kristina went to follow the girl, but he shook his head. 'I go next, you follow me,' he explained. His voice was polite but firm, and she realised that from now on she could do nothing unless he told her to. She was to take no decisions and make no choices, everything that happened this night would be dictated by Tarquin.

The room that they finally entered was on the third floor, a huge studio-type room with an enormous sky-light window. A vast bed set low to the floor dominated the room and behind it was a silk-covered screen. There were pillows and cushions all over the bed's surface and the room was scented with burning candles set in the four corners. The perfume was subtle yet erotic, with a hint of both jasmine and sandalwood.

She stood uncertainly on the soft carpet, awaiting Tarquin's orders. She was still trembling and hoped that it didn't show. It was ridiculous to be frightened by the situation when she'd chosen it, longed for it, but the fear wasn't of the man in front of her but of the total loss of control.

For what seemed to Kristina to be an endless time he stood two feet away from her studying her carefully, while the Indian girl waited in the background. 'Tell me what you're feeling,' he said at last.

'Excited,' replied Kristina.

He moved close to her and put the palms of his hands flat against the sides of her head, his grip firm but not unpleasant. 'You're meant to tell the truth,' he murmured. 'I don't like it when people lie to me.'

Kristina tried to jerk her head away and his eyes widened in surprise. 'I didn't tell you to move,' he reminded her and it was only then that she fully understood the extent of the control he had over her.

She tried to remain still, and the pressure from his hands eased a little. 'Tell me how you really feel,' he suggested, his fingers moving up into her hair and lightly massaging her scalp.

'Rather nervous,' she admitted.

'Of course; that's only to be expected. Lydia will

undress you now and then give you a bath. After that you will be ready for me.'

She assumed that Lydia was the girl who'd let her in, and the thought of another woman undressing and washing her wasn't at all to her liking. Knowing, however, that there was nothing she could do about it she simply remained where she was as Tarquin stepped away from her and the Indian girl took his place.

Kristina saw that Tarquin was watching closely as the girl began to unfasten the buttons of the lightweight coat-dress that Kristina had worn to the house, but when she tried to help the girl by drawing an arm out of one of the sleeves his voice interrupted her.

'No!' he said curtly, and he turned his head away slightly in what she recognised as a sign of displeasure.

Lydia smiled at her. 'Don't worry,' she murmured as she eased the garment off the other woman's shoulders. 'The first time is always difficult.'

Kristina wondered how many other women the girl had seen come to this house.

Beneath the top garment Kristina was wearing a cream satin body edged with lace and with very high-cut legs. Lydia stepped to one side to allow Tarquin to study Kristina as she stood there before him, feeling her nipples hardening under his gaze until they brushed against the prickly lace. This most delicate of caresses seemed almost unbearably erotic and her stomach drew in on itself with desire, the muscles tightening in anticipation of sexual pleasure.

Finally Tarquin nodded and Lydia once more stood in front of his visitor. Then, slowly, she knelt on the floor, her slim hands going between Kristina's thighs as they tried to unfasten the press-studs set there.

Lydia's fingers were light and practised, and as she undid the studs she let the pads of them trail over the cotton gusset of the garment, lightly caressing Kristina's outer sex lips beneath the material. The touch was brief, almost imperceptible, and yet Kristina heard her breath catch and felt her thighs start to shake with longing for more pressure, for Tarquin's hands at last to touch her there at the very centre of her pleasure.

If he was aware of Kristina's feelings the dark-haired man didn't show it. His eyes remained unfathomable and his expression sombre. From the look on his face Kristina felt that she could just as easily have been a patient who was posing a problem as a woman he intended to make love to.

Now Lydia moved behind Kristina and very slowly she eased the thin straps off her shoulders and let them fall down the sides of her arms, the material again teasingly brushing her flesh which was now starting to burn all over her body as though from some inner heat. Finally the entire garment was eased upwards and over her head. As Lydia pulled on it she allowed her hands to cup the undersides of Kristina's small but rapidly swelling breasts and once again Kristina was pierced with need for physical contact with the stranger standing so near and yet so far away.

Now she was totally naked and Lydia gestured for her to follow her out through a door set in the side of the room, but before she could obey Tarquin moved up to her again. Very slowly he put out a hand and to her astonishment he covered her eyes so that she couldn't see what he was doing. Suddenly his mouth was on hers and his tongue was parting her lips, thrusting in and out in an imitation of the sexual act that only fired her already fevered imagination all the more. Without thinking she moved towards him, her hips trying to brush against his upper leg or groin.

At once he stopped kissing her, uncovered her eyes and stepped away. 'I didn't tell you to move,' he reminded her in a detached voice that was in startling contrast to the sexual urgency that she'd sensed in the kiss. 'It seems that you find the rules of the society difficult to obey.'

Kristina didn't answer, feeling certain that even to speak uninvited would be wrong. At her silence he nodded in approval. 'Before the bath I will remind you of two things. One, if you wish the bathing to stop, remove the bracelet but you must then return home. Two, I do not want you to speak or indeed make any kind of sound during the bath. The time for such communication is later, when I choose. Please indicate your understanding by nodding your head.'

The frustration of not even being allowed to vocalise her agreement was unbelievable and also incredibly arousing. Normally Kristina had to make sure that she explained everything several times over. Her entire business life was made up of communication and now here was a man refusing to allow her any form of communication. She wondered if this was how Laurence behaved with Jacqueline, but then guessed that it probably wasn't. All the men, like the women they chose, were bound to be very different. At this moment she was very glad she'd been chosen by Tarquin.

'Well?' he sounded impatient and she realised that she'd been day-dreaming. Hastily she nodded, and he then indicated that she should follow Lydia through into the adjoining bathroom.

The bath, like the bed, was huge and so full that when Kristina lowered herself into the water it rose almost to the top. The bath was scented but there were no soap bubbles and when Tarquin seated himself at the foot of the bath he was able to see every inch of Kristina's body.

Lydia put a bath mitten on her right hand, poured some liquid soap on to it and then began to gently rub at Kristina's back, moving her hand in small circular movements that both cleansed and stimulated the skin.

When she moved her hand a little and started to use it beneath Kristina's breasts, Kristina looked directly into Tarquin's eyes, but because they were so deep-set and he was sitting in shadow it wasn't possible for her to make out the expression in them. She hoped that he liked what he was seeing and was just about to sit up straighter, pulling back her shoulders to emphasise her small breasts, when she remembered that he hadn't asked her to move and she managed to prevent herself from moving at all, congratulating herself on her self-control.

Lydia worked swiftly but carefully, and when she started to soap the breasts themselves she removed the mitten and used only her bare hands. She deliberately teased the pale pink nipples a little and as the soap dried round them the hardened tips felt cold despite the warmth of the room.

'Crouch on your hands and knees,' said Tarquin softly. 'Keep your legs as far apart as the bath allows. Lydia needs to be able to cleanse every part of you.'

For the first time since she'd entered the house, Kristina didn't want to obey. The idea of opening herself in such a way to another woman, allowing the Indian girl's fingers access to her most private place, was both shocking and in a way degrading. At the same time, though, she could feel her pulse quickening with excitement and with only the slightest hesitation she scrambled into the position Tarquin had requested and let her head hang down so that she was looking into the bath water and not his face as she was washed between her thighs.

She felt the girl's fingers slide between her legs from behind her, and then her pubic hair was being soaped and the massaging movements caused Kristina's highly aroused body to start to open so that her outer lips expanded. Now Lydia's fingers were moving along the inner tissue until quite unexpectedly they glided over the slowly swelling clitoris and Kristina gave a gasp of delight as a spark of hot pleasure flared in her lower belly.

'I told you to remain silent,' said Tarquin, disappointment clear in his voice. 'Tell me what happened.'

Kristina swallowed hard, wondering how she could possibly vocalise what had just occurred. 'I'm sorry, but Lydia touched . . . That is, her fingers brushed . . .'

'For a literary agent you seem to be having great difficulty with words,' he laughed. 'Please explain accurately what happened.'

Kristina bit on her bottom lip with irritation at herself, but even as she tried to find the words Lydia's fingers repeated the movement and this time lingered a second longer so that there was a slow coiling movement of pleasure deep inside Kristina's abdomen and again she gasped.

'Tell me,' repeated Tarquin insistently.

'Her fingers keep touching my clitoris!' gasped Kristina. 'It makes me feel wonderful and I can't control my breathing when it happens.'

'Then we must teach you better control during the course of the evening,' he commented.

She felt herself start trembling again at the words, and suddenly Lydia stepped away from her and Tarquin held up a large bath towel. 'Time to get out of there. I will dry you.' She expected a slow, sensuous towelling but it was brief and hurried, and she still felt slightly damp when he put one large hand on the back of her neck and pushed her in the direction of the bedroom again.

'Now we will really begin,' he murmured. She felt the bracelet caress her wrist as though it was reminding her that she was still bound to obey him and her only pleasure would be the pleasure that he allowed her.

Leading her to the foot of the bed, Tarquin then opened the intricately carved door of a wardrobe and drew out a turquoise satin kaftan which he draped round the passive Kristina. It was unlike any other kaftan she'd seen, with a high mandarin-style collar that fastened quite tightly round her neck with a velcro strip and then hung open down the front. The sleeves were conventional, long and wide, but when Tarquin's hands turned her towards a mirror set in the wall on the opposite side of the room and then gently pushed her forwards she saw that with every step she took the garment parted, revealing tantalising glimpses of various parts of her body before closing around her again.

When she was a few inches away from the mirror she felt his hands grip her shoulders in a movement of restraint, and obediently she stood quite still, but there was nothing passive about her feelings. She felt as though her entire body was buzzing beneath the skin, tiny tremors tingling with such heightened anticipation that she knew the moment he touched her intimately she'd explode into a shattering climax.

'Some jewellery I think,' he murmured to himself,

and she watched in the mirror as he reached over her to clip on a pair of gold tear-shaped earrings with a huge pearl at the base of each one. Finally he walked in front of her, momentarily obscuring her reflection, and carefully daubed her with perfume from a tiny cut-glass bottle. She didn't recognise the scent but it had fruity overtones, reminding her of apricots, and beneath that the indisputably sexy hint of musk.

'Do you know it?' asked Tarquin, allowing himself the luxury of placing one final drop on the thin skin at the back of each of her knees, a touch that made her toes curl in delight.

'No, I don't,' she admitted.

'It's *Trésor*. The moment I met you I knew that this was your perfume. When it was launched they used the slogan, *For the woman who seeks a successful life rather than success*. Under the circumstances I feel that most appropriate!'

Suddenly the swift, heart-stopping smile crossed his face and Kristina, who was already in such a state of arousal that she was almost beside herself with lust, knew that under normal circumstances she'd now take his hand and lead him straight to the bed, rubbing her aching pubic area against his thigh as a preliminary to their love-making. But tonight she couldn't; tonight she had to wait for him to decide what they would do next, and the strain was unbearable.

He moved behind her once more and together they stared into the mirror. Kristina could never remember

seeing her eyes so bright, and her dark hair was damp
and curly, giving her a look of wild sexual abandonment
despite the fact that she hadn't been given the opportunity to be either wild or abandoned.

Tarquin studied her calmly and seriously, as he
might a painting or ornament that he was considering
buying, she thought with a swift surge of indignation,
and then he nodded to himself with satisfaction and
lightly clapped his hands.

To her astonishment two young men, entirely
nude and with copper-coloured skin and strong chest
and thigh muscles, hurried out from behind the silk
screen at the head of the bed. She wondered how long
they'd been waiting there. Tarquin uttered no word of
instruction, but they clearly knew what was expected of
them and knelt down side-by-side on their hands and
knees between Kristina and the mirror.

'Turn and face me,' said Tarquin in her ear. She
twisted round, and before she had a chance to say a
word he'd grasped her by the waist and was carefully
lowering her backwards over the men's backs until they
were bearing her full weight. She bent her knees and
her toes gripped the pile of the carpet as much in fear
as for support, while at the same time her head fell back
and she looked upwards to see her own face reflected in
the mirror.

She realised that the kaftan had opened wide, leaving
her entire body utterly exposed to the tall, impassive
man waiting to make love to her for the first time. Her

breasts felt almost painfully hard and without thinking she moved her hands to caress them. Tarquin moved with the speed of lightning and she felt her hands gripped in his. 'No!' he said firmly. 'You touch yourself only when I say.'

'But they ache,' she complained.

'It's all part of the pleasure,' he assured her. Kristina wasn't sure he was right. Then, so lightly that she might almost have imagined it, he trailed the tip of one of his fingers over the rigid little peaks of her nipples and she heard her breathing quicken as a muffled moan escaped from her lips.

'You may make noises now,' he conceded. 'My only order is that you do not climax until I give my permission. It would be a pity to rush things at this stage.'

'But how can I . . .? I'm so ready to come!' explained Kristina, all inhibitions gone as she tried to explain the way her body felt. 'I don't think I'll be able to control myself.'

'I'll help you, as it's your first time,' he murmured, and then she felt his mouth on her tightly stretched stomach and she jerked upwards at the surge of electricity that coursed through her. He waited a moment for the involuntary spasm to pass and then started to kiss and lick her belly button until the scorching tendrils of pleasure started to build into a heaviness deep inside her, centred somewhere behind her pubic bone and she knew that her climax was approaching.

Tarquin saw her toes start to curl and immediately stopped what he was doing. He lifted his head and Kristina groaned aloud as the delicious sensations slowly ebbed away again, leaving only the ache of thwarted need.

She heard him move, and looking up at her reflection saw that her eyes were wide and frantic, her mouth tight with the sexual tensions wracking her body. When she felt the point of his tongue gently insert itself between the toes of her left foot she cried out with shock, and as his tongue moved firmly up over the tendons of her foot and then in tiny circles around the sensitive ankle bone she began to squirm against the naked backs of the men beneath her.

She could hear herself making strange beseeching noises as the pleasure snaked upwards until it felt as though his tongue was actually lapping much higher, on her inner thighs where the swirls of excitement were making themselves felt, and all at once her abdominal muscles drew in on themselves prior to the sexual release she craved so urgently.

Again Tarquin was alerted by her body's movements and the tiny gutteral sounds that were issuing from her throat. Once more he stopped, and lazily he let one hand trail up the centre of her body and then round each of the tiny breasts that so aroused him, but he avoided the straining nipples and surrounding tissue.

Finally, when he felt that Kristina could cope no longer, he gripped her upper thighs with his hands and pressed his mouth against her vulva. She felt the pressure on her clitoris and moaned. She could feel sweat running down her forehead and into her hair and tried desperately to stop herself from coming too soon, but now that he was actually stimulating the clitoris, even indirectly, she didn't think she could handle the situation much longer. Her body's demands were more insistent than the rules of the society and she felt her sex lips opening to allow him better access to her most sensitive tissue.

As she opened, as the wonderful feminine scent of her filled his nostrils, Tarquin too decided to end the game and with the tip of his tongue he drew a circle round the visibly swollen bud while at the same time he released one of her legs in order to insert two fingers of one hand into her vagina.

At the exact moment that he allowed his tongue to at last touch the side of the shaft of the clitoris he also hooked his fingers up and slowly massaged the little bump that he could feel on the top vaginal wall. Kristina now had the exquisite sensation of her two most sensitive places being stimulated at the same time.

The combination of the deep throbbing excitement caused by the manipulation of her G spot and the searing red-hot pleasure of the cunning use of Tarquin's tongue against her clitoral shaft sent Kristina into a paroxysm of pleasure that was so intense she almost lost consciousness.

She gave a wild cry as Tarquin lifted his head briefly

and whispered, 'Now you may come.' Then, as his tongue returned to its amazingly skilled sexual torture she at last gave herself over to her body's insistent clamouring and her legs clamped around the sides of Tarquin's head while her belly convulsed in glorious spasms of flooding liquid pleasure that seemed to go on and on for ever.

When the last tremors had died away, and the last uncontrolled muscle spasm ended, Kristina glanced up at her face in the mirror. Her lips were parted, flushed and moist, and her cheeks were equally flushed but for the first time in many weeks she looked relaxed, as though all the tensions and pressures of everyday life had been drained away by the incredible sensuality of the entire evening.

She started to sit up, only to feel a hand pressing on the middle of her chest. 'Stay there a little longer. I want to touch your breasts,' said Tarquin.

'I don't like them touched after I've come,' retorted Kristina, entirely forgetting that she was still wearing the bracelet.

'What you do or do not like is secondary to what I like,' Tarquin reminded her. 'Or do you wish to remove the bracelet?'

'No, of course not!' she said quickly, terrified that the chance of another night like this might be lost to her.

'Then do as I say.'

Her breasts felt comfortable now, the nipples soft and relaxed. Kristina didn't want them touched. She always liked to be left alone once she and Ben had both reached their climaxes, and now this man was forcing her to allow him to do something she actively didn't wish to do.

No, not forcing, she reminded herself. She could remove the bracelet and leave now, with the memory of their loveplay still fresh in her mind, but she wanted more. She wanted to have him inside her, making love to her properly. If that was going to happen then she had to follow the rules and so, reluctantly, she lay where she was and waited for his fingers to touch her breasts.

Tarquin knelt between Kristina's loosely spread thighs and leant forward over her body. Lowering his head he licked along the undersides of the globes and then drew his tongue upwards towards the nipples, moving from one breast to the other and gradually increasing the pressure of his tongue.

At first Kristina wanted to move away, to stop the irritatingly insistent caress, but slowly she found that her breasts were responding and when his tongue swirled around each of the nipples in turn she was surprised to find that they were definitely responding. Tarquin could see that they were, and he smiled to himself as the little tips stood out more proudly from the soft breast tissue.

When the nipples were at last fully erect he grasped the left one between his thumb and forefinger and then very lightly, using the other three fingers, he scored tiny marks across the surface of her breast.

Kristina drew in her breath sharply. The sensation was entirely new to her, a strange mixture of sharpness and sweetness that made her shiver with desire for more. Tarquin then repeated the process with her right nipple only this time the score marks were fractionally heavier and Kristina moaned with excitement.

Listening to her and watching her body's responses, Tarquin was greatly encouraged. This, he was sure, was a woman who would be willing to enjoy all the things he enjoyed, who would learn through the rules of the society more about herself than she could otherwise have ever hoped for, and her learning process would give him incredible excitement and hopefully a sharp desire that had been lacking for some time. With her he would cease to be jaded and his sexuality would again recapture some of the freshness of its early days.

Just watching her lying helpless and moaning beneath him drove him half-mad with desire. He wanted to take her now, to enter her moist welcoming softness and allow himself the same blissful release that she'd known, but just as the waiting had made it better for her, so it would for him. In any case, sending her away without having allowed either of them what they both wanted most would be an aphrodisiac in itself. So too would be the knowledge that Kristina, a woman who was used to being in total control, was being forced to accept rules that were, ultimately, designed for her own greater satisfaction.

She was quivering all over now, her body once more

aroused and he allowed himself the luxury of one last move before ending the evening. Using the tips of his fingernails again, he daubed a light path through the valley between her breasts, across her waist and then down the middle of her hard, aching belly and by the time he reached the top of her pubic hair she was shuddering from head to foot. Gently he lowered his head and kissed her softly at the very base of her stomach before taking hold of her arms and pulling her upright.

'Time for you to return home, Kristina. It's very late.' He pulled her up to her feet and the two men who'd been bearing her weight in stolid silence for so long stood too and then slipped silently away out through the main door.

Dazed and shaking, Kristina's head rested against Tarquin's chest for a moment and she was shocked to realise that he was still fully clothed. Suddenly she felt that she had to touch his skin, had to feel his bare flesh just as he'd been feeling hers and she reached up to unfasten his shirt buttons but he quickly stopped her. 'Time to go,' he repeated calmly.

She didn't want to go. She wanted to stay there. Wanted him to continue playing with her body the way he'd just been playing with it. She longed for the feel of his nails on her, of his mouth kissing her between her thighs as he had done earlier, and her trembling body betrayed her need.

'I thought you preferred to be left alone after a

climax,' he reminded her as he handed over her clothes and removed her kaftan.

'I thought I did, now I'm not so sure,' she muttered, pulling on her hold-ups and slipping into the satin body before Tarquin helped her on with the coat-dress.

'Next time we will try other things,' he whispered as he bent his mouth to her ear. Then he ran his fingers through her hair in a gesture that was almost possessive, before stepping away from her and holding out his hand.

Kristina stared at him, unable to believe he wanted to shake hands after the extraordinary experience he'd just given her. 'The bracelet,' he said with a half-smile. 'It has to stay here.'

She felt very silly. 'Yes, of course. I quite forgot! Here.'

As she handed it back to him their fingers touched, and she was able to look him in the eyes as an equal. She saw something stir behind his usual sombre gaze, a flicker of something that could have been surprise or excitement, but she knew that it was something far more intriguing than the indifference he usually portrayed.

'Lydia will call a cab for you,' he promised, after he'd taken her back down into the hall. Then he turned on his heel and disappeared into one of the downstairs rooms without another word.

Kristina felt a sharp pang of disappointment as he vanished from her sight. Sensual and satisfying as the evening had been, she'd expected it to end in a different way, never in her wildest dreams imagining that she'd leave his house without them making love. The promise that he'd made about doing other things the next time was reassuring in its way; at least he intended to call her again, but she still wished that he'd allowed things to progress more tonight.

And yet, she admitted to herself, the fact that he hadn't; the fact that she still had that moment to look forward to, to anticipate at her leisure as she waited for his call, would add to the sexual tension and possibly increase the pleasure of their second meeting.

As a psychologist he'd no doubt worked it all out, she thought, as Lydia telephoned for a cab, and no doubt he was as intent on increasing his own pleasure as hers. She just hoped he didn't play the waiting game for too long as she was desperate to see his naked body and feel him inside her.

At the sound of a car drawing up outside, Lydia gave her a smile and opened the front door to allow her out. The cab driver turned his head. 'Where to?'

Kristina opened her mouth to reply, and realised that her mind had gone totally blank. She felt most peculiar, light-headed and unreal, and for a few seconds she thought she wouldn't be able to answer him. Then just as suddenly as she'd forgotten, the memory flooded back again. Quickly she gave him the directions, ignoring his raised eyebrows.

When she finally got back and started to unlock her front door it was gone midnight. The entire evening's experience had totally disorientated her and she felt as though she was being forced back into a world that she didn't like very much. She wasn't the only one who was unhappy.

'Where the hell have you been?' demanded Ben from the lounge doorway. 'I thought you said you'd be back by eleven at the latest?'

'I didn't say anything of the kind. I had no idea when I'd be back.'

He frowned. 'Of course you did. Lucretia always has to catch the last train from King's Cross, and that leaves at five minutes past eleven. What happened?'

'For heaven's sake,' snapped Kristina, her thoughts still back in St John's Wood and her body yearning for the touch of Tarquin's fingers and tongue on her burning skin. 'I'm not twelve you know. I can look after myself.'

'But where have you been?' persisted Ben.

'Seeing a lover!' snapped Kristina.

Ben laughed. 'Oh, well that's all right then! Did Lucretia watch or join in?'

Stop it, thought Kristina to herself. Just stop talking now, before you say something you'll regret. 'Joined in, naturally,' she said lightly. 'Look, I'm really tired. I'll take a shower and then go to bed. Sorry if I worried you, but she decided to stay in London overnight so there wasn't the usual rush.'

Ben seemed to accept this quite happily, and a few minutes later Kristina was standing beneath the hot spray, running her hands slowly over the red marks that covered the surface of her breasts. She wondered how long it would be before Tarquin called again.

Chapter Four

'I thought we might go to the cinema tonight,' suggested Ben as he and Kristina drank their early morning coffee and Ben munched on a slice of toast. 'That new French film looks good.'

'I'm not in the mood for that,' retorted Kristina. 'Why don't we try something different? How about an exotic film, one of those Indian love stories that go on for hours?'

Ben laughed. 'Since when were you interested in Indian love stories? We might as well go to *Pocahontas*!'

Kristina sighed. 'Forget it. It doesn't matter anyway; I'm out tonight.'

'But it's Wednesday!' exclaimed Ben. 'We always spend Wednesday nights together if we can.'

'I know, but tonight we can't. Besides, that might once have been true but it isn't any more. I don't think we've managed a Wednesday night together for the past six months.'

'Well that's not my fault,' declared Ben, glancing

at his watch and putting on his jacket. 'You're the one who's got the high-powered career.'

'We've both got high-powered careers,' said Kristina calmly.

Ben seemed appeased by her reply. 'Okay, we've both got high-powered careers. And that's the reason why we find it difficult to make time for each other. Although I must say that I sometimes seem to try harder than you do.'

'In what way?' asked Kristina.

'I don't think you had to stay out quite so late with Lucretia. I'm well aware of the money she makes you, but she isn't normally a night-owl. Surely you could have got away before you did?'

'Were you planning something special then?' asked Kristina, mildly intrigued.

'Yes, an early night.'

She was pleased when she heard the front door close behind him. An early night! If he only knew what she'd really been doing, she thought with a smile. She had no doubt that Tarquin Rashid had a high-powered career, but it didn't seem to limit his nocturnal activities.

As Kristina dressed for work, she ran her fingers over the slowly fading scratch marks on her breasts. She replayed the events of the previous evening in her mind and realised that her nipples were becoming erect, and her whole body began to feel tight with desire. She wondered if she'd hear from him today. He'd looked as intrigued by her as she'd been by him, but then again he could be seeing a lot of women, in which case she might only ever be sent for one night a week.

She spent so long daydreaming that she was nearly late leaving, and pulled on a straight black skirt and short cropped red jacket with gold buttons without stopping to think whether or not the outfit was suitable for her day. They were simply the first items she caught hold of in her wardrobe.

She knew she'd made a mistake when she walked into her office and Sue raised her eyebrows. 'You're looking very smart,' she murmured. 'Have you forgotten it's Tom's day today?'

'Tom?' asked Kristina in horror. Tom was a naturalist. He wandered the world studying rare animals, returning now and again with a mass of incredible photographs and pages of notes that he turned into instant best-sellers before disappearing into the uncivilised areas of the world again.

Kristina liked him, but he took no interest in material things and always turned up for their meetings in torn cords or jeans and with a shirt that had seen better days, the collar fraying and buttons invariably missing. On Tom's days Kristina took care to dress down and they ate sandwiches in her office because he hated the hustle and bustle of London restaurants.

'I'm going straight out after work,' she explained to Sue.

'Hope you don't scare Tom off then. He's only

seen sabre-toothed tigers and pygmies for the past ten months!' giggled Sue.

'Well, I'll growl for him, if you think that will help.'

'It might have some effect!' called Sue as Kristina closed her door and shut herself away.

For nearly half an hour she stared sightlessly out of her window, trying to recall the exact way she'd felt when she'd entered Tarquin's house the night before. She could remember the sensation of Lydia's hands when she'd been in the bath, and the feel of Tarquin's tongue between her thighs, but many of the moments had vanished into oblivion and she longed to recall them in vivid detail. To her annoyance the longer the time that elapsed the more difficult this became. It was as though everything that had happened to her in St John's Wood had been a dream, and after waking the dream was slowly vanishing, as the best dreams always did.

When the phone rang she began to shake with excitement and had to take some deep breaths before she spoke. 'Kristina Masterton here.'

'Hi, it's Jackie!' said her friend. 'I wondered how you were.'

'Jackie! I was going to call you later anyway. Guess what?'

'Tell me,' said Jackie with a laugh.

'I've had my first visit, and it was the most incredible experience of my life. No wonder you said you've changed since you joined the society. I'd never have believed the way I felt last night when . . .'

'Look, we shouldn't talk over the phone,' interrupted Jackie. 'Can we meet tonight? Say straight after work, about six?'

'Of course. Where?'

'Franco's. He never minds if we only have coffee, and I can't stay long because I'm seeing Laurence at eight, and if I'm late he sends me away.'

'Right, six at Franco's,' agreed Kristina quickly. She couldn't wait to tell her friend about Tarquin, everything he'd done, and also what he'd failed to do.

The rest of the day seemed to drag by. Kristina knew that she wasn't paying enough attention to Tom, and she was aware that he knew it too because he kept frowning and glancing at his shoes for inspiration.

'What's the matter?' he asked at one point. 'Don't you think people will be interested any more? Have things changed a lot while I've been gone? I knew it had to happen one day, but the publisher seemed keen when I set off.'

'No, no honestly it all sounds wonderful!' enthused Kristina. 'It isn't you, Tom, it's me. I think I'm coming down with the summer flu or something. I'm having trouble concentrating.'

'You ought to get more exercise,' Tom told her. 'Human beings weren't designed to sit at desks all day.'

Kristina thought this was probably true. She wondered if Tarquin had ever taken a woman over his desk, and decided that he probably had. Then her mind wandered and she conjured up a scenario where he was taking her over her desk, while Sue sat outside typing away, blissfully unaware of what was happening inside the main office.

'I'll leave it all with you then,' announced Tom, standing up and dumping a mound of papers and photographs on her desk.

'But Tom,' she protested, 'that doesn't look to be in any kind of order!'

'I've been trying to sort the order out with you for the past twenty minutes, Kristina,' he said softly. 'Either your flu's worse than you're letting on or you've something else on your mind. Well, I've done my bit, and now you can do yours. Let me know how much they're willing to pay up front and then I can leave the big cities behind again. It can't happen quickly enough for me either, I can tell you.'

Kristina felt mortified. 'I'm truly sorry, Tom. I know I haven't been any help, but I promise I'll get it sorted out and you'll end up with a terrific deal. Trust me.'

'I do, at least I always have before,' he muttered. 'You know where you can contact me. Hope to hear something soon.'

'Tom!' she called, but it was too late and he'd gone without even eating the sandwiches Sue had bought that morning.

'Damn!' she exclaimed, picking up a prawn and lettuce one and taking a large bite. 'Pull yourself together Kristina, this isn't good enough.'

She spent the rest of the day trying to make it up to

Tom by negotiating with more than her usual tenacity, and when she rang him at five-thirty and named the sum she'd finally obtained for world rights he was clearly both surprised and delighted.

'I thought you were losing your touch this morning,' he confessed as the conversation drew to a close. 'But I admit it, I was wrong. Get off home now and take care of that 'flu.'

'I'm just leaving,' she told him truthfully, but despite her excitement at seeing Jackie she was more than a little perturbed that someone as unassuming and generally unobservant as Tom should have thought she was losing her touch. It made her wonder how she'd be after her next visit to Tarquin.

At six o'clock there were few people in Franco's, and he gave Kristina and Jackie their usual table, tucked away in the far corner of the restaurant area, despite the fact that they were only there for a coffee.

'You come here and eat soon?' he queried, putting the cups of espresso down in front of them.

'We certainly will,' promised Jackie, flicking her blonde fringe out of her eyes, and for once Kristina realised that Franco was more interested in her friend than he was in her. She thought that it was probably because Jackie still had the glow about her that she and Ben had noticed the night they dined with her and Laurence.

'Tell me about your date then,' said Jackie, leaning across the table and lowering her voice. 'What did it feel like when you put on the bracelet?'

'Scary and exciting at the same time,' admitted Kristina. 'He's the most amazing man. I suppose it's his mixed blood or something, but he isn't like anyone else I've ever met. There's this masculinity about him that English men seem to have lost over the past few years.'

'They don't want to seem macho any more, that's why. They're all trying to be New Men.'

'Yes, but even at the times when they are in control they aren't like Tarquin! And it was so sensuous. He took everything at such a slow rate. You won't believe this but even when I left we still hadn't made love properly.'

Jackie's eyes widened in astonishment. 'You mean he hadn't . . .'

'No! I don't think he had an orgasm himself. He probably had one with Lydia after I'd gone. They seemed to know each other pretty well.'

'Didn't you mind?' asked Jackie.

Kristina shook her head. 'Not in the least. I would, if I thought I was never going to see him again, but he made it clear that wasn't the case and it just made me even more excited about our next meeting. And I've never had such an intense climax. After all that waiting I shattered into a thousand pieces!'

At the adjoining table two middle-aged women stopped drinking their coffees and turned their heads towards Kristina and Jackie. Jackie grinned. 'Better keep your voice down. We're not here to provide entertainment! How about having to obey? What was that like for you?'

'The biggest turn-on imaginable. The trouble is, all I've done today is go over and over it all in my mind. I couldn't concentrate properly on my work, and every time the phone went I thought it was Tarquin.'

'It gets worse,' Jackie assured her. 'Sometimes I can hardly string a sentence together at work after Laurence and I have had a long session. I'm losing interest in everything but our meetings, and I keep picturing things that I hope he'll do to me. Unfortunately, I can't vocalise them and there are one or two things he's never suggested.'

'Don't you get a chance to mention them when you take the bracelet off?' asked Kristina.

'I don't take it off very often,' confessed Jackie. 'I used to of course, at the beginning. Now, I prefer to keep it on even if we're at the cinema or the health club. The other night he made me take off my bikini bottom and let him make love to me in the pool while other people swam all around us. I was terrified we'd be spotted and thrown out, but at the same time it made me come harder than ever before.'

'Does he ever do things that you don't like?' asked Kristina curiously.

Jackie hesitated. 'He's done things that I wasn't sure about to start with, but I've always gone along with them and by the end I find that I like them too.'

'Why do you go along with them?'

Jackie looked slightly embarrassed. 'I guess I'm afraid that if I don't he won't ever see me again.'

'But he's never hurt you?' persisted Kristina, remembering the thin red nail marks that had covered her breasts.

Jackie glanced away. 'It all depends on what you mean by hurting someone, doesn't it? He's tied me up and sometimes punishes me, but to be honest those are the best times. When I'm helpless and being disciplined I feel as though it doesn't matter how extreme my sexual reaction is because it isn't my fault. He's making me behave that way, and so he takes the responsibility out of my hands. If my fellow feminists could hear me they'd probably have me lynched, but it's the truth, and after all it isn't real life, so where's the harm?'

Kristina shivered. 'I think that if Tarquin ever starts doing things like that, I could very easily be totally taken over by him. You were right, Jackie. This game's like a drug, and I'm not sure that people like us should get addicted.'

'Why not? We work hard, we deserve the right to play hard as well,' retorted Jackie.

'Agreed, but suppose that by playing hard we find that we can't work as hard any more? What happens then?'

Jackie went pink and she picked up her shoulder bag. 'Who cares? It's time I was off. I would just say this though, Kristina. Your Tarquin sounds a far more subtle and dangerous type than Laurence. With Laurence I knew what I was getting right from the first moment. You've no idea where Tarquin's going to lead you, so perhaps you're right to be nervous. If you're not sure, don't see him again, because believe me once you're really involved there's no way out. I'd rather lose everything I've got than give up Laurence, and that includes my job. There, I've shocked you, haven't I?'

'A bit,' admitted Kristina.

'Well, it's the truth, so remember what I said and be warned. Keep in touch. I want to know what happens next time.'

Kristina watched her friend walk out of the restaurant and slowly drank the last of her coffee. She wanted to know the same thing, and hoped it wouldn't be too long before she learned exactly where Tarquin was leading her.

Five nights later, at nine-fifteen precisely, she was standing once more outside Tarquin's house in St John's Wood, her pulse racing as she rang the doorbell. Just as she'd thought the call was never coming he'd rung her at home, about three minutes after she'd arrived back from work, and instructed her to be at his home that same evening.

It had been very difficult making up an excuse for Ben at such short notice, but in the end she'd invented a sudden visit from an American agent who was only free for the one evening and had to see her. Ben had frowned, but hadn't questioned her story at all, and she was surprised to find that she didn't feel as ashamed as she should at lying to him.

Once again Lydia opened the door, but this time Tarquin didn't come to greet her himself. Lydia led her into one of the downstairs rooms, opening the heavy door and then standing back to allow Kristina to enter.

The room was in total contrast to the second floor bedroom. All the furniture was modern: glass-topped tables were surrounded by white wooden chairs with modern striped cushions and the curtains at the windows were cream with tiny pink rosebuds on them. Only the *chaise longue* at the far end of the room looked old-fashioned and out of place.

'I'm glad you were able to make it,' said Tarquin as he came into the room behind her. 'I think that this will be a very special night for us both. Let me take your jacket and then you can put on the bracelet.'

At last the moment had arrived again, and the minute Tarquin had removed her jacket Kristina held out her arm and he slipped the bracelet over her hand.

As soon as the tiny gold chain was round her wrist the atmosphere changed. Tarquin's eyes swept over her and he shrugged off his own jacket, placing it carefully over the arm of the nearest chair. Then he loosened the knot of his tie and undid his top shirt button without once pausing in his serious assessment of the slim figure in front of him.

'Take off your dress and all your underclothes,' he instructed her. 'Make sure that you keep your eyes down the entire time, until I give you permission to look at me again.'

Kristina didn't want to look away from him. She wanted to see his face as she removed her clothes, see his eyes light up with appreciation and desire, but the fact that she couldn't, that he wouldn't allow her even that small pleasure, merely increased her excitement.

She struggled briefly with the zip at the back of her dress and then, once that was undone, let the dress fall to the floor and stepped out of it, leaving it in a heap on the carpet. She turned slightly sideways knowing that her high heels and hold-up stockings emphasised her tight buttocks, and was rewarded by the faintest intake of breath from Tarquin.

Taking care to keep her eyes down in feigned modesty she bent forward from the waist to step out of her half-slip, and her underwired push-up bra made the most of her normally small breasts, creating what she knew must be an attractive amount of cleavage.

Her panties were bikini-style and she hooked one hand into the side nearest him and then eased them down her legs as gracefully as she could manage. Once she'd stepped out of those she was left in only her bra and stockings and the need to look at him and see what effect her slow, careful undressing was having on him was almost overwhelming, but she knew that to disobey would be fatal and with an inwards sigh rolled down her stockings, stroking her legs sensuously as she did so.

Now there was only her bra left and as she reached behind her she paused for a second, almost teasing him as to whether or not she was going to remove it, then she unhooked the clasp and dropped the garment to one side where it joined her slip and panties.

'Face me and lift your eyes to mine,' murmured Tarquin, his voice huskier than usual. Kristina was warming to the game now and she took her time over obeying but finally she was facing him, standing directly opposite him, and she raised her blue eyes to him, lifting her chin in an unconscious gesture of defiance.

'You did that well,' he said approvingly. 'I think it's time the rest of my clothes were removed too. I'll ring for Lydia.'

To Kristina's surprise he pressed a bell concealed in the fire surround and almost immediately Lydia glided into the room. She was wearing a long purple sari trimmed with gold and looked beautiful and exotic. She needed no instructions but went straight to her employer and started to remove his shirt and tie.

As she worked, Tarquin continued studying Kristina. 'Turn around slowly,' he said when Lydia was removing his trousers. 'I'd like to see what you look like from all angles.'

Kristina obediently turned around, wishing that she was just a fraction more voluptuous. When she'd turned full circle his expression was thoughtful, and she had no idea if he found her pleasing or not.

'Turn and face the opposite end of the room,' he said, and this time she wished she didn't have to obey because Lydia was about to remove his boxer shorts and she wanted to see him fully naked for the first time.

'Quickly,' he said abruptly, and unlike before there was a suggestion of impatience in his soft voice. Swiftly she turned, and remained staring at the *chaise longue* at the far end of the room until suddenly she felt his lips on the back of her neck and his hands coming to rest on each side of her naked waist. He kissed the top vertebrae of her spine and moved down the curve of her back, licking and kissing as he went, until he reached her waist. Then he squeezed her with his hands, his strong fingers pressing into her delicate flesh for an instant before she was released. Finally he walked round to the front of her and at last she was able to see him naked.

He was, by any standards, a well-built man. His shoulders were broad, his chest and upper arms muscular and his silky golden-brown skin had less hair on it than she'd expected. His waist was narrow, as were his hips, but his legs were even more muscular than his arms and chest, and his penis, which was fully erect and standing up proudly from the surrounding dark pubic hair, was huge with a very dark head. She shuddered at the prospect of him inside her, easing the ache that she could already feel between her thighs.

Tarquin let her look at him for several minutes, then caught hold of her right hand and led her over to the *chaise longue*. She expected him to lay her down on it, but instead he left her standing at the foot of it before releasing her briefly to pick up a silk scarf from a small table.

'I want to tie your hands behind your back,' he said

quietly. 'If, after I've tied you, there comes a time when you wish to remove the bracelet then you must tell me and the evening will immediately be terminated. You need have no fear that this will not happen. My pleasure comes from my partner's pleasure. If you are not enjoying yourself then neither will I. In addition, if I should break the rules of the society I would be expelled from it, and that is not something I would wish to happen. Having told you this, I shall now proceed.'

Kristina's mouth went dry. After spending so much time with her eyes downcast, and with no control over the events of the evening, she was feeling totally lost. This was a world of which she had no experience, but a world she was eager to explore further. In order to have Tarquin make love to her fully, to have him inside her, spasming in ecstasy, she was willing to allow anything to happen.

Very carefully he tied her hands behind her back, and then turned away from her and with one swift movement removed the waiting Lydia's sari from her so that she too was totally naked.

'Kristina, you must remain still,' he said, his mouth curving upwards in a slow smile. 'I'm going to touch Lydia in various ways, and if you think that such a touch would pleasure you then you may say "yes". That is the only word you are allowed to utter during this stage of the evening.'

Kristina felt like crying from frustration. His lips on her back, his hands on her waist and the sight of his nakedness had brought her to fever pitch and when he'd tied her hands she'd been expecting him to take her in some complicated way. Never for one moment had she expected him to leave her to watch while he touched another woman.

Lydia and Tarquin stood facing each other, with Kristina on Tarquin's left hand side. She watched in despairing silence as he poured some oil into the palm of his left hand and then slowly began to massage it over the Indian girl's breasts.

Lydia gave a tiny groan of delight, and Kristina had to bite on her lip to keep herself silent. She watched as Lydia's nipples hardened and extended and then Tarquin looked across at her, his eyes deceptively kind. Suddenly she remembered what was expected of her. 'Yes,' she said hoarsely.

He nodded, and now he spread his fingers wider across Lydia's ribcage as he continued to massage the oil into her flesh. When he reached the top of her pubic hair he turned her round so that her back was to him and Kristina watched as he pushed the Indian girl's upper body down until her forehead was resting on the chaise longue and then tipped some of the oil into the small dent at the base of her spine.

As Lydia gasped Kristina felt her own flesh jump in sympathy and suddenly Tarquin was kneading the oil firmly into Lydia's rounded buttocks. Then he parted the fleshy globes and very slowly inserted one well-oiled finger into the servant girl's puckered rear opening.

Lydia gave a low moan of delight and thrust her belly forward as she tightened her buttocks and drew the softly caressing finger deeper inside her. The cheeks of Kristina's bottom also tightened and her hips tilted forward while her internal muscles twitched with desire.

Tarquin glanced across at her, his eyebrows raised in a silent question. At first Kristina didn't notice him as, with flushed cheeks and throbbing breasts, she struggled to keep silent. Just before he looked away she caught his eye. 'Yes!' she shouted, and again he nodded so that she knew that in time this pleasure too would be hers.

Tarquin's free hand reached round the front of the bent-over Lydia and began to massage her abdomen. He pressed firmly, and the pressure caused the Indian girl to cry out with excitement as her desire mounted.

The watching Kristina could see the tension in the young woman's body and understood it only too well as her own was throbbing and aching with the need for a climax. She'd never watched another couple make love before, and was finding it more erotic than she'd imagined possible. Lydia's tiny gasps and moans only increased Kristina's need and when the large light-brown hand moved lower down the servant girl's stomach and began to explore her soft pubic mound Kristina felt herself grow damp and her outer sex lips began to open as her state of arousal increased.

'Yes!' she said urgently, this time not even waiting for Tarquin's question. He flicked his large dark eyes sideways at her, and then she realised that his fingers were busy between Lydia's thighs because suddenly the girl was squirming and wriggling frantically, her breathing rapid and loud in the otherwise silent room.

Despite the fact that no one was touching her, that her body was without any form of stimulation, the sight of Lydia climbing towards her climax was enough to start Kristina on the ascent towards her own release. She wished that her hands were free so that she could touch herself between her thighs in the way Tarquin was touching Lydia. Then with startling abruptness, Lydia's entire body was shaken from head to foot as she came with whimpering, gutteral sounds of gratitude.

Those were the most sensual sounds Kristina had heard in her entire life and she realised that she too was balanced on the brink of an orgasm. She concentrated on the sensations deep within her: the tight coil of sexual tension behind her pelvic bone, the bittersweet ache between her thighs and the tingling streaks of excitement from her swollen breasts, but before she could actually manage to force herself over the edge Tarquin had released the Indian girl and was standing in front of her.

'You are not allowed to come,' he warned her, allowing one finger to touch the very tip of each of her erect nipples in turn. 'Not until you too have been stimulated as Lydia was. Now, I shall untie you and then we will begin.'

'But I'm nearly there!' protested Kristina. 'I won't be able to wait until you've done all that!'

'I am ordering you to wait,' he told her, and his left hand gently tugged on the slim gold bracelet, reminding her that her wishes were of no importance.

Kristina was shaking with desire as he led her across the room to where Lydia had been standing. Then with such slowness that it was a kind of torture, he began to pour the oil into his left hand and massaged her breasts, just as he'd massaged Lydia's.

Kristina's entire body was so over-sensitive after all she'd witnessed that even the most innocuous touch felt like the final caress that her orgasm needed, and by the time he'd turned her and was sliding his finger into her tight rear opening she knew that no matter what he wanted there was no way she could obey him. She longed to do as he said, was fighting as hard as she'd ever fought to subdue her frantic flesh, but the sensations were too exquisite.

When he reached round her bent-over body and began to massage her straining belly she knew that she was lost because the deeply coiled tightness suddenly released itself into a wonderful spreading sensation and heat flooded through her as his clever finger moved against the highly sensitive walls of her rectum. Her body went rigid as every muscle contracted prior to the explosive moment of release and Kristina moaned in despair.

'Not yet,' said Tarquin calmly. 'I still haven't touched your clitoris, you must wait for that.'

Kristina heard the words, but there was no way that

she could obey them, and almost before he'd finished speaking the giant orgasm crashed over her. Her breasts were stimulated by the brocade covering of the *chaise longue* as she thrashed wildly from side to side until the final flickers died away and then she was still. Still, silent and terrified that because she'd disobeyed him she would be sent home, and never see him or feel his hands on her again.

'I accept that you tried to obey,' he remarked casually, 'but it seems that you need more practice. What do you think Estelle?'

Shocked, Kristina glanced over her shoulder. To her horror there was another woman in the room. An elegant, voluptuous woman with long brown hair and pale green eyes. She was dressed in a tight calf-length black skirt and a long white-and-black cotton top.

'I agree,' said the woman, her voice clipped and commanding. 'She's wonderful to watch though and I'm sure she'll improve with practice. Watching her tonight's been very stimulating!'

Tarquin helped the still-shaken Kristina to sit on the *chaise longue.* 'Sit up straight, with your breasts thrust forward,' he murmured. 'Estelle likes to see women's breasts when they're excited, so I'll try and do something with them.'

He lowered his head to her quiescent nipples and sucked on each of them in turn until Kristina felt them hardening between his lips. When he was satisfied with each one he tugged softly at it as he withdrew his mouth and when he stood back from her she knew that once more her breasts were firm and the pink nipples hard and pointed.

'Are you going to make love to me before I leave, darling?' Estelle asked Tarquin after looking at Kristina's body with approval. 'I'm sure your visitor would enjoy watching us, and I'm certainly ready for you.'

Kristina knew that she wouldn't enjoy it at all. She wanted him to enter her tonight, it was her turn, but because she'd failed the test to obey totally she realised that once more she was going to leave the house without him having actually entered her.

'I think not,' said Tarquin, standing in front of Kristina with his hands clasped loosely in front of him. 'I don't want to wait any longer before I possess her. Her forfeit for failing to obey will have to be paid next time.'

'But I want you now,' said Estelle sharply.

Kristina was fascinated to see that Tarquin's habitually sombre expression didn't lighten for Estelle any more than it did for her. In fact, if anything he looked irritated by her objection.

'Lie at one end of the couch,' he said to Kristina. 'Prop your shoulders against the cushions there.' When she was in position he climbed on to the *chaise longue* as well and then pushed upwards beneath her buttocks until she lifted her legs. Next he lay face down on top of her and with her knees bent she was able to hook her ankles over his shoulders while he took his weight on his hands, lifting himself off the couch until she could feel the tip of his erection nudging against her moist opening.

Estelle stood beside them and very softly stroked the side of Kristina's body, running her hand in a sweeping movement from the outer side of her breast down to her hip bone. Kristina shuddered and twitched and felt herself opening wide between her thighs.

Carefully Tarquin eased the tip of his penis inside her, taking his time so that she was slowly able to take the entire length of him. Then, once he was in place, he withdrew a little and she gave a cry of protest.

'Push against me,' he urged her. 'When I withdraw, you push upwards, then you withdraw and I'll plunge deeper again.'

Kristina found this easy to do because every time he withdrew from her, her body automatically surged up towards his, desperately seeking the wonderful sensation of fullness that he was at last giving her. After a few alternate thrusting movements she caught the exact rhythm that he wanted, and suddenly they were moving in perfect harmony and she felt the sparks of another impending orgasm smouldering behind her clitoris.

'I want you to tell me when you're about to come,' he whispered.

Kristina concentrated on the sensations as they built with glorious speed towards an orgasm. She climbed steadily towards the peak, and then at last felt the heavy fluttering pulse start to throb somewhere deep inside her, a pulse that always preceded that final rush of ecstasy.

'I'm coming now,' she whispered, and at once he changed the rhythm, thrusting himself fully into her until their pubic hairs were touching and then rocking his hips without withdrawing his penis at all.

With this deep penetration he seemed to reach some part of her that had never been touched before and after a few seconds she heard herself screaming aloud with delirious excitement as her body once more convulsed and she came in a long shuddering rush of release that left her totally exhausted.

With a smile Estelle picked up the iPod that had been lying on the table nearby and stopped it recording. She knew that Tarquin would want it for their next session.

Tarquin looked down at Kristina and as she stared up at him, her eyes wide and shining, he suddenly smiled one of his heart-stopping smiles and she smiled back at him. Then he withdrew from her, climbed off the *chaise longue* and picked up his clothes. 'I shall dress in another room. By the time I return I would like you to be gone. Leave the bracelet with Estelle.'

After the brief instant of intimacy when he'd smiled at her, and the incredible pleasure that he'd given her body, this brusque, indifferent dismissal came as a terrible shock to Kristina. She looked at him in amazement and he looked calmly back at her, almost as though he was waiting for her to speak. Then she remembered that she was still wearing the bracelet and as he saw that realisation dawn in her eyes he broke eye contact by blinking twice in rapid succession and then, picking up his clothes, he left the room.

Kristina mentally filed the blinking away in her memory. She'd noticed that he often did this, usually when he wanted to shut himself off from a moment that threatened to become too intimate. When he did it she felt that it was a small victory to her, just as his smiles were a victory, although of a different kind.

Estelle remained where she was, sitting in one of the chairs and watching Kristina closely. 'You've got a nice body,' she remarked, watching her dress. 'Rather small breasts for Tarquin's taste, but everything's nicely shaped.'

Kristina drew off the bracelet and handed it to Estelle. 'This is for Tarquin. If you don't mind I'd prefer not to have to listen to your comments about my body. They don't really interest me.'

She was surprised at how quickly she was able to return to the everyday Kristina now that Tarquin had left the room. Estelle looked surprised too.

'You're right,' she acknowledged. 'I don't belong to the society so the rules don't apply when Tarquin isn't here. He likes me to join in though, which is always fun. Most of his women haven't lasted long. They start to fall in love with him, or object to some of the things he wants to do. I've got the feeling he's chosen well with you.'

Kristina zipped up her dress, picked up her handbag and walked out into the hallway. 'If you're his mistress I'm surprised you're not put out that he needed to join,' she commented.

'Why should it worry me? It's only a bit of fun; a break from his normal way of life. We all need diversions, as you've obviously discovered. I recognised you of course, although I'm more used to seeing you with your clothes on. *The Publishing News* doesn't run a sexy agent photo page yet!'

'You read *The Publishing News*?' queried Kristina, opening the front door.

'But of course. I'm the new senior editor at Stoddart-Wades. I was appointed after the merger.'

'Fiction or non-fiction?' asked Kristina, assessing whether or not Estelle could be useful to her professionally.

Estelle smiled. 'At the moment non-fiction, but I'm beginning to think fiction might be more fun! Have you thought about writing your own novel?'

For the first time fear of discovery touched Kristina. 'This has nothing to do with my work,' she said sharply. 'I'm sure Tarquin wouldn't expect me to mention anything to a fellow psychologist.'

'Of course he wouldn't, but then Tarquin's a member of the society, and I'm not, so the same rules don't really apply. Don't worry,' she added as Kristina frowned. 'Your secret's absolutely safe with me. It's more than my life's worth to betray any of Tarquin's confidences. As you can imagine, the last thing I'd ever do is upset him. Once you find a lover like that you make sure you hang on to him.'

'I wasn't worried,' lied Kristina. 'I know that absolute discretion is assured. Now, if you don't mind I must get back home.'

'Me too,' said Estelle, closing the heavy door behind them. 'I don't live here. Tarquin hates anyone sharing his life. I've got my own pad round the corner, near enough for off-the-cuff meetings and far enough away to give him the illusion of freedom.'

'I think you're the one with illusions,' said Kristina sweetly as she hailed a taxi.

Estelle watched her go and her eyes were thoughtful. Until now she'd enjoyed all the games that had gone on at the house in St John's Wood since Tarquin joined the society, but she wasn't quite so sure about this young woman. Then she thought of some of the things that lay ahead of Kristina and shrugged her worries aside. They all took the bracelet off at some point, and Kristina – although intelligent and sensuous – would be no different in the end.

Kristina arrived back home and found that Ben had waited up for her. 'Get any good deals done?' he asked.

'She's going to try and sell three books for me that I haven't given to my usual agent in the States. I hope she comes up trumps but I'll have to see,' said Kristina.

'Well, you look pretty cheerful anyway. I haven't seen

you with such good colour since we went to Greece for those two weeks last year.'

'Must be the wine!' laughed Kristina as she fled to the bathroom to shower off all traces of her evening with Tarquin.

To her horror, Ben was obviously feeling amorous when she returned to the bedroom and the moment she got into bed he curled himself round her back and his hands started fondling her breasts through her nightdress. She remembered the way Tarquin had oiled them, and the teasing caress of his thumbs as they stroked the sensitive undersides of each globe. Ben's squeezing seemed so heavy-handed in comparison that she knew she couldn't stand it.

'Leave me alone,' she said wearily. 'I'm tired.'

'I'm not,' he retorted and she felt his erection nudging against her buttocks.

'Ben, please, I'm not in the mood,' she murmured.

He laughed. 'You're always in the mood if you try. Come on, Kristina, it's been ages.'

'It has not!'

His hands were inside her nightdress now, rubbing her legs and insinuating their way higher towards her pubic mound, which still felt heavy and slightly sore from Tarquin's enthusiastic love-making.

'I really don't want this!' she protested.

'What's the matter?' he teased. 'Don't I turn you on any more?'

She thought of Tarquin, of his tall, muscular body

with the smooth golden-brown skin and his large black eyes shining with intelligence as he studied her body. Without thinking she wrenched herself away from Ben's all too familiar advances. 'No, you don't!' she snapped.

There was a moment of complete silence. Ben immediately left her alone and turned away from her.

'Look, I'm sorry,' she murmured, 'but I hate being pressured. You know that, and it isn't like you.'

'If you weren't so wrapped up in your bloody career,' he said angrily, 'I'd think you'd found yourself another man, but you're more likely to be in love with a book.'

For a moment she felt guilty, but then he turned and held her from behind again and she felt her body tense. 'I'm sorry,' he whispered. 'I'm just being selfish. I know how hard you work, it was really unfair of me.'

Instead of feeling even more guilty, or realising how lucky she was to have such an understanding man, Kristina was appalled to discover that her first reaction was one of contempt. Never in a hundred years, would Tarquin say such a thing, she thought, before checking herself.

She didn't know the real Tarquin, she said sternly to herself. He too might behave like Ben in real life. The only Tarquin she knew was the one who belonged to the society and was her master while she wore the bracelet. It was dangerous to confuse the fiction of that man, the man who made her body tingle even at the memory of him, with the real Tarquin. After all, she, Kristina, didn't normally behave the way she did in Tarquin's presence and neither would she want to all the time.

The problem was, she was enjoying it far more than she'd expected, and rather than enhancing her real life, her two nocturnal visits to St John's Wood had made her less contented with it.

Kristina fell asleep daydreaming about what might happen the next time she and Tarquin met.

Chapter Five

Has Laurence ever let people watch when you and he are together?' Kristina asked Jackie the following Friday lunchtime as they nibbled on their barbecued spare ribs at Jackie's favourite Chinese restaurant in Queensway.

Jackie dipped her fingers in the fingerbowl and then wiped them on her large white napkin. 'I don't really think I want to discuss that. Why?'

Kristina shrugged. 'It's only that I thought if it did happen, to you or to me, then it might be a bit of a security risk.'

'Of course it wouldn't! Anyone who takes part in anything connected with sessions arranged through the society is bound by their rules. Everyone knows that. Didn't you get a list of the official rules and regulations when you were accepted?'

Kristina shook her head. 'No, I never heard anything official. It was all done over the phone.'

'Well, I can let you see mine if it will make you feel

better. Do you want any of those pancakes? If not I'll eat them!'

'Go ahead, I'm not very hungry today.'

Jackie grinned. 'Worn out by the incredible Tarquin?'

'I was, but I haven't seen him for three days. No, I'm worn out coping with work. For some strange reason it doesn't give me the same buzz it used to. I pulled off a really good deal today. One of the major publishing houses bought a book I've been trying to sell for two years, and they're going to give it a big push. I should feel as though I'm walking on air, but instead I feel sort of flat. When I got the offer I put the phone down and thought, so what? I mean, that's crazy!'

'I did warn you,' Jackie reminded her. 'Real life isn't quite so exciting once you've got the thrill of your secret life.'

'Then there's Ben,' went on Kristina. 'Obviously things weren't brilliant between us before, but now I can't stand having him around me.'

'Then ask him to leave. I got rid of William pretty sharply, I can tell you, and I've never regretted it. We only live once and we're a long time dead if you want some clichés to back me up!'

'But he hasn't done anything wrong.'

'No,' said Jackie with a laugh. 'Neither is he Mr Right, so ditch him.'

'But Tarquin isn't Mr Right. I've no idea what he's like really, and it's never going to be any more than it is now so . . .'

'So what?' demanded Jackie. 'You don't want him living with you do you? You wouldn't want to see his dirty socks or find yourselves watching TV together! For heaven's sake Kristina, this is the whole point of the society. You get what you want, what you *need* and you don't have any of the boring parts of a relationship.'

'It's only that sometimes I wish I could get to know him better. To ask him about himself, talk for a while, or possibly suggest some things I'd like to do to him!'

'I expect he'll take you out one evening when you're not wearing the bracelet. Talk to him then. That's what Laurence and I used to do. We don't any more because we both enjoy it more when I'm wearing the bracelet.'

Kristina sighed. 'I'm not sure Tarquin's the kind of man who actually wants to know me without the bracelet on. He's got a permanent mistress who presumably supplies the mental as well as physical stimulation that a proper relationship needs.'

'Look,' said Jackie seriously. 'The whole point of this is that it's an improper relationship! You've only seen the man twice, believe me he's bound to have a lot of surprises in store for you yet. Don't start getting intense about the mental side of things, make the most of the physical.'

'But he's such a fascinating person. It's the way he looks at me, as though he's trying to work out exactly what makes me tick. And last time, when we'd finished, he really smiled at me as though I meant something to him.'

'He's a psychologist isn't he? Perhaps he's going to write a paper on you! The trouble is, Kristina, you're trying to justify overwhelming lust but you don't have to justify it, all you have to do is enjoy it.'

'So, you aren't interested in Laurence except for sex, is that what you're saying?' asked Kristina.

Jackie dropped her eyes. 'No, what I'm doing is trying to stop you from making the same mistake as me. I'm crazy about the man, sometimes we do things that frighten me, they're so way out but I can't stop because I have this terrible need to keep him happy. Me, the woman who advises other women to leave their control-freak partners and get themselves a life!'

'Who needs to get a life?' asked a male voice, and both women turned their heads as Laurence appeared from the far corner of the room.

Jackie looked at him in surprise. 'What are you doing here?'

'The same as you, eating a very nice Chinese meal. You mentioned it the other night and I thought I'd give it a try. Hello, Kristina, you're looking very well,' he added.

Kristina looked thoughtfully at him, mentally comparing him with Tarquin. They couldn't have been more dissimilar. Where Tarquin was dark and muscular Laurence was fair and angular, and where Tarquin's eyes would change and soften Laurence's pale blue ones were like splinters of ice. She could well imagine that he liked very dangerous sex games, but as he ran his fingers through Jackie's hair Kristina understood why her friend was obsessed with him. Like Tarquin he was a one-off and she wondered what it would be like to spend just one evening with him.

Laurence looked pointedly at Kristina's wrists. 'Short on jewellery today?' he queried.

'I never wear much for work. I don't want my clients or the publishers to think I'm doing too well,' she replied smoothly.

'Quite, but at night the bangles and necklaces come out in full I hear.'

'Yes, they do.'

'You and your . . . friend must meet up with us some time,' he suggested, and Kristina was surprised to hear a muted sound of protest from Jackie.

'Perhaps we will,' she said levelly. 'At the moment though we don't go out.'

He smiled thinly. 'Early days! I find that going out adds a certain something to it all, isn't that right, Jacqueline?'

'Yes,' she agreed brightly. 'But I'm not sure we'd be the right companions for them.'

'I'd like to find out,' murmured Laurence. 'Anyway, I can't stop. Yet another important meeting. You both know what it's like I'm sure, being such successful ladies in your own right.'

Kristina watched him go and didn't know whether she loathed him or found him intriguing.

'He's mine,' said Jackie softly. 'Don't get involved.

You're happy with Tarquin; Laurence would spoil that for you. He likes spoiling things.'

'He isn't yours, he's a member of the society, the same as Tarquin, but I wouldn't dream of getting involved. He isn't my type at all,' said Kristina, secretly shocked by the expression on her friend's face.

'Good,' said Jackie, getting briskly to her feet. 'Time for me to go I think. I'll pay on my way out. This one's on me.'

'But we haven't had coffee!' exclaimed Kristina.

'Sorry, no time. Call me when you've had your next visit.'

Kristina realised that Jackie was hoping to catch up with Laurence, although why she needed to talk to him in the middle of the day she couldn't imagine. So this is what she meant about people getting too involved, she thought with a wry smile. Jackie was clearly besotted, and not at all anxious to let Kristina learn anything intimate about Laurence at first hand.

When Kristina got back to the office there was a scribbled note on her desk from Sue.

Someone called Tarquin rang, he said you had a meeting at four. It isn't in the diary but he rang off before I could tell him. I'm at the dentist. Hope you can sort it all out without upsetting anyone.

Kristina glanced at her watch. It was five to three, which gave her very little time indeed to deal with her work and get to St John's Wood, but she had no intention of missing the appointment.

She arrived at Tarquin's house with two minutes to spare; hot, out of breath and guilty because of all the work she'd left on her desk, but still trembling with urgent desire.

Tarquin himself opened the door to her. This time he was wearing a dark grey suit with a grey and white striped shirt and a dark red tie. He looked immaculate and so desirable that her mouth immediately went dry.

'I'm glad you got my message,' he said softly, taking her bag and jacket. 'I have something rather special laid on for this afternoon. There's no one in the house but us, so you'll be able to make as much noise as you like.'

She frowned, uncertain what he meant, but when he held out the bracelet she didn't hesitate for a moment and the second it was on her wrist she felt her body stir in anticipation of whatever delights he had in store for her.

This time they only went up one flight of stairs and into a large but almost empty room with heavy drapes across the windows. There was concealed lighting round the walls with one spotlight that centred on the middle of the room. Kristina gazed at what the spotlight revealed and was ashamed to find that she was becoming damp between her thighs.

Tarquin's eyes followed her gaze. 'I know the beam's a little high, but as long as you stand on a footstool you'll be perfectly comfortable. I think that today, I shall undress you. I have to say, Kristina, that this is something I've been anticipating with a great deal of pleasure.'

Jackie's words at lunchtime rang through her head. 'Believe me,' she'd said, 'he's bound to have a lot of surprises in store for you yet.' Well, she'd been right, now all Kristina needed was the courage to follow them through.

'Time to start,' said Tarquin, his voice soft, and very gently he began to unbutton her blouse.

This time he seemed to want her undressed quickly, and although he didn't hurry neither did he prolong the removal of each garment. However, he took care to allow his hands to caress her taut flesh at every opportunity, and when he unhooked her bra he once more kissed a trail down the length of her spine in a gesture that Kristina was beginning to recognise as his trademark, the preliminary to their times together.

As soon as she was naked he removed his own clothes and then stood in front of her. This time he looked directly into her eyes as he spoke. 'Hold out your hands, I want to cuff your wrists.' Although his tone was still quiet and his expression calm, there was a questioning look in his eyes and Kristina knew without doubt that this was the moment when some of his other women had chosen to remove their bracelets.

For her though it was probably the most exciting moment of their meetings so far. This was something she and Ben had never indulged in; she'd always said that any kind of bondage was demeaning, but now she was on the brink of a climax at the mere thought of it and without a word she extended her hands.

The cuffs were real leather, thick and adjustable so that he was able to fasten them firmly around her slender wrists. A small chain ran between them, and as he led her across the room towards the beam she saw that the loop hanging from the rope in the middle of the beam had a clip on the end of it. A clip that would undoubtedly fasten on to the chain between her wrists.

Without another word Tarquin fetched a padded footstool from the side of the room. Putting his hands on either side of her waist he lifted her easily up on to it. 'Lift your hands above your head,' he whispered. 'I'm going to fasten you to the loop now, and then your eyes will be covered by a blindfold. Remember, if you wish to remove the bracelet, tell me.'

Kristina nodded her understanding and then obeyed. He stood behind her as he clicked the loop on to the wrist chain and now she was standing with her arms fully extended upwards and very slightly back, with her spine curved in and her breasts pushed forward. She was so stimulated by what was happening that her nipples were stiff and there was a strange tingling sensation in her belly that she'd never felt before.

Still behind her, Tarquin ran a hand down the curve of her back. 'You look wonderful,' he said softly. 'I wish that I could take a picture, but the rules don't allow it. Now for the blindfold.'

The mask that covered her eyes was made of soft, thick velvet and no chink of light penetrated the fabric. It felt extraordinary to be standing balanced on a stool, naked except for cuffs and a blindfold and totally at the mercy of a virtual stranger, extraordinary and incredibly arousing. Kristina knew that the moment he touched her anywhere intimate she'd come as she'd never come before.

She didn't hear him move round to the front of her, and so the first caress across her breasts came as a total shock. It wasn't just the caress, it was the way she was touched. Tarquin wasn't using his hands, instead it felt like some kind of heavy fabric that was being drawn slowly across the surface of each of her breasts in turn. She sighed as she felt her breast tissue swelling, and then suddenly the caress changed and she was struck lightly just below the rounded mounds.

It didn't hurt, but it startled her and she wasn't certain that she liked the feeling, but before she could say anything a slightly heavier blow fell, right across her erect nipples. This time there was no room for doubt in her mind because the searing pleasure streaked downwards towards her navel and she shuddered with the thrill.

'It's a latex pleasure whip,' said Tarquin. 'Many women find it delightful, but naturally it isn't to everyone's taste.'

'I like it,' she whispered.

For a brief moment she felt one of his hands between her thighs. 'So you do,' he said, his voice amused. 'Then this will definitely be a very agreeable afternoon for us both.'

He trailed the whip down across her belly, drew it across the front of her thighs, and then walked behind her and struck her more firmly across the cheeks of her bottom. For a moment she experienced a burning sensation, but that was immediately blotted out by the feeling of his lips pressing against the mark and he licked along the line with such delicacy that once more she began to tremble and she felt the first tiny pulse beats behind her clitoris. Tarquin saw her start to rise up on her toes and knew that she was very near a climax, which wasn't his intention at this stage, so he stopped and put the pleasure whip to one side.

'Please, don't stop,' said Kristina. 'I liked it.'

'But I was bored,' he said quietly. 'Perhaps later I'll use it again. For now I want to try something different.'

A few seconds later his hands were roaming over her buttocks and she felt him spreading a cool gel there. Next he parted them and eased a little gel round her rear opening before moving round to the front of her suspended, tightly stretched body.

Just as he began to spread the gel over her belly and inner thighs she felt a glow start to spread through her buttocks and her rectum twitched with the heat, a heat that made her long for something else, something to assuage the deep need the gel was creating. She twisted her body from side to side and heard Tarquin give a soft laugh.

'I know, I know, you want me to touch you there, but first I must spread it here. And perhaps a little lower?' He hesitated at the tops of her inner thighs, but when she didn't answer he spread it there as well so that by the time he'd finished she felt literally on fire with desire and her flesh was warm and swollen.

She realised that he must have knelt in front of her, because next he parted her outer sex lips and then his tongue was gliding up and down her damp inner channel, swirling and teasing at the needy flesh without ever actually touching the swollen clitoris.

The pulse drummed harder inside her and her whole body tensed. 'I'm coming!' she screamed, only to have him remove his tongue and allow her sex lips to close. 'Not yet I think,' he said calmly.

'I want to come now!' she shouted, as her body continued to swell and pulsate.

'But I wish you to wait. I have another surprise for you. Listen, do you recognise this?' And as she twisted and turned helplessly on the end of the chain she heard her own voice, recorded at their last session and listened despairingly to her cries of ecstasy as she climaxed on the *chaise longue*. The sound of her past rapture added even more to her present state of sexual tension and it was as though every nerve-ending in her body was screaming for relief from the unendurable pressure.

Then the sounds of her last orgasm ceased, to be replaced by a soft buzzing that she recognised as coming from a vibrator. It was now that she fully appreciated the increase in tension from being blindfolded, as she waited taut with expectation for the first touch of the sex toy.

She was prepared for it to touch her in many places, but not the place that Tarquin chose. He ran it slowly on its lowest speed down beneath her arms, where the tendons were tight due to her arms being suspended above her. The gentle tingling sensation increased as he dipped the head of the vibrator into her armpit and she started to gasp. He laid a finger across her mouth, and she sucked greedily at it, drawing it inside her lips and running her tongue across the tip until he finally withdrew it.

Now the vibrator moved down the side of her body, but at the inward curve of her waist he ran it in tiny circles across the width of her stomach and her internal muscles shivered and writhed as the remorseless drumming of her hidden pulse continued.

Tarquin put a little oil on her inner thighs and then increased the speed of the vibrator before running it around the tops of both her inner and outer thighs until at last he allowed it to pulsate around the pubic area.

Kristina was poised on the brink of her climax now, every sinew in her body ready for the cataclysmic explosion that she knew would suffuse her, but somehow Tarquin managed to keep changing speed, area or rhythm at just that vital moment so that she remained suspended on the final pinnacle before the descent into ecstasy.

He ran the vibrator slowly to and fro between her vagina and rectum until she was squirming so much on her chain that he couldn't keep it where he wanted and knew that he was in danger of allowing her to come. With a soft sigh of regret he moved back to her pubic mound and with the fingers of his left hand carefully parted the lips of her vulva.

Kristina was so aroused that she was wet with her own secretions. Despite this he decided to use a little jelly on the tip of the vibrator and then, after circling it around the entrance for a few seconds, he thrust it deep inside her and vibrated all around her cervix.

No one had ever stimulated her there before and she screamed with the intense pleasure of it, then thrust her hips frantically forward as she fought desperately for the final touch that would send her over the edge and release her despairing body.

Tarquin knew that very soon now she'd spasm helplessly. He'd never managed to keep a woman balanced right on the edge for so long before and his own excitement was almost unbearable. Turning off the vibrator he moved behind Kristina and bent his mouth to her ear.

'I want to take you from behind,' he whispered. 'I want to release you, and then you'll kneel on the floor with your arms bent and forehead resting on the rug so that I can plunge into you, into the place where I've been using the vibrator. Would you like that? Would that make you come?'

'Oh please, yes!' shouted Kristina, the image vivid in her mind.

'Then beg me,' he murmured. 'Plead with me to release you and take you like that.'

Kristina had never begged a man for anything in her life, and when she opened her mouth to obey she found that the words wouldn't come out. Despite her body's frantic need and the unendurable ache of frustration she simply couldn't say it and she gave a small cry of anguish.

Tarquin had known that this would be hard, but he didn't intend to change the game. This was what he most wanted from her today, total surrender to him and a deeper understanding of exactly the kind of games he liked. Without another word he began to massage her buttocks and now and again he'd allow an oiled finger to slip inside her anus and lightly touch the thin walls of her rectum, causing yet more sparks to ignite in her belly. He increased the pleasure, had her twisting and crying out with excitement, but never once did he make the mistake of giving her enough stimulation to allow her to come.

Suddenly, when his fingers were playing gently with her yet again and she felt the tip of one of them start its diabolically knowing intrusion the final barrier that stood between her and her satisfaction was broken.

'Please, Tarquin, I can't stand it any more. Please, let me down and take me from behind. I want you inside me. I want to come. I'll say anything you want, but let me come.'

'You've said enough,' he assured her, and his hands swiftly unclipped the chain from the loop, but he didn't remove her mask. He simply lifted her off the stool, placing her on the rug in the way he'd described. Then, catching hold of her hips, he pulled her back hard against him so that he plunged deep inside her vagina, and because he was so massive he was able to stimulate her cervix in the same way as the vibrator had stimulated it. At the same time he reached round her; his searching fingers located her clitoris, already slippery with excitement, and he drummed softly against its side.

For Kristina the increase in intensity of all the sensations was so great that she could hardly contain herself, and within a few seconds her frantic body was convulsing around him as bright white lights exploded behind her covered eyelids and thousands of piercing shards of pleasure tore through every part of her.

She heard herself crying, 'No! No!' but she had no idea why she was saying no when what she meant was yes, unless it was because the pleasure was almost too great to bear.

Tarquin felt her internal muscles tightening around him as her orgasm racked her and this triggered his own release so that at last he too was able to relax his control and he heard his gutteral moans mingle with her cries of delight.

Kristina thought that her final spasms would never

end, and long after Tarquin had finished her flesh was still pulsating with tiny tremors. Feeling this, Tarquin resumed his light caressing of her clitoral area, although he avoided the highly sensitive clitoris now that she'd finally come. As he massaged it, it felt to Kristina as though a small ember in her lower belly had re-ignited and with a scream of delight she came once more, less intensely, but this time when it was over her body was still and they both knew that she was totally satisfied.

For a moment Tarquin remained slumped over her back, both their bodies damp with perspiration, but then he withdrew, removed her blindfold and helped her to her feet.

Dazed by the incredible pleasure, dazzled by the sudden light, Kristina looked up at him and saw that his head was tilted to one side as he studied her with what was almost admiration for a second, but then the look was gone and his face was again sombre.

'I'm glad you were able to make this meeting,' he said politely. 'These spur-of-the-moment sessions are often the best. I expect you have to return home now so I'll leave you. Lydia will call you a taxi when you're ready to go.'

'Wait!' called Kristina.

He turned in surprise.

'You haven't uncuffed me, and I still have the bracelet.'

He frowned. 'I apologise. I have a pressing appointment and was worried about the time.' Quickly he removed the cuffs and then slipped the slim gold bracelet off her left wrist. 'Do you live alone?' he asked abruptly.

'Not yet, but very soon I will be.'

He nodded. 'That will be more convenient for us both I imagine. Until next time then?'

'Yes, until next time.' She remembered that she was no longer wearing the bracelet. 'I was wondering if we might go out somewhere one evening. I'd wear the bracelet of course.'

To her delight his face lit up and he smiled at her. 'What a wonderful idea. I must choose very carefully where we go. I have to say,' he added as he reached the door, 'that this time I seem to have made a very good choice. I trust you feel the same?'

'Yes,' she said, careful to keep her voice casual. 'Yes, I rather think I do.'

As the next day was Saturday, Kristina and Ben had a lie-in and then breakfasted together. Kristina felt exhausted from the tension and excitement of the previous afternoon, and had spent most of the night awake, wondering how she was going to break the news to Ben that their relationship was over.

As she reached across the table for a piece of toast he caught hold of her hand and pushed back the sleeve of her kimono. 'What on earth is that mark round your wrist?' he asked.

Kristina glanced down and saw that there was a

red circle round her wrist from where she'd been handcuffed. Immediately she pictured herself wearing the cuffs, arms extended high above her head as she waited naked and trembling for Tarquin to give her pleasure, and she shivered.

'Well?' demanded Ben.

Kristina shrugged. 'I don't know. I must have slept on it.'

'Show me the other one,' he demanded.

Kristina frowned. 'What's the matter with you this morning? Can't you even have a meal without making a scene? Last night was bad enough.'

'I was annoyed last night because I'd tried to ring you at the office at half-four and Sue said you'd gone home. When I rang here there was no answer and you finally strolled in at seven saying you'd worked late. I think most men would be annoyed.'

Kristina stared at him. 'All right then, here's the other wrist. Take a good look.' She pushed back her other sleeve and Ben stared at the sight of another light red ring around her slender bones.

'What the hell have you been doing?' he said furiously. 'Where were you yesterday, and more to the point who were you with?'

'I was with a man,' she said calmly.

All the colour drained from Ben's face. 'You mean, some guy did that to you?'

'Yes.'

'And you haven't told anyone?'

Kristina smiled to herself. 'Not until now; you're the first to know!'

'But what happened? Did you know him or was he some stranger you . . .' Words failed him as he stared at her in amazement.

'I know him,' Kristina stated calmly. 'He and I are lovers.'

'Lovers?' It was clear that Ben couldn't believe what he was hearing, and Kristina couldn't blame him. She knew there must be better ways than this of telling him but somehow the conversation had taken on a life of its own and now all she wanted to do was get it over with.

'Yes, lovers. I'm really sorry, Ben. I was going to tell you today in any case. I've only been involved for the past couple of weeks, but I realised yesterday that it was something special. It's my fault, not yours. I've changed. I need something different from a relationship.'

'Are you saying that you want to be tied up? That you're into bondage and kinky sex, because if you are then you certainly have changed. You wouldn't even play out a bondage fantasy when I asked you to.'

'It isn't just bondage,' she said sharply. 'It's a totally different relationship from the one we have, and I prefer it.'

'You mean you're dumping me? Like Jackie dumped William?'

'I don't know why Jackie and William split up, and I hardly think dumping is the right term. We've come to the end of the road, Ben. You must know that. Things haven't been all that good between us for ages now. There's no spark, no excitement any more.'

'I'll tie you up if that's what you want,' said Ben, suddenly brightening. 'I'll do anything you like, Kristina. Just tell me what you need and I'll give it to you.'

'That's the whole point, Ben. I don't want to have to tell you. I want a man who knows instinctively what I want.'

'That's a lie!' shouted Ben, colour flooding back into his face. 'You hate being told what to do, in bed or out of it. You've banged on about equality and women's rights ever since I've known you, and I respected that. I've always thought of us as equals, and now you're telling me you want some chauvinist who ties you up and does heaven knows what to you. What's happened to the independent Kristina who once boasted that she'd never been used by a man, but had certainly used them herself?'

'I'm sorry, Ben, really I am. I can't explain it, and this new man isn't going to move in with me or anything like that. It isn't that kind of a relationship. I think I need to live alone again and think carefully about what I want from life.'

'What about me?' demanded Ben. 'Don't I have any say in this? I thought we were going to get married in a year or two, maybe have some children in time. That's what grown-up people do, you know.'

'It isn't what I want to do, and as it's clear that it's something you want to do then I think it's lucky we're finishing our relationship now. There are lots of women out there who'd give their right arm for a man like you, Ben. Pretty, intelligent women who'll make you much happier than I can.'

Ben jumped to his feet. 'Don't you dare patronise me! It's you I'm in love with. I don't want anyone else. You make it sound like choosing a doll, not a partner for life. "Lots of pretty women". If anything's sexist, that is. There are lots of plain ones too; perhaps they'd make me happy, or does the new, non-feminist you think men should only like blonde air-heads?'

'Stop it!' said Kristina, her voice rising as Ben got more annoyed. 'Okay, I put it badly, but you know what I mean. We aren't right for each other any more, Ben.'

'You're right for me.'

'Well, you're not right for me and I'd like you to move out within the next week,' she snapped.

Suddenly Ben sank back into his chair. 'You really do mean it, don't you? You're ending it, without giving me any chance to change or time for us to try and work it through?'

'Yes,' she said wearily. 'I'm ending it now because I don't want to work at it any more. You may not realise it but I have tried. I've been trying for months now; trying to make it more than it is, trying to convince myself that this was what I wanted, but I was wrong. I don't want this, I want something different.'

'A bondage freak!' sneered Ben.

'You don't understand any of it,' said Kristina softly.

'To be honest, I don't understand it myself but that's my problem. I'm sorry about hurting you, and sorry it didn't work out, but I can't go back to being the person I was. I'll go out for the rest of the day. There's plenty I can get on with at the office. That will give you a chance to think about what you're going to do and where you can go. I'll come back about six. If you don't want to see me you'd better go out with some of your friends. I'd like you to move into the spare room until you go. I'm sure you'd prefer that too, under the circumstances.'

'I suppose you're really going to spend the day with him,' muttered Ben.

'No, I'm going to work. You can ring me there any time if you need to talk to me. I don't see this new man very often, Ben.'

'I just don't understand it,' he repeated helplessly. 'I thought I was everything you wanted.'

'So did I,' said Kristina sadly. 'And for a time you were, but that time's passed and now I need something different.'

'Just go then,' muttered Ben. 'I'll move my stuff into the other room and ring round some of my friends. I'm sure one of them can put me up for a short time, until I can get a place of my own. But I tell you this, Kristina, I'm not going to trust another woman again for a very long time. I believed in you, in all you said and did, and now I find I don't really know you at all.'

'I don't think I know myself any more,' she said quietly.

'Then how do you know you'll be any happier with me gone?'

'I don't, but I have to try,' she said, and then she went and got ready for the office, leaving Ben sitting with his head in his hands.

The office was strange without Sue or any of the other girls there, and although Kristina had plenty to do she found it difficult to concentrate. For the first couple of hours she drew up contracts, inserting her own clauses into the standard publishing house templates, and then chased up two film options that were pending for Lucretia. Even as she wrote the emails she wondered how on earth they'd ever cast the stories. All the characters were so extreme it would be pretty difficult, but then she thought of Tarquin and Laurence and realised that there were plenty of genuinely extreme people around once you knew where to look. It crossed her mind that Lucretia would probably enjoy wearing the bracelet of bondage.

At one o'clock she rang Ben, checked that he was coping and then popped across the road for a sandwich and a coffee. She'd just sat down at one of the plastic-topped tables when she saw Jackie walk in, but it was a very different Jackie from the one Kristina was used to seeing.

She raised a hand in the air. 'Jackie! Over here!'

Jackie turned, and for a moment hardly seemed to know who Kristina was but then she smiled and brought her rolls over to the table. 'What are you doing here?' she asked.

'I could ask you the same thing!' exclaimed Kristina. 'What's happened to your hair! It looks as though you've been swimming!'

'Does it?' asked Jackie vaguely. 'I suppose I got it wet. What's the time?'

'One o'clock. How did you get it wet?'

'In the shower. I've just left Laurence's house. I got there at six yesterday evening, but I didn't realise how late it was. I thought this was my breakfast.'

'You look terrible,' said Kristina. 'Didn't you get any sleep?'

Jackie laughed. 'Of course not! Laurence doesn't believe in wasting time on sleep. Is it really one o'clock? No wonder I feel so shattered.'

Now that her friend was closer, Kristina could see that despite being exhausted and having wet hair plastered to her head, Jackie still had the strange luminous glow about her that her sessions with Laurence seemed to cause. She also saw tiny love bites at the base of her friend's throat, but when Jackie realised that Kristina was staring she adjusted the scarf that was knotted loosely round her neck and hid them from view.

'Why are you here, then?' asked Jackie. 'You don't normally work on Saturdays.'

'I've just dumped Ben. It seemed better to clear off out of the way until he'd had time to get used to it and sort himself out.'

Jackie nodded. 'Kinder to get it over now. I knew he wouldn't last once you joined the society. What have you done to your wrists?' she added. Kristina blushed. 'It happened yesterday afternoon. I was at Tarquin's.'

Jackie's eyes brightened. 'Tell me more! Was it as good as the previous time?'

'It was even better – I thought I'd die of pleasure!' said Kristina, and then in a low voice she told Jackie everything that had happened.

'He sounds very interesting,' admitted Jackie when Kristina had finished. 'If I weren't seeing Laurence I'd be interested myself! Isn't it bliss when they won't let you come? Sometimes Laurence keeps me on the edge for an entire evening and then sends me home. The last time he did that I finished myself off in the back of the taxi. Must have given the driver a treat.'

'I don't think I'd like that,' said Kristina.

'I don't like it, but it isn't up to me, and he always makes sure that the next time we meet I have so many orgasms that I end up begging him to stop. That's what happened last night. He just wouldn't leave me alone. I got to the stage where I was begging him to stop all stimulation, but he refused. He only stopped when he couldn't make me come no matter what he did, and that's never happened before.'

Kristina found she was getting aroused merely listening to her friend. 'You won't tell Laurence about what happens between Tarquin and me will you?' she asked anxiously. 'I don't mind telling you, but I wouldn't want anyone else to know.'

'Of course not! This is girls' talk, strictly confidential. I bet I look terrible, don't I?'

'Pretty exhausted, but very satisfied! Jackie, did you feel bad when you ditched William?'

'No, I quite enjoyed it, but then William wasn't like Ben. He was very smug and it gave me great pleasure to see that self-satisfied look vanish from his face.'

'He did love you, Jackie.'

'I don't think he did; I think I suited him. He soon found himself a replacement, and they're getting married in September so I didn't exactly break his heart.'

'Let's hope Ben gets over it as quickly then,' said Kristina.

Jackie yawned, and then covered her mouth. 'Sorry! Look, I'll have to go or I'll fall asleep here at the table. We must have lunch next Friday, compare notes on how our week's gone, all right?'

'Fine,' agreed Kristina.

'There is one thing,' added Jackie before she left. 'Laurence hasn't invited you over to wear the bracelet for him, has he?'

'Of course not! Anyway, I wouldn't go. I'm happy with Tarquin.'

'Yes, I know. I just thought that Laurence . . . No, forget it; I'm being paranoid.'

'Remember what you told me,' said Kristina softly. 'They run the show, and we're not meant to get involved.'

'When I get home I'm throwing my rule book away,' retorted Jackie. 'Laurence cheats anyway, he's always bending the rules. Once I wanted . . .'

'What?' asked Kristina quickly.

Jackie shook her head. 'Nothing, I'm tired and not thinking straight. I'll call you in the week. 'Night, Kristina.'

Kristina laughed as her friend walked out of the sandwich bar, clearly so exhausted that it seemed like night to her. She just wished that Jackie had finished telling her in what way Laurence had broken the rules.

When she finally returned home at six, having cleared most of the paperwork on her desk, Ben was out and she was able to eat, have a shower and then an early night. She never even heard him come in. She was fast asleep dreaming of Tarquin and, surprisingly, Laurence.

Chapter Six

It wasn't until the following Wednesday that Ben actually moved out, and the three days before that proved awkward for both of them. In some ways Kristina was pleased that she didn't hear from Tarquin, because she wanted Ben out of her life before they next met. On the other hand she found that her body craved him with ever increasing urgency and her dreams became more and more vivid. She would wake covered in perspiration, always on the brink of a climax and so aroused that she had to masturbate in order to ease the tension.

Neither she nor Ben spoke again about the reason for their parting. They spoke about where he intended to live, and whether or not they might meet up for a drink in a couple of months' time, but that was all.

It was strange, thought Kristina, how intimate you could be with someone and then all at once they were no longer part of your life. For several years she had thought in terms of herself and Ben, now it was only her. She was relieved to discover that this didn't worry her. She would rather be alone than with a man she no longer desired.

On the Thursday morning she went to work with a much lighter heart. The Chelsea house was hers again, all traces of Ben had been removed and she was once more free. Or at least free to all outward appearances, because inside her mind she was far from free. She was in truth a prisoner of the bracelet, forever waiting for the call that would summon her to escape and ecstasy.

'Nothing special on today, is there Sue?' she called as she walked through the front office.

'No, but a Laurence van Kitson has been on the phone twice already. He says that you know him and wondered if he could call in around noon to discuss an idea he has for a book on diamonds. Do you want to phone him back?'

Kristina hesitated. No doubt Laurence did have a genuine cover for his visit, but equally he probably had another reason and she wasn't sure that she wanted to see him, knowing how Jackie would feel about it. Then her professional side took over. Laurence was one of the world's top experts on diamonds, and there might well be a book that he could write, specialised certainly, but there would definitely be a market for it. She took a deep breath. 'Call him back and say that noon will be fine,' she said.

At twelve o'clock exactly he was shown into her office. His suit was a light beige, the shirt dark brown with a cream coloured tie and the entire outfit showed off his tanned blond good looks to the best advantage, which Kristina guessed he knew.

She stood up and held out a hand. 'Nice to see you again, Laurence. Sue tells me you're thinking of writing a book. Is that true?'

His very pale blue eyes bored into hers. 'Of course it's true. I'm not in the habit of lying.'

She bit on her bottom lip. Now was not the moment to tell him that he had an attitude problem, not until she'd heard his outline. 'So, what angle were you thinking of? Is this intended for the other experts, or lay people?'

'Both I thought. Details of the world's finest diamonds naturally, and the way to value them, but there's also the sexual side of it. You know what they say, diamonds are a girl's best friend. I want to show why that's true. Sugar daddies, rich old husbands who shower their young brides with stones large enough to make a river overflow its banks: I've got quite a stock of stories about that side of things.'

Kristina nodded. 'Interesting, but it could end up as neither one thing nor the other. Lay people won't want to know how to value a stone, and the experts won't be interested in the other side of it.'

Laurence smiled a thin smile. 'Everyone's interested in sex, as I'm sure you know. Experts are no different from anyone else. Diamond dealers, psychologists, they all have their little hobbies.'

A warning bell sounded in Kristina's head. 'I'm sure they do,' she said briskly.

'I must say I was a bit surprised when Jackie told me exactly what the famous Dr Rashid liked doing in his spare time, but I suppose it's a release for him after listening to neurotics all day. Just as it's a release for you to cast aside your business woman's suit and dangle from a beam without your clothes on.'

'Keep your voice down!' hissed Kristina. 'The girls might hear you.'

'It's a thick door and I don't speak loudly. I was very turned on by what Jackie told me. I've been thinking about how you must have looked ever since.'

Kristina was furious. 'She had no right to tell you. I told her in confidence.'

'But she had no choice. I waited until she was wearing the bracelet and then asked her what she knew about you and your lover.'

'She could have taken the bracelet off,' retorted Kristina.

'She'd already been waiting two hours for me to let her come. I think taking the bracelet off was the last thing on her mind.'

Kristina felt her face go hot. He was so relaxed, and yet his eyes were watching her intently, judging her reactions, and although she was the one on home ground she felt nervous.

'I think we should stick to talking about the book,' she said firmly. 'Why don't you prepare me an outline and . . .'

'How long did Rashid make you wait? One hour?

Two hours? Or was it more? Were you begging him to let you come? What did he make you say? I make Jackie crawl at my feet when she's begging. And she enjoys it, once she climaxed even before I'd touched her she was so excited by it.'

Kristina's stomach tightened and she felt her nipples brush against the body that she was wearing beneath her summerweight suit. 'I honestly don't want to hear this. It's private, and Jackie never discusses any of it with me.'

'That's because she's still ashamed to admit her true desires. But you're not, are you? You accept them as just another part of yourself. That's what I'm trying to make her do. Unfortunately it's taking a long time.'

'I'd like you to go away and do an outline for me,' said Kristina, her voice almost inaudible. 'Then, if I like it, I can show it to some people and get their opinions. You wouldn't get much of an advance, but sometimes books like this can really take off. Sometimes though, they don't!'

'I don't need the money,' he said, his South African accent thicker than usual. 'The book interests me, but you interest me more. If I ring you, will you wear the bracelet for me?'

'No,' said Kristina firmly. 'I'm too busy with Tarquin.'

'Don't you think variety might have some advantages? Who knows, I might be more to your taste than he is.'

Kristina shook her head. 'Sorry, Laurence; you're not my type.'

'I don't think that's true,' he said with a laugh. 'Still, I can wait. Tell me, had you ever been blindfolded before?'

Kristina swallowed hard. 'Would you please keep your voice down and stop talking about things that aren't strictly business. I keep my private life separate from work you know; I thought that was the whole idea of the society.'

'And so it is. I'm quite happy to take you out without the bracelet on, you know.'

'Thank you, Laurence, but I don't have any free time these days. Are you going to do that outline, or was the whole idea just a way of getting to see me here?'

He shook his head. 'No, I'll do the outline, but first I'd like to make love to you on your desk.'

Kristina smiled to herself. 'Would you really? How very unoriginal. I think perhaps you'd better go now, Laurence. I do have quite a lot to do today.'

'We could do it now; no one would know,' he said, getting to his feet. 'You're aroused, I can tell. Surely you'd like to know what Jackie's getting? After all, she knows all about Tarquin.'

'She what?' said Kristina in amazement.

'Didn't she tell you? He called her soon after she joined, but he wasn't her kind. Not sufficiently rough probably, although from what I've heard of your last session she may not have given him enough time! Come on, Kristina. You look incredibly sexy in that working woman's outfit. Why waste it?'

'Look, this is ridiculous,' protested Kristina, but to her horror she was getting more and more aroused the longer he talked, and she knew that he was right. She did want to learn what he was like. Now that she knew Jackie had been with Tarquin, she didn't see why she shouldn't, although since she wasn't wearing the bracelet it was hardly the same.

'Please go,' she said softly.

Laurence stood up and without thinking Kristina walked round to the front of her desk and stood in front of him. His hands went beneath the cheeks of her bottom and he lifted her on to her desk top, then he was feeling beneath her skirt and unfastening the poppers of her body, brushing the material aside and letting his fingers roam between her thighs.

'Just as I thought, you're ready for me!' he said with a smile.

'I'm not, really I'm not. We can't do this, the door isn't even locked,' protested Kristina, but her body was completely aroused and her desire for this swift, urgent coupling was growing with every second.

'Just don't scream out when you come,' he muttered as he unzipped his trousers and then he was pushing her back over the desk, and spreading her legs as wide as he could before lowering his head and letting his tongue roam round the entrance to her vagina.

Kristina squirmed on the desk and pushed her hips up towards Laurence, trying to open herself to him more fully. He gripped her ankles firmly and then his tongue was touching her damp inner channel with rapid flicking movements that made her gasp as flashes of pleasure streaked through her lower body.

'Do you want me now?' he asked. 'Or shall I leave and start work on my outline?'

'No, quickly, do it now. I want to feel you inside me,' she gasped, as without any further preliminaries he supported himself with one knee against the desk and thrust almost brutally into her soft welcoming warmth.

He wasn't as large as Tarquin, but the angle of penetration was such that every time he moved he stimulated her G spot and Kristina quickly felt herself tightening as her breathing grew ragged and quick.

'I wish your secretary would come in now,' muttered Laurence, thrusting rhythmically as Kristina continued to gasp with delight. 'I'd like her to see what you're like when you're about to come, and you are about to come aren't you?'

'Yes,' moaned Kristina, rotating her hips so that she could feel him touching all the walls of her vagina in turn. 'I'm nearly there, don't change your rhythm please.'

'If you were wearing the bracelet,' whispered Laurence, 'you wouldn't be allowed to tell me what to do would you?'

'No, but I'm not,' said Kristina hoarsely. 'Faster, do it faster.'

Laurence obeyed, and suddenly Kristina gave a

muffled cry of delight and then he felt her contracting around him, milking every drop of his sperm as he shuddered with the violence of his own climax.

The moment they were both finished he withdrew and straightened his clothing. 'Yes,' he said thoughtfully. 'I think you're definitely the right literary agent for me. We seem to understand each other, and that's very important, wouldn't you agree?'

Kristina couldn't look at him. The almost brutal coupling had shaken her badly, because her response had been instantaneous and uncontrollable. Now that it was over she wanted him gone. While he remained he was a reminder of the way her sexuality was starting to take over her life.

Scrambling off the desk she pulled her skirt down, leaving the body unfastened between her legs. That would have to be seen to later, in the cloakroom. 'I think you should go now,' she said abruptly.

'I agree. I got what I came for anyway. Shall I post you the outline?'

'That would probably be best,' she agreed, still avoiding his eyes.

'Fine, until the next time then.' He held out his hand and Kristina felt she had no choice but to take it. After all, he hadn't forced her; she'd wanted him as much as he'd wanted her.

'Laurence,' she said slowly. 'You won't mention this to Jackie will you? She's my best friend, and I'd hate to think that she knew anything about it.'

'I might not,' he murmured, fiddling inside his jacket pocket.

'Look, if it weren't for the fact that Jackie's been with Tarquin I'd never have agreed, but this isn't really the same as that because this wasn't anything to do with the society, which might hurt her more.'

'To be honest,' said Laurence, 'Jackie's never even met Tarquin. I only said that to ease your conscience.'

'But you told me earlier that you never lied!' cried Kristina.

He nodded. 'That's right, I did. That was a lie as well!'

'Jackie said you always broke the rules,' exclaimed Kristina. 'Why on earth did I believe you?'

'Because you wanted to, Kristina. You were frantic to try me out, and as long as I could ease your conscience a little that was fine by you. I said what you needed to hear because I wanted you. Don't blame me for your desires.'

'But there's no need to tell Jackie.'

'No,' he agreed. 'There isn't any need, although it might be fun. However, I don't think I will tell her.'

Kristina sat down abruptly as relief flooded through her. 'Good!'

'I shall just play her this,' he added, and he took his iPod out of his pocket. 'I kept it recording until we'd finished. The sounds should make everything clear, don't you agree?'

'You bastard!' shouted Kristina, quite forgetting the

girls in the other room. 'This was all a set-up job wasn't it? You wanted something new to use to torment Jackie with.'

'No, I can torment Jackie in plenty of ways without screwing you on your office desk. It was you I wanted, and you I got. But in the end,' he added softly, 'I intend to have you when you're wearing the bracelet. That will be an entirely different experience for both of us.'

'It won't happen,' she said shortly. 'I wouldn't trust myself to you.'

'We'll see,' he said tightly. 'You certainly sounded as though you enjoyed this little episode. I hope no one outside heard anything; you were far more vocal than I expected. Tarquin must have helped you shed some of your inhibitions!'

'Please go now, Laurence,' said Kristina. 'And I've changed my mind about the book. I think you should try another agent. I make it a policy never to get sexually involved with my clients.'

'Where's your business head gone? There could be money in this book.'

'Then I'll be the loser, but that's my decision. Goodbye, Laurence.'

He leant across her desk. 'It isn't goodbye, Kristina. We both know that. Let's just say until the next time.' Then he traced the outline of her lips with his finger and walked out of the room.

Kristina sat in her chair and wished with all her heart that she didn't have to see Jackie the following evening, because she was certain that by then Laurence would have used his recording. The trouble was, he'd given her an explosive climax. Their bodies had been completely in tune, and no matter what she said to Jackie that was a truth it would be impossible to deny.

'What's happening to me?' she said out loud, but there was no one to give her an answer.

As soon as Kristina walked into the restaurant the following evening and saw the expression on her friend's face she knew that it was just as she'd feared; Laurence had told Jackie all about them. Bracing herself for a difficult couple of hours she joined her at their table. 'Nice outfit,' she commented.

Jackie, who did indeed look stunning in a white silk blouse, black velvet waistcoat, black mini-skirt and thigh-high velvet boots, didn't bother to acknowledge the compliment, she just picked up her glass and drained the contents before calling the waiter over. 'Another dry martini and something for my friend.'

The waiter glanced at Kristina, who felt rather conventionally dressed in a simple short-sleeved russet dress with a scoop neckline, the fabric covered in tiny gold sequins. She smiled at him. 'I'll have the same,' she said lightly, hoping to improve the atmosphere. 'I'm not late, am I?' she asked Jacqueline.

'No, I'm early. I got my article finished and came straight here. You should get the paper on Monday, I think you'll find the article interesting.'

'What's it about then?'

'How women betray their best friends far more often than men betray theirs.'

Kristina decided not to comment, and picked up the menu. 'I'll have the salmon. I love fish, but I never cook it myself because the smell gets everywhere.'

'Rather like you,' said Jacqueline.

'What's that supposed to mean?' asked Kristina.

'That you seem to get everywhere. I'll have the lamb. You can order when he brings our drinks back. And get some wine too.'

'So, how's your week been?' asked Kristina bravely, deciding that the sooner it was all out in the open the better.

'Not particularly brilliant, certainly not as good as yours sounded when Laurence played me the recording of the pair of you.'

'When did he do that?' asked Kristina.

'Last night, very late last night by which time he'd already reduced me to a screaming, pleading mass of frustration. Your little recording was the icing on the cake for him. And do you know what?' she added furiously. 'When I heard it, I came! I hated myself for that, but I couldn't help it; I was so near and then listening to you, the noises you were making and the things you said to him, it was too much. I came and Laurence stood there and laughed at me. I've never been so humiliated.'

'Your drinks,' murmured the young waiter, who'd

been hovering at Kristina's shoulder waiting for a pause so that he could put the glasses down.

Kristina quickly gave their order and sent him off again. She thought that he'd probably heard some of what Jackie had said, but right at this moment that didn't seem to matter. What mattered was her friend's pain.

'Jackie, I know you're hurt but you have to believe that I'd never have done it if I hadn't thought . . .'

'That you'd get away with it?' asked Jackie. 'That Laurence would keep it secret? Well, you certainly don't know him very well. Tarquin may be an honourable man for all I know, but Laurence is not. What's the matter with you, isn't one incredible lover enough?'

Kristina shifted awkwardly on her chair. 'He came to me with an idea for a book, Jackie.'

'I bet he did! What was it? *Sixty-Nine Positions on a Desktop?*'

'It was about diamonds, and he really had thought it through well. The trouble was that he started talking about the things that I'd done with Tarquin, and I was annoyed that you'd told him when you'd promised me that you wouldn't.'

'I didn't have any choice!' wailed Jacqueline, her voice rising so high that nearby diners turned to stare at them.

'Sshh! I know that now, but I didn't at first, and even after Laurence explained I thought that you could have taken off the bracelet and refused to answer.'

'Oh did you? Well, as it happens I was right on the

brink of my first orgasm for two hours and taking the bracelet off was the last thing on my mind,' said Jackie, remembering to lower her voice.

'Yes, he told me that later.'

'But you still wanted to screw him in your office, to compare him with Tarquin, was that it?'

'No, of course not. The trouble was, he lied to me. He said that you and Tarquin had been lovers ages ago but you decided he wasn't right for you. That made me think that I was just evening the score if you like, especially as you'd never told me about it.'

'But I've never met Tarquin!' protested Jackie.

'I know that now, but at the time I believed him.'

'Even if I had,' Jackie pointed out, 'it would have been through the society, when I was wearing the bracelet. You didn't bother with that did you? You went and had sex with him and told him how you wanted it. "Faster, do it faster",' she mimicked, and Kristina's hands felt damp with perspiration.

'Jackie, people are listening to us. For heaven's sake lower your voice.'

'You're my best friend. I told you how much Laurence meant to me and at the first opportunity you went and had it away with him. How do you think that makes me feel? I'm so obsessed with him that I can hardly eat or sleep. I spend all my days waiting for the summons, and then when it comes I wonder what kind of a session it's going to be. Sometimes it's bliss, and sometimes it's more like hell, but hell with the greatest reward imaginable at the end of it. He's taken over my entire life, and you just lie back on your desk and try him out without sparing a thought for me. I'll say one thing, though; it helped me write a brilliant article for the first time in weeks.'

'He wasn't meant to tell you,' protested Kristina. 'I felt utterly ashamed afterwards, and begged him to keep quiet about it, but then he showed me he'd recorded us and I knew he wouldn't. He's really not a very nice person, Jackie.'

Her friend stared at her in astonishment, scarcely noticing as their food was placed in front of them. 'Not a very nice person? You've got a nerve! Are you trying to get me to drop him and leave the way clear for you? I suppose you want to visit both Laurence and Tarquin now. Perhaps I should move in with Ben so that you can have enough space to yourself?'

'I wouldn't put on the bracelet for Laurence if you paid me a million pounds,' said Kristina levelly. 'Yes, he's sexually attractive. Yes, he made love in a very exciting way and I enjoyed it. But no, I do not wish to put myself at his mercy. He's a liar, probably some kind of a sadist and in my opinion dangerous.'

'Then stay away from him,' shouted Jackie.

Kristina glanced around the restaurant. 'If you don't keep your voice down, I'm going,' she said sharply. 'How much have you had to drink tonight?'

'That's my business. Kristina, do I have your word that you'll never have sex with him again?'

Kristina hesitated. If she gave her word then that would be it. She couldn't let Jackie down twice, but for some reason she found it impossible to say the words Jacqueline wanted to hear. She had the strange feeling that she and Laurence were destined to make love again. She had no idea where, or why, but she knew it could happen and if she was utterly truthful with herself she wouldn't mind, as long as she wasn't wearing the bracelet.

'No, I can't say that,' she muttered.

'Why not? You've just told me what a dreadful man he is, and suggested that he's bad for me, so how come you won't agree never to have sex with him again?'

'Because now that I belong to the society I don't know what's going to happen. Suppose Tarquin and I met up with you and Laurence when we were both wearing the bracelets? What could I do if Tarquin told me to let Laurence make love to me? I'd have to obey, because I don't want to lose Tarquin any more than you want to lose Laurence.'

'It doesn't sound very likely,' said Jackie doubtfully.

Kristina knew that, but at least it was an explanation that her friend could understand. 'No, and I don't suppose it will ever happen but in case it does I can't give you the promise you want.'

'And that's the only reason?' demanded Jackie.

Kristina nodded. 'Of course it is. Laurence isn't my client any more. I've told him to find another agent.'

'Have you? He didn't mention that.'

'No,' said Kristina drily. 'I don't suppose he did!'

Jackie suddenly slumped back in her chair. 'Kristina, don't ever put me through another twenty-four hours like that again. I've suffered such jealousy I didn't know how to cope.'

'I can only repeat that I'm really and truly sorry,' said Kristina, reaching for her friend's hand. 'I think the entire episode was a put-up job, dreamed up by Laurence as a new and refined way of both torturing and stimulating you, and from what you say it worked.'

Jackie nodded. 'Yes, it worked. I came and came, and then he entered me and that set me off again, but once I got home all I could hear was you crying out with excitement, and it drove me out of my mind.'

'Tarquin made me listen to a recording of myself,' confessed Kristina. 'I found that a terrific turn-on. Jackie, do you ever think that perhaps we shouldn't have started this? That it's changing us?'

Jacqueline shook her head. 'My only regret is that I didn't find out about the society earlier. As far as I'm concerned it's the greatest thing that's ever happened to me.'

'I thought I'd work better because of it,' explained Kristina. 'It isn't working like that though; I'm finding it difficult to concentrate. I can't afford to let things slide; I'm only as good as my last big deal. Suppose Laurence's book gets published and becomes a bestseller? I'll have turned him down as a client because of the society!'

'But for the society I doubt if you'd ever have

heard from Laurence,' said Jackie matter-of-factly. 'If you're right and he only used the book as an excuse then without the society there wouldn't have been a book. You see how easy it is to get things the wrong way round. In this case the society might have been an advantage to you, if you hadn't got carried away by lust and ruined the entire deal.'

'Okay, I'm in the wrong. How many times do I have to apologise?'

'Hundreds!' For the first time that evening Jackie laughed. 'It's all right, I don't mean it. We'll forget it now. As for your work, the self-discipline side is up to you. I'm sure Tarquin doesn't waste his time at work thinking about you.'

'No,' admitted Kristina, ruefully. 'I don't suppose he does. As you say, it's up to me to manage my life better. At least I now know what I don't want, and that's someone like Ben in my life.'

'There you are then. You look better too, far less tense and exhausted. Think of your visits to Tarquin as a kind of sexual aromatherapy, very good for the entire system!'

'And free!' added Kristina, and they both burst out laughing. Later though, Kristina thought to herself that it wasn't truly free; there was a price for everything, and her price was the sensation that her life was beginning to run out of control.

The following Tuesday she still hadn't had another call from Tarquin, and her nerves were stretched to breaking point. She knew that he might have had to go abroad to give a talk, or could even be ill, but she worried constantly that it was her suggestion that they go out together while she wore the bracelet that had put him off.

Finally deciding that she must make the best of it and use the time to get on with some work she arranged for a new author, Peter Guard, to come round to her house early on the Tuesday evening for a bite to eat and a chat. He was writing a psychological thriller and they both wanted it to be sold to the States as well, which meant adding more characters than he'd originally allowed for. He was in his late twenties, a freelance artist and part-time photographer as well as an aspiring writer, so she felt that the evening should be interesting and helpful for her as well as for him.

He arrived at five-thirty and they had a couple of drinks as they went over his original synopsis. 'There isn't enough love interest,' Kristina pointed out. 'I know your hero has a girlfriend, but it's all a bit unreal. There's no depth to their emotions. I think if there were it would make her death at the end far more effective. What do you think?'

Peter shrugged. 'I don't know. I'm not into heavy commitment myself and that's just the way it came out. I might find it difficult writing about anything more intense.'

'Well, I can probably help a bit, but if you're really not comfortable with it then we'll leave it alone. There's no point in writing about things that aren't real to you, because if you do that your readers certainly won't believe a word of it.'

'Perhaps you'd better teach me how to get involved with a woman?' he teased.

'That would be delightful, but I never mix business with pleasure!' She laughed. 'Why not think about it a bit more and then we'll eat. I've got a lasagne in the oven. Is that all right?'

'Sure, I eat anything.'

She was passing the phone when it rang, and picked it up on the second ring. 'Hello?'

'Kristina?' asked Tarquin's soft, precise voice.

Her heart hammered against her ribs. 'Yes.'

'I have tickets for the opera tonight. Meet me in the Crush Bar at Covent Garden at seven-fifteen and wear a long dress. We're sharing a box with Estelle and one of her friends. I'll bring the bracelet with me.'

'Tonight?'

'Yes. I'm sorry it's such short notice but a friend passed the tickets on to me late this afternoon. Is there a problem?'

She thought of Peter Guard sitting in her living room. 'I'm afraid there is,' she admitted.

'Please, don't apologise. I quite understand. Perhaps some other time then. Enjoy your evening,' he said smoothly.

'No! Wait!' exclaimed Kristina, her mind racing feverishly. 'It's only work, I'm sure my client will understand. I'll be there, don't worry.'

'Are you sure?'

'Yes, yes absolutely sure.'

'Good,' he said and she could hear the pleasure in his voice. 'It's *Tosca*. I thought you'd enjoy that. You're the kind of woman who probably finds herself drawn to Scarpia!' He laughed, more to himself than to her, and then hung up, leaving Kristina standing with the telephone in her hand wondering what on earth she'd done.

Slowly she put the phone back on the wall and walked into the living room. 'Peter, I'm terribly sorry but something's come up that means I have to go out,' she said awkwardly.

His face grew concerned. 'No one's ill I hope?'

'No, not exactly, but it is a bit of a crisis. I feel terrible about this but I really don't have any choice.'

He smiled reassuringly at her. 'Please, don't apologise. I hope you can sort things out. Perhaps you could ring me at home and we'll arrange another meeting. Things were just getting interesting. What you said made a lot of sense.'

He was being so polite about it all that Kristina felt even worse. She could hardly believe that she was driving a client away like this, but the prospect of a night at the opera wearing the bracelet of bondage was just too arousing to pass up, and she couldn't wait for Peter to be gone. 'Of course I'll ring,' she promised. 'And thanks for being so understanding.'

The moment the front door closed behind him she turned off the oven, took out the lasagne and stood it on the side then raced into the bathroom for a quick shower. After that she put on a long, black, crushed velvet gown, sleeveless with a huge white shawl-style collar, threw a black lace stole over her shoulders and called a mini-cab. She arrived at the Crush Bar at Covent Garden with one minute to spare.

'You made it,' said Tarquin as he walked towards her from the bar. 'Here, let me put this on you. The dress is beautiful,' he added and then he was tenderly slipping the gold bracelet over her hand until it was once more nestling against her skin.

'It should be a wonderful night,' he said gravely.

Kristina nodded. 'Yes, it should.'

'We'd better make our way to the box. The curtain goes up in fifteen minutes and Estelle and Sam are already in their seats. One thing, I'd prefer it if you removed your panties before we take our places.'

She looked round the crowded bar. 'Here?'

He nodded. 'No one will notice. Ease them down through your dress and then step out of them.'

'I can't!' she whispered. 'I'll pop into the cloakroom.'

'There's no time. Do it here.'

Kristina's hands trembled but she managed to roll the panties down beneath her dress by rubbing against the sides of her legs and when they were at last round her ankles she stepped carefully out of them, then picked them up and put them in her evening bag. As she closed the clasp she saw that several men and women were watching her out of the corners of their eyes, and her face went scarlet.

'That's better,' said Tarquin with a half-smile. 'Now for the entertainment.'

When they walked into the box, Estelle glanced round from her seat and smiled at Kristina. 'What a gorgeous dress! Sam, I'm sure you've heard of Kristina but I don't know if you've actually met each other?'

The man next to her stood up and smiled warmly at Kristina. He was about sixty, but a well-preserved sixty and his grey eyes were warm with appreciation as he held out his hand. 'I'm sure we haven't met; I'd certainly remember such a lovely young lady.'

'Then I'll introduce you,' said Tarquin, standing behind Kristina with one hand resting lightly on her shoulder. 'Kristina, this is Sam Martin, chairman of Stoddart-Wades. Sam, meet Kristina Masterton, literary agent *extraordinaire*!'

'Of course I've heard of you,' said Sam, smiling even more broadly. 'But I don't think we've had any business dealings. Now that you're representing young Laurence though, that will all change. Estelle here's been telling me about his proposed book on diamonds and I really think we could make something out of it, but then you're famous for picking winners!'

Kristina felt like a goldfish as her mouth opened and closed helplessly. First of all it was a nightmare to find that the man who was sharing their box on the night she

162

FREDRICA ALLEYN

was wearing the bracelet turned out to be the chairman of Stoddart-Wades, and then to learn that Laurence had talked to Estelle about his book and claimed her for his agent was too much to take in. She saw Estelle, who was dressed in a long red brocade sheath dress with elbow-length gloves, watching her closely and knew that she was taking great delight in Kristina's discomfort.

'It's very nice to meet you, Sam,' she said with her most professional smile. 'Your publishing house has had a very good year.'

'And next year will be even better. Estelle here is going to make our non-fiction list the strongest in the country. There won't be a coffee-table in the land that doesn't have one of our books on it in twelve months' time, you mark my words.'

Much to Kristina's relief, at that moment the lights dimmed and she was spared having to answer that even if Laurence's book was one of those, she wouldn't be representing him.

Tarquin had been right in thinking that Kristina liked *Tosca*, but she didn't like the soprano very much and when the first act ended she turned to him and pulled a face. 'If that's the new Maria Callas, I'm the new Sharon Stone!'

'Your lack of underwear probably qualifies you for that rather more than our soprano's voice qualifies her!' he retorted with a grin. She smiled back at him, forgetting for a moment the thin gold chain that was encircling her wrist. Then he bent closer to her. 'When the second act begins I want you to go down on your knees in front of me and give me oral sex,' he whispered. 'Don't stop until you feel my hands cup your face.'

Kristina stared at him. 'What about Sam?'

'He'll be very envious,' said Tarquin placidly.

'But he's in my line of work. I mean, he and I are likely to meet again. I can't possibly . . .'

'Then take the bracelet off,' said Tarquin casually. 'Make up your mind though. The lights are going down again and I want you to join them!'

Kristina didn't even smile at the joke. She felt frantic with fear. Normally what he'd asked of her would have been exciting and erotic, but the presence of Sam added another dimension and she knew that this was why he'd been invited. The additional danger that his presence added made the entire episode far more meaningful, but if she did as Tarquin asked, then she would have passed yet another test.

Except that it wasn't a test, she thought wildly. This was meant to be an escape, sexual fantasies played out in the safety of a society where anything was possible and pleasure was all that mattered.

'Give me the bracelet,' said Tarquin, his voice very low.

All at once a surge of desire coursed through her and without replying she waited until the theatre was dark and then slid to her knees between his parted thighs. The long velvet dress rustled as she moved, and she knew that Sam Martin must be aware of what was happening, but the moment she took Tarquin's huge penis into her hands and felt the soft skin of the glans she was so hungry for him that nothing else mattered.

Carefully she licked all along the shaft of his erection, spreading saliva everywhere in order to make her movements easier. His erection strained upwards at the touch of her tongue, and this made it simple for her to lick along the underside of the shaft before pressing her lips against it and rubbing them up and down towards the head. His thighs spread further apart and although he kept his eyes fixed on the stage his breathing was becoming audible in the confines of the box.

Warming to her task, Kristina licked very lightly on his frenulum, that highly sensitive place where his glans joined the shaft on the underside and as he caught his breath she rose a little higher on her knees. Then, after sliding a finger inside her mouth, she drew his glans between her lips so that she could stimulate it with both her tongue and her finger even as she sucked in a slow steady rhythm.

Tarquin was having trouble sitting still and, once, a tiny groan escaped from between his clenched lips. When she heard that, Kristina used the fingers of her free hand to stimulate his shaft while she continued to suck on the head of his erection, and she felt a tiny rippling sensation beneath her fingers as he neared his climax.

Frantically Kristina began to suck harder on his glans, but suddenly she felt his hands cupping her face and she could have wailed with disappointment when she realised that he wasn't going to come in her mouth after all. Reluctantly she released him, her body shaking with excitement and arousal.

Tarquin's hands tilted her face up and he bent his head down to her. 'Raise your dress and sit on my lap,' he whispered. 'I want to come inside you.'

Kristina was driven frantic by his words, but when she glanced round the box she realised that both Estelle and Sam were watching her, although Sam quickly looked back to the stage when he saw her head turn.

As quietly as she could, Kristina manoeuvred her dress upwards, and then she was struggling to rise sufficiently for Tarquin to pull her on to his lap. For a moment the tip of his penis remained poised at the opening of her vagina, and then he pulled her down on to him with one quick movement and suddenly he was deep inside her, filling her totally and immediately easing the ache of frustration that her manipulation of him had caused.

She sat quite still, waiting for his instructions as she felt his breath, warm on the nape of her neck. 'Use your internal muscles to bring me to a climax,' he muttered. 'Keep quite still, do it all internally.'

As she tightened her pelvic muscles the pressure inside her pelvic area increased and she felt a spiral of tight pleasure spread through her lower abdomen. When she released the muscles the spiral died away, but the more she worked the greater her own pleasure grew and soon she was very close to a climax herself. Greedily she worked at Tarquin's enclosed penis, tensing and releasing her muscles in the rhythm that suited her best until at last the pleasure was constant and the ache of the approaching climax almost overbearingly sweet.

Then, just before she reached the point of no return, she felt Tarquin's hips jerk helplessly and when she tried to continue contracting her muscles around him he lifted her upwards from the hips, forcing her to climb off him and return to her seat, her whole body swollen and heavy with the thwarted orgasm.

'*Vissi d'arte, vissi d'amore*' sang the soprano, looking up towards the top circle. Kristina shivered, not at the beauty of the music but at the words. *I have lived for love*. It was like her life now, and she knew it, although in truth it was probably less romantic. She was living for lust.

When the opera was finally over Sam Martin and Estelle left separately. Sam was unable to look Kristina in the eye, but Tarquin kept a firm hold on Kristina's elbow.

'You did well,' he said pleasantly. 'I imagine that you'd like a reward. After all, we are both meant to get pleasure from our meetings.'

'I did get pleasure from it. I enjoyed every moment,' replied Kristina honestly.

'But you didn't manage to come, did you?'

'No, not quite.'

'Then we must rectify that. My car's just round the

corner, we'll go back to the house and continue the evening there. What did you think of the opera?'

'The bits I saw were quite good, and yes, I liked Scarpia best!'

Tarquin lightly touched the bracelet round her wrist. 'Sometimes, you know, I think I'd like to spend an evening with you without this bracelet for company, but then I tell myself that perhaps that isn't such a good idea. Maybe it would change things too much. What do you think?'

'When I'm wearing this bracelet I don't think very much at all,' replied Kristina, anxious not to fall into any trap and give the wrong reply, although the very fact that he'd mentioned such a thing gave her a warm glow.

He nodded. 'Absolutely, I can see that would be the case. Well, I shall think about it further another time. For now we'll go home. I have another surprise for you there. I hope it adds to your evening's pleasure.'

Kristina hoped so too.

Chapter Seven

Tarquin let them into the house and then preceded Kristina up the stairs. This time they returned to the room they had used for her first visit, only someone was there before them. Sitting in one of the lattice-backed chairs, settled deep into the soft cushion, was Sam Martin.

Without thinking, Kristina began to finger the bracelet round her wrist. Sam ran a large publishing company, and they were interested in Laurence van Kitson's book. Even though she wasn't going to act as Laurence's agent there was still a tenuous connection, and this clash between her real life and the fantasy world of the society troubled her.

Sensing her inner turmoil, Tarquin stood to one side leaving the doorway clear. She looked at him, and once again his head was tilted to the side as he considered her response with interest. She searched for some hint of reassurance in his eyes, confirmation that this was safe, but she could read nothing from his expression except curiosity.

Then, very slowly, he bent down and began to drop light kisses on her parted lips. Kristina's body reacted instantly, and she went up on her toes, silently begging him to use his tongue. He did, but not in the way she'd expected. Instead he cupped the back of her head with one hand, bent it backwards and then with a firm tongue licked along the length of her mouth in a slow sensuous movement that quickly had her moaning with desire.

'Take off your dress,' he whispered. Quite forgetting the watching Sam, she let him unfasten her zip before removing the long velvet gown and placing it over the arm of the nearest chair. Because she'd removed her panties before the opera she was now wearing only black silk holdups and high heeled black suede shoes. 'Now the rest,' he commanded.

When she was naked, Tarquin moved behind her, and his hands clasped her lightly on each side of her bare waist. 'I gave an interview to a journalist friend of yours earlier today,' he whispered. 'It was about friendship and the differences between men and women in this area. Your name came up, and she let slip that you'd confided in her that you'd always wanted to make love to two men at once. Of course, she had no idea that I could make that come true for you, but I thought it was a very fortunate coincidence. I hope it proves as exciting an experience as you've always imagined.'

Kristina knew at once that he must have been interviewed by Jacqueline, and she knew too that it wasn't any coincidence. Jackie had sought him out on the excuse of getting an interview, and then deliberately let drop something that she knew was the exact opposite of Kristina's true wishes.

It was a brilliant piece of revenge, but Kristina wasn't in the mood to appreciate it. Here she was, naked and frantic for Tarquin, and there on the other side of the room was a second man. A man who would watch them and was one of the worst men Tarquin could have chosen.

She shivered. If she took off the bracelet now then Jackie would have won. Jackie must have been certain that Kristina wouldn't go through with it, knowing how strongly she felt about the risks of one woman with two men, and would have been equally certain that by creating this situation she would end Kristina's relationship with Tarquin.

'Sam,' called Tarquin softly. 'Would you like to touch her?'

Sam Martin got out of his chair. He was still wearing his dinner suit and seemed unable to believe that this was happening to him. Tentatively he reached out and ran the fingers of his right hand in a line down the centre of Kristina's breasts until he reached her pubic hair. She shivered with a mixture of excitement and fear.

'Stand quite still, Kristina,' continued Tarquin, walking round to join Sam. Then he flicked at her quiescent nipples with the tip of his tongue until they were erect. Once they were fully extended he turned to Sam. 'Suck them gently, Sam,' he said with a half-smile. 'I want her to come just from that.'

Sam looked at Kristina's tense, aroused body and without any further instructions hurried to do as Tarquin had suggested. As he sucked carefully on the highly sensitive tissue, occasionally running his tongue round the rigid peak, Kristina stared deep into Tarquin's eyes and she felt the first tremors of an orgasm beginning deep inside her.

Tarquin continued to watch silently, and then he nodded in encouragement as despite his instruction for her to stand still her head went back and then she was shuddering as her body was overcome by a small but intense climax.

'Very good!' exclaimed Tarquin. 'Remain there Kristina while we both undress and then we can start to satisfy you more fully.'

She watched each of them undressing and her body felt more sensuous than ever before. She was no longer worried about the fact that Sam was a publisher, or that this might affect her work, all she could think about was the look on Tarquin's face when Sam had made her come, and the delights that she was about to experience.

'Sam, would you lie on your back on the bed?' asked Tarquin politely. 'I want to position Kristina on top of you, then with Lydia's help we should be able to stimulate almost every part of her at once. How does that sound, Kristina?'

She smiled at him. 'It sounds incredible.'

He moved close to her. 'Was this really something you'd always wanted to do?' She shook her head, and to her surprise he smiled in satisfaction. 'I thought not. In that case, it will be all the more exciting for everyone. We must make quite sure that it works out well.'

Sam Martin was already lying on the bed. Kristina saw that his body was in very good shape for a man of his age, with no trace of any spare flesh, and he had an extremely impressive erection.

'Lie face down on top of Sam,' said Tarquin. 'Support your weight slightly on your forearms and spread your legs out on each side of his legs. Then rub your pubic bones together in order to stimulate yourself, but don't come.'

Kristina felt as though she was in a dream. Although she obeyed him promptly it seemed that her limbs were moving in slow-motion, like an erotic love scene in an art film. The fact that she had only been introduced to the man beneath her earlier that evening was no longer of any importance. All that mattered was the thrill of obeying Tarquin's instruction, and the fierce consuming need driving her on towards the pleasure that awaited her.

The other Kristina, Kristina the brisk, no-nonsense literary agent, ceased to exist as raw sexuality took over and she revelled in the freedom that the so-called bondage of the bracelet gave her. Because she wasn't allowed to make decisions herself, she was able to lose herself in the freedom Tarquin's orders gave her. Freedom to do things that she would otherwise never have done, and freedom to enjoy them. Jackie had been right, she realised. By removing all responsibility from the women, the bracelet allowed free reign to their natural sensuality without any feelings of guilt.

'What are you thinking about?' asked Tarquin, looking down at her as she prepared to spread-eagle herself over the publisher.

'What a strange paradox the bracelet is,' she replied honestly. 'It doesn't really enslave me, it frees me.'

He nodded. 'Precisely. Not all women find that to be the case, but for many, and particularly women like you, it is the truth.'

She wanted to ask him what he meant by women like her, but that would not be allowed while she was wearing the bracelet. If they ever went out as equals though, she would ask him.

Once she was in position she pressed urgently down on the supine form beneath her. His penis was rubbing against her lower stomach, and when she pressed he caught his breath and moved slightly, clearly afraid that he'd climax straight away. The knowledge of the power she had over him increased Kristina's excitement and she ground down harder, and was rewarded by tiny, satisfying tingles of growing pleasure. The tingles spread and she started to feel a heat between her thighs. At the same time her breasts were rubbing against Sam's chest and they too tingled and swelled with arousal.

'That's enough,' said Tarquin quickly. 'Lydia's here now. She's going to spread your legs wider so that I can touch you from behind. You must keep facing Sam, don't look round at all.'

Kristina felt a slim hand grip her right ankle and then her right leg was being pulled out as far as it could go. 'Now lift your hips,' murmured Tarquin. 'Open yourself to me.' She raised her buttocks and her breasts squashed down against Sam's nipples, which made his penis move against her hip as he started to thrust upwards.

'Please don't move, Sam,' said Tarquin in a slightly bored voice. 'You'll only make it more difficult for me.'

Now that she was fully open to him, Tarquin reached beneath Kristina and very gently started to pull on her curly pubic hair. He used both hands and worked his way up towards her pubic bone, teasing at each side of the labia. The result was a delicious pricking sensation that travelled directly from where he was working to her clitoris, causing the tiny bud to swell until she could feel it stiffening. He refused to hurry, and each time he reached her pubic mound he would return to the far end of her sex lips and begin again until she was frantic for him to pleasure her further.

Eventually his fingers left the sensitive pubic hair and instead began to gently pull on both the sex lips at the same time, pulling and releasing in a steady rhythm that caused her to squirm and try to press down on Sam's body.

'Keep yourself raised up,' said Tarquin brusquely. 'Lydia, push her knee in a little, that should help her stay higher.' Lydia stroked the soft skin of Kristina's calf muscle for a moment and then pushed the leg in. She envied the dark-haired young woman this prolonged pleasuring that she herself had sometimes experienced from her employer.

After he'd worked steadily on the sex lips, Kristina's body felt ready to burst and she was gasping and moaning as her excitement mounted but failed to reach its peak. 'Turn over,' whispered Tarquin. 'I want to work on the front of you now. Sam can easily take your full weight, can't you Sam?' He seemed to take the strangled sound that Sam uttered as assent and, helped by Lydia, Kristina was turned and then her legs were again spread, but this time Sam spread his legs as well and she felt his erection nudging between the cheeks of her bottom.

'Bring me the warmed oil,' said Tarquin to Lydia. Kristina's breathing grew even more ragged as the ache inside her deepened. She looked longingly up at Tarquin, into the dark, enigmatic face that even now, when he was giving her such exquisite pleasure, showed nothing of his own feelings.

When Lydia returned he flexed the fingers of his left hand until they were pointing down just above Kristina's clitoris and then, as Lydia carefully prised open Kristina's sex lips, he poured the warmed oil over his own fingers so that it slowly seeped through them and ran down over Kristina's entire vulva.

The warm flooding sensation was like nothing she could ever have imagined. It felt as though it was actually filling her, flooding her internally with the strange heat, and the full, hot feeling was so intense that for a second she was afraid.

'Just wait a little longer,' he whispered reassuringly, gazing into her frantic eyes. 'Relax, enjoy the feeling. Give yourself over to it.'

Kristina discovered that she had no choice. As the oil seeped into every crevice, so her nerve endings were suffused with heat and seemed to shed a layer of protection so that everything she was experiencing was more intense than ever.

'Spread her legs still wider,' Tarquin ordered Lydia.

'I can't bear it,' groaned Kristina. 'The feelings are too much.'

'In a moment you'll come,' he promised her, and she felt Sam's hips jerk at the other man's words as his penis rubbed between her buttocks. She knew from Sam's breathing and the tension of his body beneath her back that he too was very near, but she didn't care about him. All she cared about was herself, the increasing need of her own wanton body.

At last Tarquin allowed a finger to slide up her oiled channel and then to Kristina's almost hysterical relief, he was circling the head of her clitoris at an even pace. After about a dozen circling movements he reversed the action, circling the other way as Kristina's body drew in on itself in preparation for the climax that was approaching.

Kristina was groaning now, thrusting her hips

upwards, virtually out of her mind with the frantic need for satisfaction. She heard Tarquin laugh gently, and then his finger stroked the side of her throbbing clitoris, moving lightly up and down, and this movement was the one that finally allowed her release from the delicious torture of the past half hour.

She felt the pulse behind her clitoris increase in intensity; there was a drumming in her ears, her face grew hot and then with a scream of relief she felt her body tighten yet more and finally shatter as the warmth flooded through every particle of her flesh and she writhed helplessly in the throes of the blissful muscular contractions that went on and on.

It was only when she was still that she realised that Sam had climaxed between the cheeks of her bottom, and that her continued thrashing on his lower body had been causing him some discomfort, but Tarquin was in no hurry to release the pinioned man and gently stroked Kristina's face for a moment.

'Was that good?' he asked.

'Better than ever,' she gasped breathlessly.

'Then I think it's my turn,' he muttered.

Kristina heard a faint sound of protest from the man beneath her, but Tarquin ignored it and the next thing she knew he was lying on top of both of them, his massive penis sliding easily inside her thanks to the oil he'd poured on earlier.

He took his weight on his hands and thrust in and out, slowly at first but then faster, and as his eyes grew

hooded and the sinews of his neck tightened she knew
that she was about to come again, and she cried out with
delight as another climax swept over her, less intense
but wonderfully warm and relaxing, and at last the ache
deep inside her was stilled.

Once again Tarquin removed himself from her
within a few seconds of his own climax, but this time
he did hold out a hand and pull a dazed Kristina to her
feet. Just for a moment he held her naked body against
his, and then he moved her to one side and looked down
at Sam.

'I trust you enjoyed the experience as well?' he asked
politely.

Kristina looked at the publisher and was surprised
to realise that he didn't want to look at anyone in the
room. He muttered a reply that could have been yes,
then got off the bed and started to dress.

Kristina looked at Tarquin, and to her joy he smiled
at her. 'A wonderful end to the evening,' he said, his
voice more affectionate than she'd ever heard it. 'You
were better than I dared to hope. I'll leave you to get
dressed, and Lydia will call you a taxi when you're ready,
as usual. At least now you've proved your friend wrong.'

Yes! thought Kristina triumphantly. She'd managed
to enjoy herself despite Jackie's efforts to spoil the
evening, and now Tarquin seemed keener on her than
before. At that moment her life looked very good.

The next morning, life didn't look quite so rosy. Kristina

hadn't got to bed until three and even then had slept fitfully, her mind and body still tuned to a high pitch that refused to allow her much rest. When she went into her office at nine a.m. she hoped that this wasn't going to be a difficult day, but Sue stopped her before she could reach the sanctuary of her own room.

'Kristina, I've had Sam Martin of Stoddart-Wades on the phone twice already. The second time he said he was about to go into a meeting, but would you ring someone called Estelle as she knew what it was all about. It sounded urgent.'

'Yes, I expect it did,' said Kristina with a sinking heart. She'd wondered when she'd hear from Sam, but nine o'clock this morning was far quicker than even she'd anticipated.

'Lucretia's been on as well. It seems that her royalty cheque doesn't tie in with the statements Alice sent her and she's got some queries she'd like to go through with you.'

'Can't she go through them with Alice?' asked Kristina.

Sue looked surprised. 'Well, she could, but you always like to deal with Lucretia yourself.'

Kristina nodded. 'Sorry, you're right. Give her a ring and say it will probably be this afternoon but I'll definitely get back to her, okay?'

Sue nodded. 'I've also got a message from Tom. He met with his new editor yesterday and isn't happy. Apparently the woman seemed more interested in the plight of the rainforest than the people of the village. He says he'd like you to speak to her.'

'What's the matter with people this morning!' exclaimed Kristina. 'Do I have to deal with every detail myself? The next thing you know they'll be asking me to write their damned books.'

'But this is the way you like to operate,' pointed out Sue. 'It's what makes you so successful, the personal touch that the large agencies can't supply. If you lose that you won't have much of an advantage over everyone else.'

Kristina scowled at her assistant. 'Are you saying I'm not doing my job properly?'

'Of course not; I'm only reminding you why you're so successful. Aren't you feeling well? You look a bit tired.'

'I'm fine, although I did have trouble sleeping,' admitted Kristina, wishing she could snap back into her business persona more smartly.

'Missing Ben?' Sue's voice was sympathetic.

'No, I am not missing Ben. Not having Ben around is possibly the best thing that's happened to me in a long time,' retorted Kristina. 'I've got to call Jackie, then you'd better ring Estelle for me.'

Sue nodded. 'Right. Remember you're lunching with Greta, our Dutch agent, that's one o'clock at Franco's.'

'Am I? Better check out exactly how many books she's sold for us over the past two years, then. If it's as few as I think this is the last free lunch she's getting.

Next time I'm at Frankfurt I must look for a different representative for her area.'

'I'll get the sales figures for you,' promised Sue, and at last Kristina was free to go into her office and shut the door on the sound of clattering keyboards. She sank down into her chair, rested her elbows on the desk and put her chin in her hands. It was proving more and more difficult to get involved in her work after sessions with the bracelet, and this worried her. Reluctantly she picked up the phone. Jackie sounded surprised to hear from her friend, surprised and a little defensive. 'Hi, I thought we weren't meeting up until next week. Is there a problem?' she asked.

'What kind of a problem could there be?' demanded Kristina. 'Surely I've rung you before without something being wrong?'

'Naturally, only I happen to be busy, so if it isn't important . . .'

'What are you doing? Another interview with a psychologist?'

There was a long silence. 'You've seen him, then?' asked Jackie.

'If by "him" you mean Dr Tarquin Rashid, yes I have seen him. I saw him last night. He arranged a very special evening for me, a bracelet evening naturally, and tried to make it one of the most memorable yet by acting on a suggestion that you'd "accidentally" let drop during your discussion on female friendships.'

'It was the merest hint of a suggestion,' said Jackie

defensively. 'I didn't know if he'd pick up on it or not, especially as I didn't let on that I belonged to the society, or that I knew you did and were seeing him. He could easily have ignored it all.'

'He's a psychologist, and, I understand, a good one. He was bound to pick up on anything, as you well know.'

'So what?' demanded Jackie, switching abruptly from defence to attack. 'You made love to Laurence without even the excuse of the bracelet. Did you really think I'd sit back and take that? That I'd be quite happy for you to continue your wonderful relationship with Tarquin and screw around with Laurence too?'

'I didn't mean Laurence to tell you; I've already explained that it just happened. It wasn't pre-planned, not like your little scheme.'

'Well, what did you do?' demanded Jackie with interest. 'Did you take off the bracelet?'

'No,' said Kristina, unable to hide the satisfaction she was feeling. 'I kept it on, did everything he asked and had a night that I'll never forget. All in all, you did me a favour. That's really why I'm ringing.'

'Meaning what?' asked Jackie, suddenly subdued.

'I thought I ought to thank you for helping me learn something new about myself. Now I know that it's sometimes best to throw aside old prejudices. If you don't try things how can you know if you like them or not?'

'You'll see Tarquin again, then?'

Kristina laughed. 'He was more eager for our next

meeting than I've ever known him. Look, Jackie, can we let it go now? Forget what's happened and carry on the way we used to?'

'I don't know,' replied her friend. 'I will say this though; you weren't exaggerating Tarquin Rashid's charms, I fancied him myself. With any luck he might go through the computer again some time and see me there. We got on very well.'

'Good; I hope he interviewed well?'

'As a matter of fact he did. I tried to interest him in a regular piece but he said he was too busy. Perhaps he'd like to write a book, then you could represent him and Laurence,' she added tartly.

Kristina sighed. 'I am *not* representing Laurence, Jackie.'

'According to him you are, and according to his would-be publisher. Strange that you're the only one who doesn't know! Sorry, I have to go now. I'll call you some time.'

The line went dead and Kristina felt a pang of loss. She and Jackie had been close for so many years that even a temporary hiccup in their relationship was difficult to take, and she had a nasty feeling that if they weren't both careful it would be more than temporary.

Before she had time to think about it further her phone buzzed. 'I've got Estelle from Stoddart-Wades on the line for you, Kristina,' said Sue.

Kristina tensed. 'Put her on,' she said.

'Kristina? You're in at last. Sam told me he'd been

ringing you ever since he arrived at the office. Long night was it?' asked Estelle, her voice amused.

'I don't start work until nine, however long or short my night's been,' replied Kristina calmly. 'What can I do for you?'

'It's not really for me, it's for your author, the divine Laurence van Kitson. Sam's very interested in his book and wants to make an offer for it.'

'Laurence will be delighted, but I'm afraid I'm not his agent,' retorted Kristina. 'He did come to me with the idea and I thought it a good one. The problem was, I didn't think he and I would work well together. I suggested he tried a couple of other very good agents.'

'He did, and he preferred you!' laughed Estelle. 'You know, Kristina, Sam is going to make an extremely generous offer for this book. You'd be rather foolish to turn it down. After all, your reputation's been built on deals like this.'

'What does it matter to you who his agent is?' queried Kristina. 'You'd be much better off if he didn't have an agent at all.'

Estelle made a sound of mock-indignation. 'I hope you're not suggesting we'd cheat an author who didn't have an agent? That isn't the policy here at Stoddart-Wades. We think of every author as a friend.'

'Only while they're making you a lot of money. I'm sorry Estelle but I'll have to pass on this one.'

'Sam will be very disappointed,' said Estelle smoothly. 'He was most impressed with you last night. Said he'd never seen a girl with such a head for business!' She laughed and Kristina gripped the receiver tightly.

'Sam will get over it,' she muttered.

'I'm not sure he will. Well, yes he'll get over it but he can be pretty ruthless when he doesn't get what he wants and there's always the possibility that he might shall we say "talk" about you if you don't prove to be part of the package.'

'Talk about me?' snapped Kristina. 'He's in no position to talk about anyone.'

'Perhaps "position" isn't the best word under the circumstances,' suggested Estelle. 'There's no need to be coy, I know all about it. Sam can't keep anything to himself. That was one of the reasons I suggested him for your little threesome last night. To be honest, I'm surprised you took the risk of going ahead with it. Mixing business with pleasure isn't wise, is it?'

'I thought he was your idea,' said Kristina. 'I admit I hesitated, but in the end I decided he had as much to lose as I had by talking out of turn.'

'Not quite as much. In the first place, he's a man. They're expected to enjoy sexual excesses, women aren't, even in these liberated times. In the second place, he doesn't belong to the society. That means he isn't bound by the society's rule of secrecy.'

'Yes he is. You told me that anyone who takes part in an evening's pleasure has to keep silent.'

'No, I said that it was more than my life was worth to talk about it because of offending Tarquin. Sam isn't bothered about offending Tarquin, all he's bothered about is seeing you again.'

Kristina's mind raced. 'But I was told that sessions with the bracelet were totally safe. That there was no risk of anyone ever using it against you in your other life.'

'But there's always a risk in things like that,' murmured Estelle, as though she were talking to a child rather than an intelligent business woman. 'You must have known that, deep down.'

'No, I didn't. I believed what others told me.'

'Of course, Sam hasn't said to me that he'd ever make things difficult for you,' said Estelle quickly. 'I'm only saying how it looks to me. Maybe Tarquin got some kind of promise from him about his silence before the evening began. All I'm saying is, there's a tiny chance he could talk and why take even a small risk over something like this? You could make a lot of money through Laurence. Quite apart from your secret life, think of the business side. Why are you so reluctant to represent our handsome South African?'

Because I don't trust him, thought Kristina. Because my best friend is madly in love with him, and he's exciting, sexy and dangerous. Aren't those enough reasons? The trouble was, she couldn't say any of them. They were all related to the society, not the real world.

She knew really that she had no choice. Quite apart from the danger of Sam talking, and that was something she could easily check with Tarquin, she knew that under normal circumstances she wouldn't dream of letting someone like Laurence slip through her fingers. Business was business, and she had to remember that.

What Jackie thought mustn't be allowed to sway her, not over a book contract, and it wasn't as though Estelle could have any devious reason for wanting her to represent Laurence.

'All right,' she conceded. 'I'll ring Laurence and arrange for the pair of us to come over and talk to Sam some time. Does he have any particular date in mind?'

'Tomorrow at two,' said Estelle. 'I must say, Kristina, I think you've made the right decision.'

'I hope so. What sort of sum are we talking here?'

'Five figures,' Estelle assured her.

'So I should hope, after all this fuss. Well into five figures?'

'I imagine so. Sam hasn't discussed the fine details with me. I'll be editing the book of course.'

'Good luck to you. I think you and Laurence should get along very well,' replied Kristina before she hung up. She hoped she hadn't made a mistake, but common sense told her that she hadn't. In the past she wouldn't have hesitated for a second. Things mustn't change because of the delights of the bracelet. That was already in her mind far more than it should have been, creeping into her thoughts whenever she had a spare moment. She could not allow it to creep insidiously into her work too.

In her office in Bloomsbury, Estelle smiled and

picked up her phone. 'Laurence? It's all arranged. Kristina will represent you. I hope I get a reward for this, it was hard work.'

'You'll get a reward,' promised Laurence at the other end of the line. Then he sat in his own office and smiled to himself. Meeting Estelle at a party a few weeks ago had turned out to be very useful. Now he was assured of seeing Kristina again, and with any luck at the next meeting of the male members of the society he'd also manage to have a few words with Tarquin Rashid. Eventually, no matter how long it took him, he was going to have Kristina and Jackie together with him in the same room at the same time, both wearing their bracelets of bondage.

That night, Kristina didn't get back from work until eight, but she still rang Tarquin the moment she got in. He was clearly surprised to hear from her, but as soon as she started to talk she knew that she'd done the right thing.

'You mean, Estelle implied Sam Martin would talk about last night to people in the publishing world?' he asked in astonishment when she'd finally poured out all her fears.

'Yes, she thought he might.'

'She knows perfectly well that isn't true. I would never have allowed him into my house had I not known that he was the soul of discretion. I'm not saying that he might not wish to see you again. Who could blame him after such an exciting evening? What I am saying is that no one you meet through me would ever threaten your position in the literary world. You must remember, Kristina, that I too have a vested interest in choosing participants very carefully. I could hardly continue in my line of work if such things were a matter of common knowledge.'

'It isn't the same for men!' protested Kristina, remembering what Estelle had said.

'Not some men, perhaps, but for anyone connected with the medical world it would be the end of his career. No, you must believe me, nothing we do together presents any kind of security risk.'

'I'm very pleased to hear it,' said Kristina with relief.

'I hope your day hasn't been ruined by this inference?'

She smiled to herself. He used the English language so quaintly and she found that very endearing. 'No, not ruined, but there was a dark cloud on the horizon.'

'I trust it's now been dispersed?'

She laughed. 'Totally dispersed.'

'I will contact you very soon,' he promised before he hung up.

All in all, thought Kristina when she went to bed, she'd done quite well for herself. She'd kept Laurence as a client, and that was going to bring in good money, and she'd also shown Estelle up as a less than truthful trouble-maker.

Her last thought of the day, before sleep claimed her, was that in the end she'd thrown off the effects of the bracelet and acquitted herself well as a literary agent again, which was the way she'd intended it to be from the start. Jackie was wrong. The thrill of sexual obedience didn't have to take you over to the extent she'd implied. You really could have it all.

Once again, Kristina's confidence was misplaced.

Chapter Eight

Because Kristina's house was on the way, it had been arranged that Laurence should call round there at one o'clock the following day and then the two of them would go on to the meeting at Stoddart-Wades. He was fifteen minutes late, but the comment that Kristina intended to make was stifled when she saw that he had someone with him.

His companion was a tall blonde woman in her early thirties. She was very striking, with immaculate make-up and large, long-lashed blue eyes that seemed far more innocent than the rest of her.

She was vaguely familiar to Kristina, but before she had a chance to try and place her, Laurence and the woman had walked into the house. 'This is Hester,' he said with a thin smile. 'Don't worry, Hester won't be accompanying us to our meeting. She'll wait quietly here until we return. Isn't that right Hester?'

'Of course,' replied the blonde in a surprisingly meek voice, and it was then that Kristina looked down and saw the thin gold bracelet on the other woman's wrist.

Laurence noticed Kristina's glance and without taking his eyes off her, pushed firmly on Hester's shoulders until she was sitting on the sofa. Then he stood at the back of it and ran his hands caressingly round the blonde's full breasts, which were tightly encased in a black lycra dress. He massaged them firmly, moving the globes in circles until Hester's breath quickened and colour rose in her cheeks.

'She's very responsive,' he said laconically to the astonished Kristina. 'That's one of the things I like best about her. Unfortunately she's abroad on business a lot, but today she happened to be free and neither of us wanted to pass up the opportunity to meet. I hope you don't mind if she stays here until we get back? She could provide a lot of very good references.'

'I don't mind,' said Kristina, trying not to look as though the scene was having any effect on her. 'There are plenty of books on the shelves, Hester. Feel free to browse through any of them.'

'I'm afraid Hester won't be free to do anything,' said Laurence sharply. 'Where's the spare bedroom?'

Kristina frowned. 'It's on the left at the top of the stairs, but we've got to go now. We're late as it is.'

'This won't take a moment,' he assured her, his clipped South African vowels sounding more pronounced than usual. 'Hester, this way.' The blonde rose and followed him, as she had to while she continued wearing the bracelet, and Kristina found that she couldn't resist following them.

Once inside the spare room, Laurence pulled the black Lycra dress off over Hester's head, revealing a lush naked body with soft womanly curves. Then he laid her naked on her back on the bed and pulled some silk cord out of his jacket pocket.

Kristina stayed in the doorway, watching intently as he tied Hester's ankles and wrists and then covered her eyes with a dark blue silk scarf, adjusting it carefully in order to leave her ears uncovered. Fleetingly he allowed his right hand to brush against her rounded hips and cross the softness of her belly, then with a regretful sigh he perched on the edge of the bed.

'Don't move until I get back, Hester,' he ordered. 'I'm sorry about this meeting, but since I can't pay you the kind of attention you'd like right now, I'm going to leave you a little something to listen to in my absence. It might help pass the time.' Kristina stared as he laid an iPod in the middle of the bed, put the headphones over Hester's ears and then pressed play.

'What was that?' asked Kristina as they left the house.

'Oh, just a little something I put together this morning. It's a very intimate conversation really. I tell her all the things I'm going to do to her when I get back, and remind her of how it will feel. Once we return she should be more than ready for me, don't you agree?'

Kristina did. By blindfolding Hester, Laurence had

made sure that her mind, with nothing else to focus on, would create its own scenes as his arousal tape played on and on.

'What about Jackie?' she asked curiously.

Laurence raised his eyebrows. 'What about her?'

'I thought that you and she spent most of your time together, that's all.'

'We do, but Hester and I go back a long way. She's very big in the fashion industry and spends most of her time abroad. When we can meet up, we do. It makes a nice change for her. Most of the time she's telling her men what to do and how to make her come. Wearing the bracelet gives her a holiday! How did it make you feel watching me prepare her?'

'I was worried we'd be late,' said Kristina shortly, refusing to admit to him that she was very aroused herself, and that she kept imagining how Hester must be feeling lying helplessly on the bed with Laurence's silkily suggestive voice in her ears.

'Is that all? I could have sworn it had turned you on too! Let's hope Sam Martin doesn't keep us too long or Hester will go mad with frustration!'

Sam was waiting for them in the entrance lobby. He greeted Kristina with a kiss on both cheeks and an arm that rested just a shade too familiarly on her waist, but his expression was strictly business-like.

'Come up to my office,' he said warmly. 'Let's hope this is the first of many such meetings.'

'I expect Hester would like that too,' whispered

Laurence to Kristina, and sparks of arousal stirred inside her at the thought of the helpless, even more aroused blonde waiting for Laurence to return.

For the first half hour they talked about the construction of the book, and how specialised Sam wanted it to be, before moving on to their advertising plans and personal publicity by Laurence.

'You're a good-looking young man,' remarked Sam. 'Women will flock to buy it if we can get you on something like *The One Show*. What do you say, Kristina?'

'Women certainly seem to like him,' she agreed, although she couldn't help wondering if 'like' would be quite the right word to describe how Hester must be feeling at that moment.

'Yes, you and the book are a good package. Try not to be too intelligent though; we don't want to put the average reader off, if you know what I mean!' He laughed, but Laurence didn't.

'I'm afraid I can't act the fool, even to sell my own book,' he said shortly.

'No, no! I didn't mean act the fool, I meant try not to seem too superior. There's a big difference, and if you're going to attract the ordinary reader then there has to be a warm side to you. Sure, there's an attraction about men who seem remote and hard to catch, but it's not the kind of attraction that sells books. Isn't that right, Kristina?'

'Yes, and I think I can probably help Laurence on

that before we get to the publicity stage,' Kristina promised him.

Sam nodded. 'I'm certain you can. Kristina's a very friendly girl underneath that professional business woman's exterior, Laurence. Believe me, I know that better than anyone.'

Laurence turned his pale blue eyes on Kristina. 'Is that a fact? I didn't realise you two were that well acquainted.'

'We haven't know each other long,' said Kristina, far more calmly than she felt. 'It's just that we got on very well when we did meet up one evening. Isn't that right, Sam?'

He nodded enthusiastically. 'One of the best nights out I've had in years.'

Kristina knew that Laurence had guessed something had gone on that was connected with the society, but she was determined to put a stop to that line of thought. 'We went to Covent Garden's new production of *Tosca* and it was a memorable performance for all of us,' she said with a tight smile. 'It's just a pity Mrs Martin couldn't be there as well.'

Sam recognised the veiled threat and the gleam in his eyes died away. 'Sadly my wife doesn't enjoy the opera.'

'Neither do I,' said Laurence. 'Ghastly noise. I'm always waiting for the intervals and the next bottle of champagne. So, when do you want the manuscript delivered?'

'I think you can safely leave the contract details to me, Laurence,' said Kristina lightly. Laurence went very white, and for a moment an expression of anger crossed his lean face, but then it vanished and the realisation that he was more dangerous than she'd thought flashed through Kristina's mind.

'Naturally I'm not expecting to draw up my own contract,' he assured her. 'But as I'm the one who has to write the book, I thought I should know how long I've got.'

'How long will it take you?' asked Sam.

Laurence laughed. 'As long as I want.'

'Let's say twelve months,' suggested Kristina. 'If you deliver early I'm sure Sam won't mind, but that allows for delays if your day-to-day business affairs hold it up.'

'Sounds fine to me,' agreed Sam.

After that they talked for another twenty minutes and then, much to Kristina's relief because she'd been horribly aware of Hester throughout the entire meeting, she and Laurence were free to leave.

'How about a cup of coffee somewhere?' he suggested.

Kristina shook her head. 'I have to get back to the office, and you have to collect Hester.'

He smiled with his mouth, but once again his eyes were cold. 'I hadn't forgotten her. Anticipation works wonders. She won't mind waiting and the recording is on repeat.'

'I still don't want coffee.'

'You'll come back and let me in to get her though?'

Kristina looked at her watch and sighed. 'I'll have to, but I've got loads left to do at the office, and very little time to do it in.'

The minute they were back inside the house, Laurence went into the kitchen and started to fill the kettle.

'What the hell do you think you're doing?' demanded Kristina. '*I'm* not wearing a bracelet, you know. I want you and Hester out of here, fast.'

'I'm thirsty. You go; I'll lock up carefully if that's what's worrying you.'

'I want to see you both leave,' replied Kristina. 'Now would you go upstairs, untie your friend and take her back to your own place.'

For a moment Laurence stared at her, then without another word he brushed past her and walked slowly up the stairs. Kristina waited in the hallway. The moment Laurence opened the door to the spare bedroom she heard Hester start to scream at him.

Her threats as to what she intended to do when she was free and what she thought of him for leaving her listening to the tape were far from subservient, and Kristina smiled to herself, but then she saw Laurence descending the stairs on his own and the smile left her face.

'Where's Hester?'

'She can't wait. I'll have to let her come now or she'll keep screaming all the way to my flat. It won't take more than a few minutes. You can watch if you like.'

Astounded, Kristina saw him pick up Hester's shoulder bag and then carry it back up to the bedroom. Part of her wanted to tell him to get the hell out of her house and take the blonde Hester with him, but the other part, the part that enjoyed belonging to the society of the bracelet, wanted to see what was going to happen in the spare room. Almost without realising what she was doing, she too climbed the stairs to the spare room.

Hester's ankles and wrists had been untied, but she was still wearing the blindfold. She heard the sound of a second set of footsteps in the room and turned her head blindly towards the noise.

'It's only Kristina,' said Laurence. 'As my agent she's like one of the family. Besides, we are using her bed! Time to carry out all my promises, I think. Kristina, do you have a spare pillow? I may need it later.'

'There are two on the bed, that will have to be enough,' retorted Kristina, unwilling to leave the room for even a moment.

'Right then, Hester. On your hands and knees, just like I said on the tape,' ordered Laurence, and Hester, who was now totally silent, obeyed without question.

Kristina looked at the blonde woman's full smooth buttocks and then Laurence began to massage them, just as earlier he'd massaged her breasts. He moved the cheeks of her bottom around, and kneaded at the flesh with his fingers, pressing up hard from underneath.

Out of Hester's bag he drew some massage lotion and a pair of thin rubber gloves and soon he was spreading the lotion over the blonde's upper thighs and bottom and then across her lower back and down the crack at the base of her spine, where the cheeks of her bottom met. When he reached that highly sensitive area Hester wriggled and shouted at him to hurry.

'Hester, remember the bracelet,' said Laurence warningly. 'I'm not one of your toy boys. I call the tune here.'

'I'm sorry,' she murmured, and Kristina's stomach lurched at the remembrance of similar, delicious subjugation. Her body longed for Tarquin.

'So you should be,' Laurence replied, and then he was parting her buttocks and carefully rimming the opening of her rear entrance with the lotion, easing a little of it inside the opening of her rectum and swirling his finger around in a featherlight teasing caress as he worked.

Hester was frantic for her climax now. She was groaning and gasping, thrusting her buttocks provocatively towards him and trying to twist her hips around in order to stimulate herself, but Laurence sharply ordered her to keep still.

When she obeyed he put his hand back into her bag and drew out a pronged instrument that Kristina realised was a double-headed dildo. Smothering both ends with the lotion he then indicated with his head that Kristina should move nearer the bed.

She did, walking as lightly as she could, but Laurence wanted Hester to know Kristina was there. 'My agent's watching you now, Hester. She's anxious to see you come. I think she's been worrying about you all the afternoon. Is that right, Kristina?'

'I was concerned,' admitted Kristina, relieved to find that her voice sounded steady despite the sexual turmoil she was feeling at the sight of the curvaceous blonde so obviously desperate for a climax with her glistening flesh and twitching muscular spasms.

'Spread your knees a little wider,' said Laurence. Hester whimpered with excitement and moved as he suggested. Then, when she was steady again, he carefully inserted the prongs of the dildo into her two openings and began to move them in and out in a slow teasing movement, only penetrating a little way at first, causing Hester to thrust back with her hips.

'Wait!' he snapped. 'I choose when to penetrate you fully. Tell me how near you are.'

'I'm right there!' shouted Hester. 'I feel as though I'm going to explode. My breasts are aching, my stomach's cramping and I ache between my thighs.'

'You certainly sound ready,' he admitted, glancing at Kristina. 'Right then, here we go. You have thirty seconds to climax. After that, I stop and we leave. We've taken up enough of Kristina's valuable time already.'

Kristina looked at him with a mixture of surprise and admiration. It was a very clever touch at this stage. A few seconds earlier Hester must have felt she'd come the moment he gave her enough stimulation, now she had the psychological fear in her mind that if she didn't then she'd have to wait much, much longer for her satisfaction.

Hester recognised the diabolical quality of the trap too. 'No, not a timed climax, Laurence,' she begged. 'Not after all this.'

Ignoring her, he started to move the two heads in and out of her pulsating openings, working her with consummate skill so that she was shouting and panting as her excitement grew to fever pitch, but all the time he worked he counted off the seconds aloud as well and this distracted her so much that when he said 'thirty' she still hadn't quite come.

Without any comment, Laurence removed the dildo and pulled Hester upright. 'Bad luck. We'll start again back at my flat.'

As he tore off the silk blindfold, Kristina saw the dazed, disbelieving frustration on Hester's face, but there was nothing the blonde could say because she was still wearing the bracelet.

Then, as she clambered off the bed, Laurence abruptly reached between her thighs and squeezed her swollen clitoris between his thumb and forefinger. 'No!' cried Hester, but she was too late and Laurence and Kristina watched as her body bent double on itself and the delayed release caused her to momentarily lose control of herself and her muscles.

She half-fell back on to the bed as her belly continued

to ripple and the contractions swept over her while she whimpered helplessly for forgiveness.

'It seems you've forgotten how the discipline of the bracelet works,' said Laurence dispassionately. 'Perhaps you need another lesson. I think we'll go straight back to my flat and have it now, before you forget the error of your ways today.'

Hester gasped, and Kristina saw her right hand move to the bracelet, but then she let her hand fall back to her side and nodded. 'I think we should,' she agreed, her voice docile.

After they'd left and Kristina was on her way back to the office, Kristina couldn't help wondering exactly what Hester's lesson would involve.

'Jacqueline's called three times while you've been out,' said Sue the moment Kristina walked through the door. 'She asked you to ring back as soon as you got in. Apparently it's very urgent.'

'Right,' sighed Kristina, who could guess what the call was about.

She was right in her guess; Jacqueline was very angry. 'You told me you weren't going to be Laurence's agent,' she shouted down the phone. 'But you are, aren't you?'

'Yes,' admitted Kristina. 'I was going to tell you, but I haven't had the chance. It all happened so quickly.'

'And you've been out with him today, too. Was there time for anything intimate before you parted company, or will that happen later? He told me he wouldn't be in touch for a few days; I guessed immediately it was you.

How could you do this to me again? After we talked I believed you. I honestly thought you meant what you said, but it was all lies wasn't it? Why, Kristina? Are you on some power trip that means you have to have everyone in the society?'

'Will you listen for a moment,' said Kristina sharply. 'I took Laurence on because I got myself in a bit of a mess through the society, and in the end it made more sense to represent him than to pass him on to someone else.'

'Business sense, or sexual sense?' asked Jackie tartly.

'Believe it or not, this was a business decision. I realised that I was allowing my private life to interfere with my work. Laurence is a very good proposition from a financial point of view. I thought about turning him down because I knew you'd be upset, but that wasn't a good enough reason, not where work's concerned. You wouldn't miss a journalistic scoop involving Tarquin simply out of consideration for my delicate feelings, would you?'

'Am I meant to deduce from all this that you're not sexually involved as well?' asked Jackie, her voice tight with anger.

'Hard as you might find this to believe, that happens to be the truth. We are not sexually involved any more. Last time was a one-off; it won't happen again.'

'Then why isn't he free to see me?' demanded Jackie.

'I don't know,' lied Kristina, aware that it wasn't her place to tell her friend what Laurence chose to do.

'But you must know. He and I had something special going. It was perfect until you joined the society.'

'For the last time would you get this into your head, Jackie. I have *never* had any contact with Laurence through the society of the bracelet. I've never worn the bracelet for him, and I never intend to. What you seem to forget is that he's perfectly free to see other women through the society apart from you. Perhaps he feels afraid you're becoming too involved. That's one of the things we're supposed to be trying to escape from ourselves, come to that!'

'Is this what Laurence has been telling you?' demanded Jackie. 'Does he think I'm trying to take him over?'

Kristina wished that Jackie would get off the line and leave her alone. She had work to do, and she also kept thinking of Hester and the way Laurence had played with her, physically and mentally, in such an erotic way. It had left Kristina thoroughly aroused, and longing for a call from Tarquin. She was certainly in no mood to listen to her friend's accusations, especially this time, when they were largely unfounded.

'He never discusses you with me,' she said shortly. 'Sorry, I've got to go now. The other phone's ringing.'

'I know he wants to have you under his control, wearing the bracelet,' hissed Jackie. 'And if you're honest, you know it too. That's why you took him on as a client, not because of his boring book. Well, when he gets his way you might find you don't like it as much as you think you will.'

'I've never given it a moment's thought,' lied Kristina, and she hung up.

The rest of the afternoon passed far too quickly. There were books to look at, manuscripts to chase up from tardy authors and equally tardy publishers and the usual number of desperate authors suffering from sudden attacks of writer's block.

'It's a good job I don't get agent's block!' laughed Kristina when Sue brought in some letters to be signed.

'It isn't the same,' Sue pointed out. 'You're dealing with sensitive, creative creatures, not ordinary mortals like you and me!'

'True, but it's a shame they have to be quite so temperamental. I suppose you need to be mad to become a writer in the first place. Is this the lot?'

'Yes, all done. Is it all right if I go now? It's after six and I'm due to meet Greg at seven. We're seeing the new Ryan Gosling film. That's the penalty he has to pay for going to football every Saturday of the season!'

Kristina smiled. 'That's fine, go ahead. I'll lock up as soon as I've sorted out tomorrow's work. Remind me to chase Lindsey Price about her children's book. She's way overdue and her editor's getting a bit nervous.'

'Will do,' promised Sue.

Once she was alone, Kristina found that there was more work to sort through than she'd thought and it was seven thirty before she was ready to leave. She'd just reached the outer office when the phone went. After a brief hesitation she picked it up before her voicemail cut in.

'Kristina Masterton.'

'I thought you must still be at work,' said Tarquin's voice. She drew in a sharp breath, praying that he was going to suggest seeing her. 'I tried your home number a couple of times and this was my last attempt.'

'Lucky you caught me; I was about to leave.'

'Are you free tonight? Estelle and I are having a literary evening; you seemed the ideal guest for the occasion.'

Kristina's excitement faded a little. She didn't want a literary evening; she wanted, needed, eroticism and sensuality, but more than that she needed to see Tarquin and so she didn't hesitate. 'That sounds like fun. What time?'

'Come now,' he suggested. 'You can eat here.'

'But I'm wearing my office clothes!' she protested.

'That doesn't matter in the least,' Tarquin assured her gently. 'By the end of the evening you won't be wearing anything at all.'

Her pulse quickened and once again her excitement rose. She should have known, she thought to herself. Tarquin wouldn't bother to ask her to an ordinary literary dinner party. This was something special, and even the fact that it included Estelle didn't put her off.

'In that case, I'll be there in the next half hour,' she promised him.

'It's nice to know that you're always ready to try new things,' he murmured. 'I find that I'm beginning to look forward to our meetings more and more. All you need to bring with you tonight is yourself and your undoubtedly considerable depth of knowledge about the plays of William Shakespeare.'

'Shakespeare?' asked Kristina blankly, but he'd already hung up on her. She shrugged to herself. Shakespeare had never been one of her favourite playwrights, and you could put what she knew about his plays on the back of a postage stamp, but she didn't think that was likely to spoil the evening.

In Tarquin's house Estelle looked at him as he replaced the receiver. 'Well?' she asked eagerly.

He half-smiled. 'I got the feeling that our attractive literary agent is not the greatest admirer of the Bard.'

'All the more fun for us then!'

He shook his head. 'All the more fun for me, Estelle.'

She pouted. 'Surely I'm allowed to enjoy it too? After all, I'm seeing far less of you since Kristina came on to the scene. This is my compensation.'

'We see plenty of each other,' he murmured. Estelle wondered why it was that she couldn't ever get really close to him. Her only comfort was that no other woman could either.

'I'll set up the room,' she said quickly.

'Good. I'll prepare the questions. Easy at first I think, in order to lull her into a sense of security, then the more difficult ones. Make quite sure to set the scene exactly as I said. Atmosphere makes such a difference to an evening like this.'

Estelle pressed herself against him and he took her face between his hands and kissed her lightly on the mouth. 'It's strange that the society's never tempted you,' he murmured.

'I'd never wear a bracelet that meant I was helpless, some kind of sexual toy for a man to use as he chose,' she retorted. 'I've far too much self-respect for that.'

He nodded. 'I thought that was what you believed.'

Estelle frowned. 'What do you mean, "believed"?'

'I think your reasons are actually more profound than that.'

'Is this a professional assessment?' she asked.

'Yes, it is.'

'Then please let me have the benefit of your expert knowledge. Why don't I want to join the society?'

'Because you're afraid of finding out what would happen if you ever allowed yourself to lose control of a situation. It takes a very special kind of self-confidence to do that, you know.'

'You don't think I've got much self-confidence?' she asked in disbelief.

'Not in your personal relationships, no. Most people haven't, Estelle. You're not in the minority.'

Her temper flared. 'I suppose that means Kristina is more confident and liberated than I am?'

'I don't think I want to answer that. This isn't the time for a quarrel, and in any case the remark wasn't meant to be a comparison between you and another woman. It was an analysis of your personality, nothing more.'

'It's a pity you can't stop analysing everything,' she snapped as she walked away.

Twenty-five minutes after she'd received the phone call, Kristina rang Tarquin's door bell. It was Estelle who opened the door, and she smiled pleasantly at the newcomer.

'Hi, glad you could make it. How's Laurence? Sam seems very impressed by him and his book.'

'I think that's because Sam knows the family and has an interest in diamonds. I'm not sure that the book will do as well as he imagines, but that's not my problem,' replied Kristina.

'Of course not. Anyway, we mustn't talk shop. Tarquin would be very annoyed. This evening is meant to be an escape from all that, isn't that right?'

'Yes,' agreed Kristina. 'It's a very good form of stress-relief!'

'I hope you feel the same after the evening's entertainment. We're using the back room. I don't think you've been in there before, have you?'

Kristina shook her head, and went with Estelle down the hallway. When they reached the door to the room Tarquin appeared from what she assumed to be the kitchen area. He was wearing light blue slacks and a white short-sleeved shirt, a far more casual outfit than Kristina had ever seen him in before, and yet he somehow still managed to look formal. He nodded in greeting, then handed over the bracelet.

'Perhaps you'd like to look in the room before you put this on?' he suggested.

Behind her ribs, Kristina's heart thumped. 'No,' she said firmly. 'I trust you enough to put it on now.'

'Excellent. As usual you can remove it at any point in time. Shall we go through?' and he pushed open the door.

Kristina hadn't been sure what she was expecting, but it certainly wasn't the scene that met her eyes. The room was in semi-darkness, the thick curtains drawn to shut out the evening light. Dimmed lamps provided an eerie glow. But it was the furniture that astonished her; in the middle of the room was a large, comfortable-looking leather chair with the beam from a suspended spotlight trained on it, while in the shadow directly opposite the chair were two straight-backed tapestry chairs with a small table in front of them. In the dim recesses of the room she could see that other pieces of furniture had been pushed out of the way, but she couldn't make out any of them clearly, and in any case she wasn't interested in them. The layout of the room made her think of an interrogation scene from a film, and her throat tightened.

'Does it remind you of anything?' asked Tarquin, his hand stroking softly through her dark, curly hair.

'Yes, an interrogation room at a police station,' she responded.

'Do they really have such comfortable leather chairs for their suspects?'

Kristina turned her face up to his. 'I suppose not. I've never been questioned by the police.'

'You're not frightened, are you?'

'Yes,' she admitted. 'I am a little.'

'There's no need. I did tell you this was to be a literary evening, remember?'

'But I can't see what this has to do . . . Wait a minute, it's like *Mastermind*!'

He nodded. 'Exactly, this is our own quiz room for the night. I shall be the question master, Estelle will be the timekeeper and you, naturally, are the contestant.'

'Only me?' asked Kristina.

'Yes, there's only you because the rules are not precisely the same as on the television show! Every time you make a mistake, you'll be punished. The punishments vary in severity according to the difficulty of the question. Sometimes we won't stop until you've incurred a few penalties. That way we can have one punishment session for a group of errors.'

'And the questions are on the plays of Shakespeare?' asked Kristina.

'Yes, not too taxing for a literary agent I'm sure. Now, let me see what you're wearing.'

He stood back and looked at her. She was dressed in a knee-length cream linen skirt with a blue jacket that was nipped in at the waist, then flared out over her hips. On her feet were blue high-heeled shoes and her holdups were navy blue silk.

'You're dressed for the part,' he said with satisfaction. 'I think it's time you took your seat. Estelle, get the stop-watch ready and sort the questions for me please.'

Kristina began to walk towards the chair and then stopped. Suddenly her legs refused to move and she started to tremble. Tarquin came up behind her and she felt one of his long-fingered hands in the small of her back. 'I'm told all quiz show contestants suffer from last-minute nerves. I do hope you're not going to run out on me?'

'No,' she said hastily. 'Of course not.' He reached out and tugged softly on her gold bracelet. 'The delights of obedience,' he whispered, and immediately she shivered with desire and hurried to the chair.

Once she was seated she stared straight ahead of her. She could just make out Tarquin's face, but Estelle was virtually invisible in the shadows. He picked up a card.

'You have to name the play from which each of the quotations I give you comes, Kristina. Here's the first. *"To be, or not to be, that is the question"*?'

Kristina smiled in relief. The game wasn't going to be as hard as she'd feared. *'Hamlet,'* she said confidently.

'Correct. *"I will do anything, Nerissa, ere I will be married to a sponge"*?'

Kristina stared blankly at him. 'I've no idea,' she said honestly.

'You're meant to say Pass. That's two mistakes. Please stand and take off your skirt.'

Kristina obeyed, and her legs were trembling so much they would hardly support her. The whole atmosphere in the room was charged with erotic electricity, and she knew that all three of them were in a state of high sexual tension that Tarquin's measured tones only increased.

When she sat back in the chair she was very aware of the soft leather against her bare buttocks as her blue G-string style panties rose up high between them. She glanced down and saw that her jacket just covered her pubic area at the front.

'*"Now is the winter of our discontent"?*' asked Tarquin briskly.

'*Richard the Third,*' she said with relief.

'Correct. *"O thou weed"*?'

'What?' asked Kristina in astonishment. Tarquin repeated the words. 'But that's not a full quote. It could come from anything!' she protested.

'But it doesn't, and arguing with the quiz-master is an error. Answer please.'

'Pass,' she whispered helplessly.

Tarquin sighed. 'It's from *Othello*. Remove your jacket.'

Again Kristina stood, and as she peeled off the jacket she heard Tarquin's sigh of pleasure at the sight of her small breasts thrust upwards by the cleverly wired bra she was wearing.

She sat again, and the next question was easy, but

after that she was totally lost. As pass followed pass she felt her hands grow damp and there was a sheen of perspiration on her forehead because, despite all her mistakes, he continued to ask questions, and she knew that her degree of punishment was increasing all the time.

At last he stopped. 'Fifteen passes to date. Not very good for a literary agent. Time to administer some appropriate punishment. Please rise and stand to the right of the chair.'

When she was in place, Tarquin came over and sat in the leather chair himself. 'You do know you deserve to be punished, don't you?' he asked gently.

Kristina remembered the bracelet, and understood what she had to say. 'Yes,' she agreed submissively.

'Good. Then bend over my knee, but first remove your bra. The panties can stay in place for the moment.'

She felt incredibly vulnerable as she took off her bra and then bent face-down over his knees, keenly aware that Estelle was watching them from the darkness. She tensed her buttocks, but to her surprise he started to stroke them with a gentle hand.

'You have lovely buttocks,' he said quietly. 'I adore your body, it's so soft and smooth. For perfection I'd like larger breasts, but that's a very small quibble.'

As he continued to stroke her bottom and talk soothingly and admiringly about her, Kristina started to relax. She still felt humiliated because Estelle was watching, but it wasn't as bad as she'd feared. Surprisingly this almost disappointed her. After such a high degree of sexual tension it was something of an anticlimax.

Then, with no warning at all, Tarquin spanked her hard on the buttocks with the flat of his hand. She felt a burning sensation and gasped with surprise, but immediately he began to run his hand over the area he'd just struck until once more she relaxed against his knees.

As soon as her body was limp and pliant again, he struck once more, but harder this time and along with the stinging sensation Kristina felt other nerve ends reacting. Her breasts began to swell and her nipples hardened, while her stomach muscles tightened and ripples of pleasure ran from her navel down to her pubic bone.

This time Tarquin bent his head and licked the burning area he'd previously struck, and the feeling was so delicious that her whole body felt swollen with desire and she wriggled against his knee to stimulate the tight little bud that was throbbing between her thighs.

'Keep still,' he warned her, and then he slapped her a third time, causing her whole body to jerk with excitement, and one of her shoes fell to the ground. She was incredibly aroused, the contrast between the slaps and the soothing that followed was driving her mad and she knew that she could climax easily if only he'd touch her in the right place.

'Say you did badly,' he whispered against her ear. 'Say you're a disgrace and must try harder next time.'

Kristina gabbled out the words. 'Louder,' he commanded, his fingers kneading at her sensitive bottom until she thought she'd go out of her mind with frustration as she teetered on the edge of her climax.

'I must try harder next time!' she screamed and then, just when she was certain she could take no more, he reached beneath her and softly stroked between her sex lips until the tip of his finger brushed her swollen clitoris. She climaxed instantly, her body convulsing over his legs, squeezing them together with the force of her muscular contractions.

She heard herself moaning with delight as the wonderful melting heat swept through every part of her and the desperate tension of the previous half hour was at last dissipated.

'Good,' said Tarquin, standing up so quickly that she almost fell to the floor. 'Sit back in the chair and we'll try again.'

It wasn't until Kristina sat down that she realised how sore her buttocks were, and they burned as they touched the chair. She winced, but then the coolness acted as a balm and slowly she became comfortable again.

She was so caught up in the sensations that she failed to hear the first question, and had to ask Tarquin to repeat it. 'That's an error,' he stated, before giving her the quote for the second time.

The words meant nothing to Kristina. 'Pass,' she whispered, and as she spoke she was startled to feel a sexual thrill pass through her, tightening her breasts and quickening her breathing. It was the realisation that she was once again storing up a punishment for herself that was so arousing.

'"*Love is blind, and lovers cannot see the pretty follies that themselves commit*"?' quoted Tarquin, and Kristina almost smiled.

'*Merchant of Venice!*'

'Correct, and very apt too, I feel! "*Villain and he be many miles asunder*"?'

'Pass,' she murmured, and again the thrill of sexual excitement lanced through her tight, swelling body.

After six more passes Tarquin stopped. 'Eight passes, time for the punishment. Estelle, it's your turn to sit in the chair, but first you must be naked too.'

This was something entirely new, and Kristina watched as Estelle walked into the glare of the spotlight and with easy grace discarded her ankle length crinkle-cotton overdress, then peeled off the T-shirt that was beneath it. She was wearing no underwear, and her lightly tanned legs were also bare.

'Stand up and let Estelle take your place,' said Tarquin, watching Kristina's reaction to this new development. As soon as Estelle was seated he pressed a release lever at the side of the chair and partially reclined it, which meant that Estelle was lying back at an angle.

'Perfect! Now you sit on her lap and then lie back against the front of her body,' he ordered Kristina. She looked at him and wondered whether to do as he asked or not. She'd never been involved sexually with another woman before, and wasn't certain it was her scene, but she reminded herself that if she didn't try she'd never know. Without further delay she slid on to the other woman's lap and lay back carefully, feeling Estelle's full breasts pressing against her naked back.

The two women's legs were one on top of each other and Tarquin knelt down and parted them both. This meant that the muscles in Kristina's buttocks were pressing hard on Estelle's pubic bone at the same time as she herself was opened up to Tarquin's attentions.

He pushed the front of Kristina's panties to one side and slid his right hand inside, pushing down on the fleshy area to the side of her pubic mound. The pressure sent sparks through her entire vulva and she felt her clitoris begin to tingle and swell. Tarquin's hand eased further inside the panties and now he slowly massaged over the outer part of her vaginal area, skilfully stimulating the sensitive tissue beneath until she could feel the clitoris throbbing behind the covering of her sex lips.

Tarquin was in no hurry to progress further, and the longer he kept stimulating her the more Kristina's need for a climax increased until she began to make whimpering sounds in her throat and her body moved restlessly.

'Remember, this is a punishment,' pointed out Tarquin, watching her breasts swell and the veins in them become more prominent as a pink sexual flush suffused her upper chest. 'You have to wait for your orgasm until Estelle's had hers.'

'Estelle?' gasped Kristina.

Beneath her, Estelle smiled. Already her nipples were hard from the movement of Kristina's body during Tarquin's clever manipulations of her body, and she too was very near to climaxing, but she was determined to postpone the moment as long as possible in order to keep Kristina waiting.

'You have to help,' said Tarquin. 'Press down harder with your buttocks. Grind against her pubic bone, and move yourself up and down. That will tug on the skin around her clitoris and should give her some delicious sensations, sensations that I'm sure are familiar to you.'

His words were an aphrodisiac in themselves, and Kristina felt she was going to burst, she was so full and needy, but she remembered the bracelet and knew that she had to obey.

Estelle felt the other woman's buttocks moving as instructed, and now it was her turn to feel the delicious hot tingles of an approaching climax as all her pubic area became suffused with heat and she too started to whimper.

The whimpering almost drove Kristina mad. She knew the feeling of being close to orgasm so well that to hear another woman's cries of desire was unbearable.

As Estelle pressed her aching breasts harder into Kristina's back, Tarquin ran a finger over the outside of Kristina's panties, along the line between her outer sex lips, and he laughed to himself. 'You're very damp, Kristina. I wonder how damp Estelle is? Reach between your thighs and find out for yourself. I want you to tell me if she's moist and ready for me.'

Kristina wriggled harder. She felt that this torture was unbearable, to have to touch Estelle when it was her own aching, throbbing clitoris that needed to be touched, but just the same she reached tentatively down between her spread-eagled thighs and then hooked her fingers back towards Estelle's body. This meant that she put more pressure on her own pulsating clitoris but she fought frantically to ignore that as her fingers parted Estelle's sex lips and slid upwards to the tiny bud, slippery with Estelle's excitement.

'Good,' said Tarquin approvingly as he heard Estelle's sharp intake of breath. 'Now circle it with your finger, but slowly. Tease it, torment it like I'm tormenting you.'

Kristina wanted to rush, wanted to feel Estelle spasm beneath her so that she too could come, but Tarquin's wishes were what mattered and she slowed her finger movements so that she was doing as he wanted. When Estelle uttered a gutteral cry of excitement Kristina began to take pleasure in what she was doing.

Suddenly she was enjoying making Estelle wait. Her own need was still there, but the thrill of feeling Estelle's thrusting, aroused body heaving helplessly beneath her as she encircled the slippery nub was incredible. When she felt Estelle's hips rise higher she knew that the other woman was close, and so she stopped circling her clitoris and turned her attention to the side of the shaft instead.

Estelle groaned aloud with thwarted need, and Tarquin sighed with delight. 'Excellent! Take your time, let her come when you're ready.'

'No!' said Estelle fiercely. 'I want to come now, Tarquin. Tell her to make me come, please.'

'But the longer you wait the longer she has to wait. That was what we planned, Estelle, remember?'

'I don't care about that,' cried Estelle. 'I'm ready now.'

'I still care,' he said calmly. 'Carry on, Kristina.'

Kristina had never felt such power. She massaged the side of the exquisitely tender shaft until Estelle's hips rose once more, and then she managed to push her fingers lower and swirl them round the entrance to Estelle's vagina, driving Estelle into a frenzy of fury as the elusive climax kept ebbing away just as it was about to peak.

Estelle's body movements grew more and more jerky as her tormented nerve endings went into overdrive and she twitched and writhed silently as Kristina continued to take her to the edge and then reduce the level of stimulation.

Finally, when Estelle was more slippery and swollen with excitement than she could ever remember, Kristina's own need for an orgasm forced her to allow Estelle to come. She drummed lightly beneath the stem of Estelle's clitoris until Estelle was gasping and moaning, then suddenly flicked at the tip of the clitoris itself.

When Estelle's rigid, frantic clitoris received that flick it exploded into a paroxysm of pleasure and Estelle's legs shot out in front of her, lifting Kristina's legs higher too, and she sobbed with relief and gratitude as the cruelly delayed climax finally crashed down on her.

She was still shuddering beneath Kristina when Tarquin pulled off Kristina's panties and then used his tongue on her. He licked slowly at first, moving upwards from the entrance to her vagina, but once he reached the rigid clitoris he began to lick across its tip in a series of swift brushing movements that so stimulated her that the clitoris retracted. Carefully he eased back the hood, drew the little hard nub into his mouth and sucked rhythmically until with a cry of ecstasy Kristina too was convulsed by a fierce, muscle-wrenching orgasm.

Tarquin watched the two women lying in the chair with their heads back and their eyes closed, their bodies finally at peace and he nodded to himself with satisfaction. Then he lifted Kristina off Estelle, laid her on the soft carpet and took Estelle upstairs with him, so that he could at last have his own climax in the privacy of his bedroom.

Watching them leave, Kristina felt a terrible ache of loneliness. She was physically satisfied, and had revelled in the whole evening, but with a shock she realised that she'd have traded it all if only she could have been the one to leave with him and share his night.

She was still lonely and confused when she fell into the taxi that Lydia got for her after she'd dressed again, and she spent the rest of the night sleepless in her own bed. She knew then that she had fallen into the same trap as Jackie. Her feelings for Tarquin were becoming too personal. She loved their adventures, and the absence of responsibility that accompanied their times together, but she also wanted to get to know him as an equal. She wanted to play both parts, to be both the women in his life. Estelle seemed like an intruder, and Kristina resented her.

Chapter Nine

Three nights later, after a particularly difficult day at work when Kristina, for the first time ever, had lost a client to another agent, she was preparing to go to a publishing party the prospect of which didn't excite her in the least.

Lucretia's publishers had moved offices, and tonight they were throwing a party to let everyone see how tastefully they'd wasted their money. There would be over a hundred people there, many of whom Kristina didn't know and had no interest in knowing, but she had to attend because Lucretia was their most successful author, and Lucretia herself was unable to go.

Kristina had tried hard to persuade Lucretia to go with her, but had met with no success. 'I'm finishing my new novel,' explained Lucretia. 'They'll understand. After all, a lot of the money that's gone on the new offices has come through me, so I'm sure they'd rather I kept writing and missed the *canapés*!'

'But I'd rather you came with me,' protested Kristina.

'Take a nice young man, or better still a young man who isn't nice!' laughed Lucretia, and that was that.

After spending fifteen minutes debating what she should wear, Kristina settled on a wine-coloured, velvet dress, mid-calf length, dressed it up with a pearl choker and pearl earrings, slipped on a pair of matching high-heeled shoes with straps that crossed over the arches of her feet, and decided that would have to do. She guessed that most of the other women would either be in the obligatory little black dress or wearing long, ethnic-style skirts and shapeless tops, but tonight she didn't feel like conforming.

What she really felt like, she realised on her way there, was seeing Tarquin again. Ever since their sexual version of *Mastermind* she'd longed for him to call her, but there had been total silence.

She arrived late, having had considerable difficulty parking her car, and after she'd tasted the cheap champagne and tried one of the mini cheese biscuits with two tired-looking prawns on it, she wondered how long she'd have to stay.

'Kristina!' called Lucretia's editor. She was a rather formidable young woman who, as far as Kristina could remember, had graduated from one of the big universities three years earlier and had fully expected to be editing the Booker Prize winner by now, rather than Lucretia's pot-boilers.

'Robbie, lovely to see you,' exclaimed Kristina,

kissing the air on either side of the editor's face. 'Adore the new offices.'

Roberta smiled. 'Really fabulous aren't they! So much better than those clingy old rooms we all had before. Where's Lucretia?'

'She couldn't make it, too near the end of her novel,' explained Kristina.

Roberta raised her eyebrows. 'I had no idea she was such a workaholic.'

'Those massive hundred-thousand-word tomes don't write themselves,' pointed out Kristina. 'They may not be literature, but they're still hard work.'

'Of course,' said Roberta quickly. 'And where would any of us be without them?'

'Probably not in this divine new building,' said Kristina sweetly.

'Well, quite! Did I tell you I'm moving on?'

'Moving on?' asked Kristina stupidly. 'What, leaving here?'

'No, not moving to another publisher, just another area. Much as I love your Lucretia I have felt a tiny bit stifled lately, and as Jilly's going . . .'

'Is she?'

Roberta nodded. 'She was asked to go,' she murmured, lowering her voice carefully. 'Not quite up to the job in the end. So, with a vacancy there, I'm taking over.'

'You're moving from fiction to non-fiction?' queried Kristina.

'Not exactly. You see, Jilly had set up this rather

special, top-secret project before she left, and that's what I'm going to take over.'

'Is it any good?' asked Kristina.

'Wonderful!' enthused Roberta.

'But Jilly wasn't any good at her job?'

Roberta flushed. 'Let's say there were inter-departmental problems, shall we?'

Kristina nodded. 'Go on then, do tell me what this project is.'

'If you turn round,' whispered Roberta, 'you'll see the most *divine* man standing behind you. He's tall, wearing a grey suit, blue shirt and red tie and is absolutely the most gorgeous man in the room.'

Kristina started to turn.

'He is also,' continued Roberta, her cheeks flushed with excitement, 'one of the country's most famous psychologists, and he's going to write a book for us. It's the most incredible scoop because he's been approached by loads of publishers in the past and refused them, but we gave him the chance to write whatever he liked and . . .'

She was still talking when Kristina's eyes met and locked with Tarquin's. His lips curved in a slight smile and he nodded a greeting before turning his attention back to the man talking to him.

'Are you by any chance talking about Dr Tarquin Rashid?' asked Kristina, her heart racing.

'You mean you know him?'

'No!' said Kristina, far too loudly. As Roberta

blinked in surprise she rushed in to repair the damage.
'That's to say, I know *of* him but I've never actually
met him.'

'Well, when I did it was lust at first sight,' confessed
Roberta. 'Those eyes, they're so dark and deep, you
could drown in them.'

'You'll be writing poetry next, Roberta! I can see he's
a more attractive proposition for you than Lucretia.'

'That had nothing to do with me taking on the job,'
said Roberta sharply. 'I hadn't met Dr Rashid until after
I accepted the new position, and I'll miss Lucretia, she's
such a sweetie, but . . .'

At that moment Tarquin came up behind them and
stood at Roberta's elbow. 'Is this your assistant?' he
asked her, glancing at Kristina.

Roberta laughed. 'Good heavens no! This is the
famous Kristina Masterton, literary agent and the
fiercest driver of hard bargains any publisher has to
contend with.'

'Indeed? Then perhaps I should try and get her to
take me on?' suggested Tarquin smoothly.

'I'm afraid my list's full,' retorted Kristina.

'Indeed? What happens? Do you wait until someone
dies and then replace them?'

Kristina struggled to suppress her laughter. 'No, I
wait until one of them stops being creative.'

'Presumably death has that effect?'

'Presumably, but in my experience most authors stop
before that moment arrives.'

Tarquin held out his hand. 'I'm pleased to meet you, Kristina, even if you don't have room for a struggling author attempting his first novel.'

'Novel?' Kristina was astonished.

'Yes,' gushed Roberta. 'Dr Rashid's writing us a psychological thriller, fiction with erotic undertones.'

Kristina stared at him thoughtfully. 'Are you really, Dr Rashid? I hope you're not using any of your real life cases in the book. I'd have thought that somewhat unethical.'

'It would be,' he agreed. 'Fortunately I have a vivid imagination, and some experience of eroticism that's entirely my own.'

Kristina felt herself growing warm beneath her velvet dress, and was grateful when Roberta was called away to greet another guest. 'Why didn't you tell me you'd be here?' she hissed at Tarquin the moment they were alone.

'I had no idea you would attend. We do not discuss our business lives when we're together, as I recall.'

'But you know I'm in publishing!'

'Does it bother you then, meeting me here?' he asked with interest.

'Yes, no, that is . . . I suppose it does,' she admitted.

'Why?' he asked softly.

'Because it makes me think about the other times we've met.'

'It has that effect on me too. However, there's one big difference this time.'

'Yes, we're in the middle of a party!'

'I meant, you're not wearing the bracelet,' said Tarquin quietly.

'More's the pity,' murmured Kristina.

'Why?' asked Tarquin, gazing at her intently. 'Can't you relate to me unless you're wearing the bracelet?'

'Yes, but I can't do anything about it!' she muttered, wishing that her body would stop its insistent clamouring for the feel of his hands on her skin and his body against hers.

'On the contrary, for the first time ever you can do anything you like. I'm no longer in charge. We are on equal terms.'

'I don't know what you mean,' protested Kristina.

'I think you do. If there's something you want from me, then you can tell me, unlike the other times when we meet. I do not, I admit, have to accede to your wishes, but the chances are I will!' He smiled at her then, a proper smile, and she was overwhelmed with physical desire.

'I want to make love to you,' she said hoarsely.

Tarquin glanced around them. 'Let's slip away and find a quieter room. I'm sure we won't be missed.'

Kristina's eyes opened wide. 'You mean, we do it here?'

'The idea rather appeals to me,' he confessed. 'But perhaps considering your standing in the publishing world it's a little too dangerous for you?'

Kristina's excitement was now almost uncontainable,

especially as Roberta was watching them from the far side of the room. 'No, I like a little danger,' she assured him.

'Let's go then. Where do you suggest?'

They walked out of the room and along the corridor. Kristina glanced at various doors and name-plates. 'I've no idea of the layout,' she explained when he hesitated at one of the doors and looked at her. 'Remember, this is the first time I've been here too.'

'Well, who's Martin Frost?' asked Tarquin, glancing at the name of the door.

'I've never heard of him,' admitted Kristina.

'In that case I can't believe he's very important. Let's use his room.'

Kristina looked back down the corridor and saw Roberta pushing her way through the throng. 'Quickly then,' she urged him, and they slipped into the room, closing the door softly behind them. Kristina hoped there might be a lock on the door, but she was disappointed. 'Shall we wedge a chair up against it?' she suggested to Tarquin.

He leant against the leather-covered desk and shrugged. 'It's up to you. I'm not bothered either way, but I thought you liked a little danger.'

'Fine, then we'll leave it,' whispered Kristina, crossing the carpeted floor until her body was touching his. 'You've no idea how much I want you,' she murmured as her hands reached up and removed his tie.

Tarquin's eyes were unfathomable and he didn't

answer, he simply stood where he was and waited to see what she intended to do next.

Luckily Kristina had a very clear picture of precisely what she intended to do, and the fact that there were over a hundred people less than a hundred feet away from them and that any one of them could walk into the room at any time only increased her excitement.

She drew his hands in front of him and then lightly tied them with his tie. 'I know you can get out of that,' she said, 'but if you do then I'm going to stop making love to you, so the choice is yours!'

When he continued to remain silent she unfastened his trousers and let them fall to his ankles, then drew down his boxer shorts, leaving his penis and testicles totally exposed to her.

Tarquin's breathing grew more rapid and his penis started to swell. Swiftly Kristina opened her shoulder bag. From it she pulled her hairbrush and then very lightly she brushed the thick dark hair that covered his lower stomach. She brushed it towards his penis and the penis rose up to meet the brush, the glans swelling and darkening with desire.

When he was fully erect, Kristina knelt down and took him into her mouth for a few seconds, sucking on the glans with her hands flat against the base of his belly until she felt the muscles there start to tighten. Then, knowing that he was building up to a climax, she released him and rising to her feet ran her hands up beneath his shirt, her fingers pinching at his nipples until she felt them grow hard. He gave a soft moan of pleasure.

Suddenly he moved his head forward and his lips covered hers in a fierce, bruising kiss that took her by surprise with its passion and scarcely suppressed violence. She knew then that he was as desperate for release as he'd often made her, and this knowledge only made the game, and the sensuality of the moment, all the sweeter.

Kristina stepped back from him. 'Naughty!' she chided him, squeezing his nipples harder. 'No moving. This is my treat, and we do it my way.'

Tarquin nodded, his eyes shining more fiercely than she'd ever seen them shine before, and his lips were parted as he struggled to control his reactions to her stimulation.

Glancing down she saw that his penis was no longer quite so hard and tight, as his erection started to subside. Encouraged she drew from her bag a tiny silk scarf that she'd left there from an evening out and she slipped this over his penis, covering the head and the sides with the soft material.

Then, after a quick smile up at him, she dropped to her knees again and cupped her hand over the head of his penis. She squeezed very softly and slid her hand over the silk down the shaft, but before she reached the base she brought the other hand up to cover the head. Like a child playing the hand-over-hand game, she kept up a continuous series of movements so that his glans was almost constantly covered as she moved both hands swiftly and rhythmically up and down.

Beneath the silken scarf Tarquin's erection swelled until he felt that it must burst if he didn't climax and his hips jerked spasmodically towards Kristina in an involuntary movement that brought the delicious torture to an end.

'Not yet,' she whispered. 'There's more I want to do to you before you come, much more.'

His upper thighs were shaking with tension, and when she grasped the middle of his aching erection with one hand and then began to rub the palm of her other hand around the glans he gave a cry of fearful excitement. Her hand circled him very gently, moving first one way and then the other and all the time he could feel his testicles drawing up tighter and tighter, but she was incredibly skilled at keeping him on the edge of his climax and just as he felt certain that he was going to come her hands stopped moving.

'Not much longer,' she promised him as his belly shook with frustration and he bit on his lower lip. Then he felt her reach beneath his aching testicles, palm uppermost, before drawing her left hand slowly towards the root of his shaft, her nails scratching lightly against the incredibly sensitive skin of his perineum.

He wanted to pull his hands free of the tie, grab hold of her head and take her on the carpet, driving into her with a ferocity he'd never imagined before, but although it would have been easy to do he remained as

Kristina had positioned him, because he – like her – was finding their role reversal incredibly arousing.

'How much do you want me, Tarquin?' murmured Kristina, suddenly releasing his tormented penis and letting the silk scarf fall to the floor. 'Tell me, I want to know.'

'I want you more than I've ever wanted any woman,' he said hoarsely. 'I want to fill you, to feel you spasm beneath me just before I come.'

With a smile she tugged the tie off his wrists. 'Then do it,' she begged, all pretence at total power gone. 'Show me what you mean.'

Tarquin struggled to remove his shoes, then stepped out of his trousers, pulled off his boxer shorts and grabbed Kristina by the shoulders. For a moment he held her face tightly, staring at her as though trying to imprint her on his memory, and then he was pressing her face down on to the carpet.

She lay there, her whole body tingling with desire, as his hands tugged at the zip that ran the length of the back of her dress. Finally it was undone and then she rolled on to her back and he tore it off her arms and pulled it down her body before throwing it across the desk.

Beneath the dress she was naked except for her stockings and bikini briefs. He lay slightly to the side of her and she felt one of his hands pressing against her already moist and swollen vulva through the silk of the briefs. He massaged her for a time, moving his hand in small circles that made her ache all the more for him and soon she, like him, was making frantic noises of need as her body arched off the carpet and up towards him.

Unable to wait a moment longer, Tarquin tugged her panties down her legs and then he was on top of her, his shirt rubbing against her breasts. 'Put your legs closer together, so that they're inside mine,' he muttered as he thrust into her, and she obeyed, feeling herself tighten around him, and feeling too the wonderful full sensation that meant he was finally deep inside her.

Taking his weight on his elbows, Tarquin moved his hips in circles, teasing around the nerve endings just inside Kristina's vagina, and jagged streaks of pleasure started to spread through her pelvis and behind her pubic bone.

'Massage your breasts,' he whispered. 'Tease your nipples. I love to see them when they're dark and erect.'

It was all the encouragement Kristina needed, and gratefully she began to caress her swollen breasts, pulling at the nipples with her fingers until she felt them harden, and the streaks of excitement from her breasts met up with the increasingly strong currents of excitement from her lower body until it seemed that every part of her was pulsating with electricity and she started to twist and turn beneath him.

Tarquin's rhythm changed, he thrust deeper inside her, so deep that she felt him against her cervix and shouted out with pleasure. 'That's right,' she cried. 'I love that! I love it!'

Tarquin's top lip was curled back from his teeth as he moved fiercely against her. He knew that she was almost there, and wanted to come just after her. The tension in his testicles increased, and then he felt the first tiny prickles in his glans that meant his orgasm was very near.

Now he thrust harder than he could ever remember thrusting before and although he was vaguely aware of Kristina screaming with delight he was concentrating so much on his own, long-delayed, pleasure that it meant little to him apart from adding to his excitement.

'I'm coming!' cried Kristina, and her words, coupled with the sudden pulsations of her internal muscles around him, were the trigger for Tarquin to come as well. He heard himself utter a deep groan of satisfaction and then his body was caught up in the most intense paroxysms of pleasure he'd ever had in his life.

Even after Kristina was still, Tarquin continued to heave and shudder above her and her arms instinctively went round his neck so that when it was finally over she was able to draw his head down against her breasts and they lay silently together, drenched in sweat and totally sated.

It was then, in the first moment of utter silence that there'd been for a long time, that they both heard the gentle click of the door closing.

'Who was that?' gasped Kristina, trying to struggle free of Tarquin's weight.

He kept his head between her breasts. 'I've no idea, and as they're never likely to tell us I'm not going to worry about it.'

'But it might be someone I know!' cried Kristina.

'I'm sure it was!' he laughed. 'We both knew that was a risk. At least we put on a good show for them. That was incredible, Kristina, out of this world.'

She'd never known him so relaxed, but all she wanted to do now was get dressed and leave the building.

Idly, Tarquin traced the outline of each of her breasts in turn. 'I adore the way your breasts swell when you're close to coming. It's much more noticeable with you, because they're quite small to start with. Look, the nipples are growing again.'

'They're not!' protested Kristina, pushing at him with her hands. 'Or if they are, it's because I'm cold. I've got to get dressed, Tarquin. That person might come back.'

'Why? They surely don't expect an *encore*!' he laughed, but he rolled off her and watched as she struggled into her dress again. 'It doesn't matter who it was,' he assured her. 'We didn't break the law.'

'But suppose it was Roberta?'

'Why should that matter? I thought having people around was part of the turn-on.'

'She fancies you herself,' Kristina blurted out.

Tarquin raised his eyebrows. 'Really? I must

remember that. I certainly don't think she's my type, do you?'

'I've no idea what your type is. Someone like Estelle?' asked Kristina, tugging at her zip.

'Let me,' said Tarquin, finally standing up and helping her fasten the dress. Then he turned her towards him and kissed her softly on the lips. 'You're an incredible woman, Kristina. I wish I'd decided to write a book a long time ago. I had no idea publishing parties were like this!'

Kristina giggled. 'Nor had I! It must be your influence. Come on, I want to leave now.'

'I'd better stay. I've still got people to meet. I'll call you soon,' he said calmly.

Kristina was shocked. 'We're not leaving together?'

'Why should we? We didn't arrive together, and I'm here to discuss my novel. Roberta might feel slighted if I left without talking to her a little more.'

'Yes, of course,' Kristina murmured, knowing he was right but still desperately disappointed. 'Fine, well I'll see you sometime.'

He nodded. 'Yes, you will.'

When she crept out into the corridor it was deserted, and she left the building without meeting anyone she knew, but in the main room Roberta stood by the window and stared out over London, her mouth a thin tight line of anger and frustration.

Two days later, Sue put Lucretia through to Kristina.

'I know you're busy working on Simon's new contract, but it's the third time she's called in the past hour and she sounds pretty annoyed,' explained Sue.

'Okay,' agreed Kristina wearily, then she changed her tone. 'Hi, Lucretia! Lovely to hear from you. How's the book going? Finished yet?'

'Yes, it is finished,' said Lucretia, her voice far cooler than Kristina had ever heard it before. 'It would have been nice to have heard from you though, rather than having to ring myself.'

'Was I meant to call you?' asked Kristina in surprise, racking her brains to think why that might have been.

'I'd have thought it would have been polite,' responded Lucretia.

Kristina began to feel worried. This was not the Lucretia she knew. 'Whatever's wrong?' she asked gently.

'I rang Roberta,' explained Lucretia frostily. 'I wanted to check out the ending with her before I posted off the manuscript. As you can imagine, it came as quite a shock to learn that she isn't my editor any longer, and that you've known that for several weeks. I felt a complete idiot, although obviously Roberta realised it wasn't my fault.'

Kristina took some slow, deep breaths as she tried to repair the damage done by Roberta. 'I only heard about it myself two days ago,' she explained. 'It was at that party you couldn't make and . . .'

'Why didn't you ring me yesterday then?' asked

Lucretia. 'Don't you think it's something I needed to know?'

'Yes, of course you needed to know, but as we don't have the name of your new editor yet I was waiting until things were a little more straight and then . . .'

'It's a man called Martin Frost,' snapped Lucretia. 'Roberta says he's written to you twice suggesting a meeting, but so far you haven't replied.'

'Martin Frost!' exclaimed Kristina, remembering the name on the door of the room she and Tarquin had used. 'So that's who he is!'

'Don't you read your emails any more?' asked Lucretia. 'I don't quite know how to put this, Kristina, but lately . . .' Kristina tried to concentrate, but she found that she couldn't. In her mind she was back at the party again. She could feel the carpet beneath her bare back as Tarquin finally thrust into her, his swollen penis desperate for release after his long slow torment as she'd brought him tantalisingly close to a climax time after time, her hands busy on his purple glans, her lips soft around his hardness.

'Kristina!'

She jumped as her mind spun crazily, trying to reorientate itself. 'Sorry, what was that last bit?' she asked desperately.

For a long time there was silence at the other end of the line. Then Lucretia spoke again. 'You haven't been listening to a word I've said, have you?'

'Of course I have!' protested Kristina.

'Then tell me what I was talking about.'

'Well, you were saying that you'd miss Roberta, and quite rightly pointing out that I've been totally remiss in failing to let you know what was going on,' said Kristina, guessing wildly.

'My goodness, I think you should be the writer, you have a wonderful imagination,' said Lucretia, and Kristina's heart sank. 'I was actually saying that I didn't wish to work with a male editor, and that I felt you weren't quite so involved with my work as you used to be,' continued Lucretia. 'It seems I was absolutely right on the second count.'

'God, I'm so sorry,' gabbled Kristina, wishing she could push away the image of Tarquin leaning against the desktop, his testicles drawn up tightly against the base of his erection and his face twisted in an expression of frantic desire.

'So am I,' said Lucretia, and suddenly she sounded very sad. 'I'm sorry, Kristina, but perhaps I ought to think about changing to another agency. I know we've been together ever since we both began, but Roberta explained that you're more interested in non-fiction now and with the way publishing is at the moment I can see that makes sense, although I feel I'm still doing well enough. I'll go away and think about it some more, then drop you a line.'

'Roberta doesn't know what she's talking about!' said Kristina, her voice rising with panic. 'I'm not doing more non-fiction. I've taken on two new fiction writers in the last three months. Honestly Lucretia, this is all a terrible mistake.'

'Yes, by you,' said Lucretia shortly and the line went dead.

Stunned, Kristina sat with the receiver in her hand listening to the humming noise on the line in total disbelief. She couldn't afford to lose Lucretia. Lucretia's work sold all over the world. They made cheap TV movies out of her books, they serialised them, they put together collections and now there was even talk of a big-budget Hollywood movie in the offing. If she lost Lucretia her agency would be in desperate trouble, and Roberta must have known this only too well.

There was a light tap at the door and Sue came in. 'Is your phone off the hook? I can't put . . . What's wrong, Kristina? You look terrible!'

Slowly and carefully Kristina replaced the receiver. 'I feel terrible. Lucretia's thinking of leaving us.'

Sue's mouth opened in shock. 'But she can't!'

'Of course she can, and I'm not surprised she wants to either. I've made such a mess of things, Sue. You wouldn't believe how stupid I've been.'

'Nonsense, you're never stupid. What was it? An argument over the plot again?'

Kristina shook her head. 'I wish that *was* all it was. I can't explain, Sue, but believe me she's got every right to be fed up. What annoys me most, apart from my own stupidity, is that Roberta Mitchell's the one who put the idea of going into her head. If she walked in here now I think I'd strangle her.'

'But why would Roberta want to damage you? I thought you got on pretty well, and she'd always worked reasonably well with Lucretia.'

'Yes, that's the point. She's no longer working on Lucretia's book, and I forgot to tell Lucretia.'

'But why is Roberta involved in suggesting a change of agent?'

Kristina closed her eyes for a moment, remembering how Roberta had drooled over Tarquin at the party and remembering too the soft click of the door closing just after she and Tarquin had finished making love at the party.

'Please, Sue, drop it will you?' she asked wearily. 'I can't think straight at the moment and I've got a ghastly headache coming on. I'm going for a walk. When I come back I'll start composing an email to Lucretia, and we'll get that off by mid-afternoon. If I grovel enough maybe, just maybe, I'll keep her.'

'Whatever you say,' agreed Sue.

After she'd gone Kristina stared sightlessly out of the window. This was what she'd feared most as she was drawn more and more into the world of the society of the bracelet. Real life, her work, and her everyday friends, were no longer so interesting. She was losing touch with reality and however hard she tried she didn't seem able to stop it.

'I must talk to Jackie,' she said aloud. 'She'll

understand.' Then she remembered that Jackie was no longer the close friend and confidante she'd once been and she hesitated, but finally she dialled the number. The worst that could happen was that Jackie would tell her to get lost.

Jackie didn't. She listened in total silence to Kristina's almost hysterical tale and then spoke quietly and reassuringly. 'Meet me tonight at my place. We'll talk about it then,' she promised. 'I know what you're going through. It's the same for me.'

'Thanks, Jackie,' exclaimed Kristina. 'I was afraid you might still be annoyed with me.'

'No, I've talked to Laurence and he said the same as you. In my more rational moments I do realise that he needs an agent for his book, and I also realise you're the best there is. See you tonight.'

As Kristina smiled with relief, Jacqueline too smiled and then began to dial another number on her mobile phone. She was very glad that Kristina had rung her, very glad indeed.

Chapter Ten

Kristina arrived at Jackie's ten minutes early. Wearing a pair of black leggings, a cream lace-trimmed sleeveless tunic and flat cream pumps she felt more than ready for a long girls-only evening, and hoped that the bottle of wine she was carrying would help get the conversation going. Certainly she was in need of something if she was going to relax. Her neck muscles felt as though they were locked together and her spine seemed to have an iron bolt running through it.

She was a little startled when Jackie opened the door wearing a black, stretch-velvet dress that ended on the knee and had a startling cut-out neckline that was linked with tiny gold chains. At the front of the dress was a deep slit that extended more than halfway up her thigh. High-heeled black stiletto shoes completed the outfit and Kristina wondered if she'd made a mistake and was meant to come another night.

Jackie smiled cheerfully. 'You're early, but it doesn't matter. As you can see, I'm ready.'

Kristina looked down at her own outfit. 'I don't think I am. Are you having a party? That dress is incredible, but I imagined we were having a girls' night.'

'So we are,' Jackie assured her. 'I just felt like dressing up.'

'You look terrific, but I have the feeling Laurence would appreciate it more!'

Jacqueline turned away to hide her smile. 'I'm sure he would too, but these days I find that even when I'm on my own I like to wear these kinds of clothes. They make me feel sensuous.'

'Right now it would take more than a black velvet dress to make me feel sensuous,' said Kristina fervently. 'I've sent off my email to Lucretia, but I've no idea if it will do the trick. If it doesn't I honestly don't think I'm going to be able to survive, at least not with my present set-up. I could cut back on staff, even work from home I suppose, but that wouldn't do much for my image as the best agent in the country!'

'I shouldn't worry about that,' murmured Jackie, pouring them each a glass of wine. 'The last time I spoke to someone in publishing they were full of that new agent, Francesca Morley is it? I think she's the new Girl Wonder. Never mind, we all have our day.'

'Francesca? But she hasn't got anyone big on her list! She's done one or two useful deals and seems to be building up quite a nice little stable of promising writers, but . . .'

'No more talking shop,' said Jackie with a smile.

'We're here to discuss the impact of the society on our lives, remember?'

Kristina sighed. 'Sorry, yes of course I remember! Cheers!'

'Here's to the society,' said Jackie, raising her glass.

'Yes, the society,' murmured Kristina, and immediately she thought of Tarquin, and the way he'd sat asking her questions as she squirmed in the large leather chair in the middle of the darkened room in St John's Wood.

'You're still seeing Tarquin are you?' queried Jackie.

'Yes, more than ever now. How about you and Laurence?'

'Well, as you know we had a bit of a hiccup, but he's calling me up regularly again so I'm not sure what that was about.' Kristina remembered Hester but said nothing.

As Jackie went into the kitchen to fetch them some food Kristina glanced through one of the magazines lying on the coffee-table, and to her astonishment she saw Hester's face staring out at her. She was accepting an award from a minor member of royalty, and looked very smart and in control, not at all like she'd been with Laurence.

'Who's that?' Kristina asked Jackie when she returned.

'That's Hester Franks, one of Europe's top fashion designers. She's won loads of awards this year, and recently ditched her second husband saying all men are wimps. Perhaps she should try the society of the bracelet!'

'Perhaps she should,' agreed Kristina, trying hard not to smile.

'So, why d'you ask?' went on Jackie.

'I thought I recognised her face, but I was wrong. Jackie, how do you cope with your business life these days? I know you said you were finding it difficult to work properly. What did you do to force yourself to get interested again?'

Jackie gave her a strange look. 'I didn't do anything.'

'You mean, after a time you adjust, is that it?' asked Kristina eagerly. 'I did wonder if that might happen. I suppose once the novelty wears off you learn to keep the two parts of your life quite separate, which is what's intended, I know!'

'I don't mean that at all. I've given up my job,' said Jackie defiantly.

Kristina stared at her friend. 'Given it up? But what do you do all the time?'

'I see other men than Laurence, so that keeps me pretty occupied. The rest of the time I watch videos, read books, have long sensual baths, it's amazing how time passes.'

'You watch videos? Are you mad, Jackie? You were one of our top journalists. You've got a brain, you can't just sit indoors and watch rubbish on your television!'

'I didn't exactly choose to stop working. I've been

fired. You see, I don't have your advantage in that I'm not self-employed. Once my work went off I was in trouble, and the bosses began to watch me closely. I failed to keep up to the mark and so I was asked – very politely – to go.'

'But I haven't heard anything about this. Didn't you make a fuss? You're well-known, and you were still working when I last spoke to you. You'd done that exclusive interview with Tarquin. Wasn't your paper pleased with that?'

'Sure, but then I failed to meet several deadlines, and that's one thing journalists are not allowed to do. As for a fuss, the truth is I didn't want any fuss. I knew it was all my fault, and after my "Pursuit of Truth" award last year it was a bit embarrassing.'

'Have you looked for work on other papers or magazines?'

'There's no point. I'm busy making sure I get Laurence to marry me,' said Jackie calmly.

'Marry you?' Kristina nearly laughed aloud, but then she realised that she was secretly harbouring much the same idea about Tarquin and suddenly it didn't seem so funny any more.

'Why? Don't you think that's likely? Has Laurence told you – as his agent naturally – that he isn't going to marry me?'

'No, of course not. We never talk about the society of the bracelet,' said Kristina quickly. 'It's just that, well this wasn't why we joined, Jackie. We wanted good, uninvolved sex with virtual strangers. Sex that was safe, satisfying and discreet.'

'Maybe we were fooling ourselves,' said Jackie softly. 'Perhaps what we really wanted to do was find the right kind of man and then hope for more commitment from them.'

Kristina shook her head. 'No, that wasn't how it was. I remember the way I felt very well indeed. I wanted something that was totally different from the sex I had with Ben but left me free to pursue my career. I wanted a man who wasn't afraid of my success, who was able to take the lead in bed and then step out of my life and let me take the lead in all other respects. I wasn't looking for a permanent partner, I know I wasn't.'

Jackie shrugged. 'You didn't think you were, and I didn't think I was, but I am now. All I think about, all I want, is Laurence. Wouldn't you like to know that Tarquin was exclusively yours, rather than sharing him with other women from the society, and that girlfriend of his, what's her name?'

'Estelle. Yes, I would rather not share him, and I hate it when he goes off with Estelle, but that's part of the price you pay. No one can have everything.'

'Precisely, which is exactly where we came in,' said Jackie triumphantly. 'We were always hearing that we had it all, and we knew we didn't. Now we've got what we thought was missing, but we still haven't got it all, so I don't think we've done ourselves much good, do you?'

'Yes, I do! I'd much rather have Tarquin, even on the

terms of the society, than not have met him at all. The sex is fantastic, and he makes every other man I've met seem like a total nonentity.'

'Even Laurence?'

Kristina sighed. 'Jackie, please! That was nothing, a mistake, a simple case of lust. You can't compare Laurence with Tarquin!'

Jackie's eyes narrowed. 'Really? I'm not sure Laurence would find that very flattering.'

'Who cares?' retorted Kristina, 'I'm telling you, not him.'

'To return to what we were saying a few moments ago,' said Jackie slowly. 'Would you honestly rather have Tarquin and all this wonderful sex but lose Lucretia and possibly your entire career?'

'No, of course not.'

'But that's what's happened, isn't it?'

'It's what could happen,' said Kristina carefully. 'That's the reason I came here tonight, to try and see if you could help me sort things out. Now I know you're not working at all, I'm beginning to think you're the last person I should have consulted!'

'Then you don't care for Tarquin in the way I care for Laurence,' said Jackie fiercely. 'If you did, you wouldn't care about Lucretia, or being "Agent of the Year", which if you want my opinion made you sound like some kind of female James Bond.'

'No,' agreed Kristina, ignoring the jibe. 'I don't think we are alike.'

'I suppose you think I'm pathetic and you're still "in control"?' demanded Jackie aggressively, refilling her wine glass.

'I don't think anything of the kind. But I do think it's a pity you're not working.'

'I am,' said Jackie, her eyes bright again. 'I'm working at becoming the perfect partner for Laurence. That's why I go and see other men, to get new ideas, and that's why I watch videos and wear these kinds of clothes. I want to be permanently aroused, permanently ready for him.'

'I don't see how watching videos is going to make you more interesting for Laurence,' said Kristina. 'Since he joined the society because he wanted dynamic business women who were willing to be dominated on the odd occasion, I think you're in danger of becoming a total turn-off for him.'

'Do you really?' said Jackie softly, and suddenly Kristina felt nervous. Her friend looked different, almost feverish and strangely triumphant.

'Well, you must admit you're not the same as you were when the pair of you first met,' she said gently. 'Maybe that suits him, how would I know?'

'I'll tell you what suits him,' said Jackie. 'It's having you here, tonight.'

'Having me here?' asked Kristina in bewilderment.

'Yes, because tonight is one of *our* nights. Tonight I'm wearing the bracelet for Laurence and he asked me to get you here so that you could watch us.' As she spoke she pulled the familiar gold bracelet out of her handbag and slipped it over her right wrist. At the same time Laurence appeared in the doorway.

Kristina stood up. 'I'm leaving. I'm not wearing a bracelet, and I don't want to stay. Please get out of the way, Laurence, and don't ever try this again.'

As she drew level with him he put out a hand and caught hold of her wrist. 'Please stay,' he whispered. 'You'll enjoy yourself, and later we're having another guest, someone you'll definitely want to see.'

Kristina's mouth went dry. 'Who?' she asked breathlessly.

Laurence gave a thin smile. 'Why, the good doctor Tarquin Rashid of course.'

Kristina looked from Jackie to Laurence, and then back to Jackie again. 'Did you know about this?' she asked.

Jackie smiled, fingering her slim bracelet tenderly. 'Of course I did. I was the one who arranged it all. I had to, Laurence made me when I last wore the bracelet.'

Kristina nodded thoughtfully. 'And you never considered taking off the bracelet and refusing?'

'Why should she?' demanded Laurence. 'There's nothing wrong with what I asked her to do. Tarquin belongs to the society, and he was delighted to be asked to join us later.'

'Does he know I'll be here?' asked Kristina.

Laurence's pale blue eyes were cold. 'Naturally; I'm sure that was the main attraction, although he admitted that the idea of two women wearing bracelets in the company of two men was very exciting in itself.'

'But I'm not wearing the bracelet,' she protested.

'Not at this moment. Doubtless Tarquin will request you to, later on. For the moment all that you're required to do is act as a spectator at our show. Are you willing? Or are you going to leave before your lover gets here?'

Kristina didn't know what to do. She desperately wanted to be there when Tarquin arrived, but she wasn't sure that she wanted to wear the bracelet in the company of the other two. Neither was she certain that she wished to watch them until he arrived, although deep down there was a part of her that had always wanted to know what went on between Laurence and Jacqueline during their times together.

'I should go if you're not sure,' said Jackie with a half-smile. 'This isn't for the faint-hearted.'

It was the smile that decided it for Kristina. Jackie wanted her to leave; wanted her to quit and leave her alone in the company of both men. This would show Kristina up as being inhibited and, worse still, unwilling to share. Tarquin might very well lose interest in her if he thought that she was involved with him on a personal level rather than with the thrill of the society itself.

'I don't mind staying,' she said casually. 'But I'm not putting on the bracelet until Tarquin arrives, if then.'

Laurence smiled his cold smile. 'That's fine by us. We don't want you to join in, we just appreciate an audience. Jackie, get changed in the other room, then bring the DVD in with you when you're ready.' As Jackie disappeared to carry out his orders he turned back to Kristina. 'We've filmed ourselves during our last few sessions,' he explained. 'It turns Jackie on to watch them when she's on her own, and I find it pretty exciting as well. This evening, we're going to play a video to you and re-enact it at the same time. You'll be seeing both the film and the performance simultaneously, quite a novelty I imagine.'

'Is there a storyline?' asked Kristina with amusement. 'Or is it simply the usual French maid being seduced by her wicked employer?'

Laurence shook his head. 'Give me credit for a little more ingenuity than that, Kristina. No, this is merely a record of the way we both like to spend our time. It may surprise you, but it won't bore you.'

'Nothing about you would surprise me, Laurence,' she said softly. 'I'm beginning to realise that you're totally ruthless when in pursuit of something you want. It doesn't matter whether it's an agent, a publisher or a particular kind of sex, nothing's going to stop you, is it?'

'No,' he admitted. 'But so far I've failed to get you.'

'I seem to remember us enjoying each other,' she murmured.

His eyes brightened. 'Yes, we did, but I want more. I want to see you the way you'll see Jackie tonight. I want you wearing the bracelet for me, bending to my will rather than being on equal terms with me. When I see you at work, or listen to you being briskly efficient in your business life, I can hardly stop myself from dragging you off and forcing the bracelet on to your wrist. Don't you see, you're exactly the type of woman we men join this society to meet and control?'

'I know that, but the bracelet's meant to be for mutual pleasure, not just yours.'

'Believe me, it would be,' he promised her but as he reached out a hand to touch her she drew back.

'I'm not part of the entertainment,' she reminded him forcefully, trying to calm herself as his words conjured up disturbing images that were surprisingly erotic.

'Sorry, I forgot. Jackie! How good you look. Give me the DVD, I'll put it on while you show yourself to Kristina.'

Slowly, Jackie walked into the room. Her head was bent submissively and her blonde fringe obscured her eyes, so Kristina couldn't see her expression, but she thought it must be one of embarrassment or shame because never in her entire life had Kristina imagined either of them wearing such an outfit.

Jackie was dressed as a slave girl. The lower half of her torso was encased in tight black leather, the narrow crotch of the garment pulling up so tightly between her thighs that her sex lips spilled over on each side. A long zip ran from between her buttocks round the front and then up to her breasts. There the leather suit ended and each breast was encircled by thick shiny leather straps that separated the breasts before joining at the back of her neck in a halter collar. There was a matching black leather collar round her neck and once Laurence had put the DVD into the machine he came and stood in front of her, one hand fingering the thin chain hanging from the collar.

'What do you think?' he asked Kristina, but she didn't know how to answer and remained silent. Nonchalantly, Laurence flicked a finger at Jackie's left nipple, which quickly grew red and stiff. 'Your friend doesn't seem to know how to talk,' he murmured. 'That's a pity. Each time she fails to respond, you will be punished. That's fair, don't you think?'

'Yes, master,' whispered Jackie, and Kristina's stomach muscles tightened with a mixture of shock and dark excitement.

'She looks very strange,' she said quickly, 'like a different person.'

'Quite,' said Laurence. 'Hold out your hands, Jackie. It's time to put the cuffs on, and then we can start.'

Slowly Jackie held her hands out in front of her, and Laurence placed soft padded leather cuffs around her wrists, adjusting the chain until her hands were close together. As she stood motionless in front of Kristina, Laurence switched on the television.

Kristina looked at the screen, and suddenly images of Jackie and Laurence appeared, Jackie wearing the same slave girl outfit that she was wearing now. As the girl on the screen knelt at Laurence's feet, so Jackie slid to the floor, lowering her upper body until her forehead was resting on Laurence's shoes.

He sighed with pleasure and then, reaching down, raised her up once more. At the same time the figure on the screen was raised to its feet. Kristina's eyes moved from the unfolding video to the two people in the room and she found that she was in a high state of sexual tension, waiting to see how the scene would unfold.

Hooking a finger through the chain round Jackie's neck, Laurence drew her across the room. On the opposite wall was a small metal ring, clearly set up in preparation for such sessions, and there was a sharp click as the collar was fastened to the ring. Now Jackie was standing with her back to the wall, facing Kristina. Her breasts were thrust upwards by the boned curves of the black leather body that ended beneath them, and their tight roundness was emphasised by the leather circles that were suspended from the halter-neck top.

The video that was playing on the screen was now ahead of the performers in the room, and Kristina realised that if she wished she could anticipate what was going to happen by watching that, but she preferred to stay in suspense, only occasionally glancing at the screen, when gasps from the soundtrack caught her attention.

'Move to the other chair,' suggested Laurence. 'You'll have a better view of what we're both doing from there. Otherwise my body will obscure your view of Jackie's responses.'

Without a moment's hesitation, Kristina obeyed. She wanted to see it all, to watch her friend's excitement and the way Laurence used her when she was totally helpless. Laurence smiled at her. 'I told you you'd enjoy yourself, tonight. Perhaps I know you better than you thought.'

Kristina didn't answer him and with one final penetrating look at her flushed cheeks Laurence turned back to Jacqueline. For a few seconds he stroked her breasts gently, lifting and massaging them until they were hard with desire. Then he picked up a drink that he'd brought into the room with him and dipped his finger into the iced glass. Jackie couldn't move more than an inch away from the wall, but she pushed her breasts forward beseechingly as he lightly drew his finger, now coated in iced vodka, across the middle of each breast, carefully rubbing the chilled alcohol into each rosy nipple, then he bent his head and licked it off while Jackie groaned with pleasure.

Kristina's throat felt dry, and she wished that she had a drink. The room suddenly seemed very warm, and she could feel the heat from her own body burning through her clothes.

As Jackie squirmed and pushed her breasts into Laurence's mouth there was a startled cry from the television, and Kristina quickly looked at the screen. There Jackie was pressing herself hard against the wall her eyes wide and frightened as Laurence busied himself between her thighs.

In the living room of Jackie's house Laurence looked at Kristina. 'That's still to come,' he murmured, stepping away from Jackie. Kristina shivered, but not with fear. She wanted to know what he'd been doing to produce such a sound from her friend and, worst of all, she wanted it to be done to her as well.

Next Laurence drew the centre zip of Jackie's bodysuit down, gradually exposing her stomach, but he left it fastened from just above her crotch. As Jackie whimpered with desire he began to cover her naked belly with kisses and tiny nips while his hands pressed against her sex lips where they spilled over the sides of the strip of leather between them.

Kristina watched his hands working busily between her friend's thighs and to her astonishment felt tingles of excitement rising from behind her clitoris as she imagined the delicious sensations Jackie must be experiencing. She imagined the tightness of the leather strip, the stimulation of her outer sex lips being squeezed and rotated so that the clitoris beneath was moved and aroused, and finally Laurence's mouth working at the tender skin of her belly.

Kristina pressed her thighs tightly together, trying to increase her own pleasure as Jackie's breathing became louder and she started to pant with excitement.

'Are you near?' asked Laurence softly. 'Tell us both, are you going to come soon?'

'Yes!' gasped Jackie, and Laurence's hands moved, so that one of them was now pressing against the area just above her pubic bone, pressing firmly to increase the pressure on the engorged area. Jackie drew in her breath sharply and her eyes widened, while her leg muscles grew taut and she started to rise up on her toes.

'I think you should wait a little longer,' said Laurence, his voice gently apologetic. 'You *are* my slave, and I don't want you to think you can have everything you desire.'

'Don't stop now,' cried Jackie. 'You know I'm close, let me have just one.'

He shook his head in mock regret. 'No, not even one. Soon, but not yet.' Carefully he zipped her up again, but immediately he unfastened a second zip that ran between her legs and up behind her so that at last the pressure on her sex lips and clitoris was eased.

Jackie's blonde fringe was turning dark with perspiration and her whole body glistened with arousal. On the screen things were moving at a different pace, and suddenly the silence in the room was shattered by the sounds of Jackie having an orgasm on screen. She moaned and gasped, sobbing with pleasure, and all the time she writhed in ecstasy Kristina watched Jackie herself, unable to move or do anything at all to bring about the same bliss at this moment when it was all she desired.

Laurence walked away from Jackie and swiftly stripped off his clothes and then, totally naked and with a huge erection, he walked back to stand in front of her. Carefully he parted her sex lips and then picked up a tube of gel that he massaged into the tissue between the lips.

Jackie cried out in a mixture of delight and fear.

Delight at the sensations, and fear that she'd climax from the wonderful feelings. Ignoring her, Laurence proceeded to position his penis against her swollen and throbbing clitoris and then he rested his hands against the wall on each side of her tethered body and slowly rotated his hips so that the yearning mass of highly sensitive nerve endings was stimulated in the most wonderful way.

'Don't come,' he warned Jackie sharply. 'If you do, I shall punish you, even in front of Kristina.'

'Then stop, please stop,' Jackie begged him. 'It isn't fair, I'm so close.' Then she stopped talking and instead began to moan softly, frantically trying to subdue her own flesh, which Laurence was arousing to even greater heights than usual.

For Kristina it was unbearable. She couldn't imagine how Jackie had ever learned such sexual discipline. Simply watching the scene was driving her to the edge of orgasm, and as Jackie continued to whimper and protest Kristina clenched her internal muscles tightly together and this stimulation, along with what she was witnessing, was enough to topple her into an orgasm. Without realising it she gave a tiny moan of pleasure, and Jackie's head turned towards her in horror. 'No, Kristina, don't. Keep quiet, please!'

'Enjoy yourself, Kristina,' said Laurence. 'That's why we're all here. Just think, Jackie. Kristina's already had release. Her body's relaxed and quiet now, but yours isn't. Yours is tight and tense, you ache between your thighs and your nipples are painful. Isn't that right?'

'I won't listen,' shouted Jackie, but with her hands cuffed she couldn't shut out his words, and when he moved away from her for a moment she knew that in a few seconds she would lose the battle. He wasn't going to give her permission to come, but he was going to make sure that she did, so that he could punish her in front of Kristina.

She was right. Deftly he inserted a pair of pulsating Chinese love balls into her vagina, and as soon as she felt them throbbing she gave a cry of despair as her tormented nerve endings refused to be subdued and her orgasm started to mount. Then, Laurence inserted two fingers inside her vagina and softly massaged her G spot, rubbing it firmly with the circular movements that she loved the most. His penis was once more pressing against the area around her clitoris and as her lower body filled with the unbearable pressure of sexual frustration he bent his head and grazed her left nipple with his teeth.

'Now I'm going to bite your other nipple,' he whispered, so softly that Kristina couldn't hear. 'I know you love it, but you still mustn't come. Not until I've finished and removed my mouth, then you may. Do you understand?'

Jackie nodded. She understood, just as she understood that it would be impossible, but despite that knowledge she thrust her right breast greedily into his mouth and then he was nibbling hard at the swollen nipple and searing lines of crazed excitement coursed down through her body, just as the tight muscular spasms of her belly and vulva erupted into a cataclysmic explosion that tore up through her. As it joined with the blissful shocks searing from her breast, her entire body convulsed and she writhed against Laurence's lean, hard body, shuddering and sobbing in a mixture of mind-shattering ecstasy and fear of what would happen next.

Perched on the edge of her chair, Kristina watched as Jackie gave herself over to the wracking spasms of her orgasm and deep inside her she felt not only rising desire again, but also a terrible satisfaction – that now her friend would be punished, and she would be able to watch that punishment.

When Jackie was finally still and silent, Laurence unfastened her collar from the ring on the wall and then removed her handcuffs. She stood in front of him, her eyes fixed on his face, and waited to hear what her punishment would be.

Laurence looked calculatingly at her, and Kristina couldn't help but contrast his expression with the way he'd looked at Jackie the first time she'd seen the pair of them in the restaurant. Then, despite the fact that Jackie had been wearing the bracelet, there had been respect and admiration in his eyes. Now there was nothing apart from sexual excitement and power. Somehow the balance of the relationship had changed, Jackie had lost something, something that Kristina felt was important and she knew that she must be careful not to alter her relationship with Tarquin in the same way.

'Before I name your punishment, do you agree that it's deserved?' asked Laurence.

'Yes,' whispered Jackie, lowering her eyes.

'Very well, what I've decided is that since you were unable to control your orgasm as I wished then I shall allow you to come as often as you wish, and for as long as I wish. Do you understand?'

Jackie raised her eyes again, and this time there was a trace of fear in them. 'You mean, you'll make me keep coming until I can't come any more?' she asked softly.

'Precisely, just as I did once before. If you don't wish to play that game again then please remove the bracelet now.'

Kristina watched as various emotions crossed her friend's face. Excitement, desire and need battled with fear and something else, something very close to resentment, but then her face was calm again and she merely nodded in submission as she fingered her bracelet lovingly.

Kristina was startled to hear something that sounded very like a sigh from Laurence, but then he was grasping Jackie by the hand and leading her out through the hall and into the conservatory at the back of the house. He gestured for Kristina to follow and as she walked into the airy room she saw that there was another man sitting on a cane two-seater chair waiting for them, a man she knew very well indeed.

'Tarquin!' said Laurence, with obvious delight. 'I didn't hear you let yourself in. You're just in time to see Jackie disciplined.'

Tarquin rose to his feet and his deep-set eyes met Kristina's. She stared at him, uncertain what her role was now. Slowly he moved towards her and then from his pocket he removed the familiar thin gold bracelet. 'Put this on, Kristina,' he said gently. 'I want you to sit with me and watch. If at any time there's anything I wish you to do then I'll tell you. You only have to obey me, not Laurence. Is that acceptable?'

Kristina hesitated. She still wasn't sure that she was ready for this step. So far she'd only been involved with threesomes, and Estelle didn't belong to the society. The prospect of being with two men who were members, and another woman wearing a bracelet, was daunting but she was so aroused by all that had gone before that she knew that if she refused and walked away she'd regret it for the rest of her life.

'Trust me,' urged Tarquin, seeing her doubt.

'If you're not happy, just go,' said Laurence sharply. 'I want to get on with this.'

Kristina looked to Jackie for guidance, and was astonished to see an expression of triumph on her friend's face. Clearly Jackie expected her to leave, and was delighted at the prospect of being left alone with both Laurence and Tarquin. Her last lingering doubts vanished immediately and without any more hesitation Kristina stretched out her right arm and Tarquin slipped on the bracelet. Then he smiled at her and she ached for his touch.

'I knew you wouldn't let me down,' he murmured. 'Sit here, next to me, and we'll watch together. First though I think I should undress you.'

With surprising speed he removed her leggings, overblouse and silk underwear so that when she finally sat down she was totally naked, and for the first time felt as vulnerable as Jackie. 'Carry on,' murmured Tarquin to Laurence. 'This should be very interesting.'

Laurence, who was still naked and aroused, moved behind Jackie and pressed himself up against her back before reaching round and covering her eyes with his right hand. Instinctively Jackie's right hand reached down to caress the top of his right leg but he ordered her to place both her hands between her thighs and then, with his right hand still covering her eyes, moved his left to caress her stomach, his fingers moving slowly across the softly rounded belly.

'Right, Jackie,' he murmured against her ear. 'Now use your hands to give yourself an orgasm. I'm going to uncover your eyes, but you're to keep them closed all the time. If you open them then you'll have to be blindfolded, and I think it's better that you discipline yourself for the punishment.'

'Why can't I open my eyes?' protested Jackie.

'Because I want you to lose yourself in the sensations, give yourself over to the pleasure and let nothing else intrude. I shall stay behind you for this first orgasm. I'm sure you can feel me.'

Kristina was sure that Jackie could as well. His erection was nudging between her buttocks and now and again the swollen head would disappear into them causing Jackie to breathe more rapidly with excitement. 'Begin,' said Laurence crisply. Kristina's lips were dry and she moistened them with her tongue as Jackie's fingers got to work. At first she rubbed the fingers of her right hand in circular motions on the area just above where her sex lips began, moving her pubis against her fingers in slow forward-thrusting movements that increased in speed as her desire grew.

'Kristina, put some massage oil on her fingers,' said Tarquin suddenly, and he handed her a small glass bottle. Startled, Kristina crossed the floor to where her friend was still rotating her hips and pressing her pubic area, with her eyes tightly closed, while Laurence continued to stroke her belly and occasionally her breasts.

'No, I've a better idea,' called Tarquin as Kristina was about to take hold of Jackie's free hand. 'Open her sex lips and pour the oil down between them.'

Jackie began to tremble with excitement at his words and suddenly Kristina was trembling too as she gently parted the other woman's labia and then allowed several drops of the sweetly scented oil to dribble down over the exposed tissue.

With a cry of pleasure Jackie's hands moved lower and now her fingers moved far more rapidly. She used her right hand to massage around her clitoris while at the same time she inserted two fingers of her left hand just inside the entrance to her vagina until she located her G spot.

Her breath was now coming in loud gasps as her body began to reach the peak of excitement. She was whimpering, the fingers of her right hand moving even more quickly but still very lightly as they circled round and round the hard nub of her clitoris until suddenly, as her belly tightened and the red flush of excitement spread over her breasts and neck, she flicked at the clitoral shaft and immediately she bent forwards with a cry of pleasure as her climax flooded through her.

'Very good,' murmured Laurence, kissing her exposed spine before pulling her back up against him. 'I'm sure you could manage another one very quickly.' Without another word he sank to the floor, drawing Jackie down with him so that he was kneeling and she was also kneeling with the backs of her thighs resting against the front of his. He kissed the side of her neck, nibbled at the corner of her mouth and then wrapping his arms around her began to stimulate her again between her thighs.

'Give me a moment longer,' pleaded Jackie, but Laurence ignored her. He looked over at Tarquin and Kristina. 'She can easily come twice in quick succession, watch.'

For several minutes his fingers were busy and then, as he'd predicted, Jackie started to whimper and moan again and her breasts swelled while her nipples stood out in rigid peaks.

Kristina could feel her friend's excitement, her own body was equally aroused and when Tarquin brushed a hand across her breasts she realised that they too were tight and swollen.

'When Jackie comes, I want you to come as well,' he murmured, pushing her back against the cane chair before kneeling on the floor between her thighs.

She was so ready for him that the moment he opened her up and she felt his tongue making long raking movements up her inner channel she began to quake with sexual tension and heard her own whimpers mingling with Jackie's.

Suddenly she heard Jackie give a sharp cry of ecstasy and immediately Tarquin circled her clitoris with his tongue and then flicked against it rapidly before drawing the whole nub into his mouth and sucking on it.

She'd never climaxed that quickly before but her orgasm was already very close and she felt the explosion of heat somewhere deep inside her. Then she was crying out and her legs gripped the sides of Tarquin's head as her muscles went rigid with the force of the climax.

'I think it's lucky you stayed,' he commented drily as he sat back beside her. Still breathless and trembling Kristina couldn't reply, but instead she looked across at Jackie who had now been drawn upright again and was facing them both but with her eyes resolutely closed.

'Tarquin's going to stimulate you now,' Laurence informed her, and Kristina felt a moment's disquiet. She hadn't anticipated sharing her lover with Jackie. 'While he does that, I'm going to take you from behind, so you need to bend forward from the waist.'

'I need a rest,' protested Jackie.

'You rest when I say so and not before. Tarquin?'

Tarquin rose to his feet and now he too removed his clothes and Kristina saw that he was as aroused as Laurence, his penis huge, the purple tip tighter than she could ever remember seeing it.

For the next half hour, Kristina watched as the two men worked their sexual magic on Jackie. Tarquin stimulated her breasts with hot soft cloths and ice packs. He massaged her belly with a silk mitten and then a soaped loofah and she cried out with delight, squirming frantically at every delicious torment while Laurence took her from behind, or sat in one of the cane chairs and pulled her on to his straining penis. Time and again she was brought to a climax, and to the watching Kristina each one seemed even more intense than its predecessor until finally the exhausted, sweat-soaked girl sank into a heap on the floor protesting that she was unable to come any more.

Tarquin touched Kristina lightly on the shoulder. 'Can you make her come one last time?' he asked, his head tilted to one side as he looked down on her.

Kristina shivered. 'I don't think so,' she whispered. 'Not now, after all the pleasuring she's already had.'

'I want you to make her come again,' he said. 'We'll hold her legs apart, then you caress her the way you'd like to be caressed. I'm sure you can think of something that will push her over the edge.'

'What if I don't?' asked Kristina.

His eyes were unfathomable. 'Then you don't,' he said tonelessly, but Kristina felt sure there was much more at stake than he was telling her. Slowly she rose to her feet and watched as Laurence drew Jackie up on to a low, glass-topped table so that her back was supported by him. Tarquin then grasped each of her ankles and spread her legs wide. 'Kristina is going to make you come, Jackie,' he said in his deep, slightly accented voice. 'I'm sure you'll enjoy it.'

'No, Kristina, don't,' begged Jackie, her voice husky and her body limp. 'There's no point. I'm finished for now. Please, leave me alone.'

'I can't,' said Kristina. 'Tarquin's told me to do this, and I'm wearing the bracelet.'

Jackie sighed and Kristina watched as Tarquin tied each of Jackie's ankles to the legs of the table with soft cord, leaving him free to assist Kristina in what he thought would be the best way, by exciting her.

As she started to lightly caress her friend's inner thighs, stroking the soft skin with the most delicate of touches, Tarquin sat on the floor behind her and suddenly she felt herself being lifted from the hips and then brought down on to his erection.

'We'll work in unison,' he said softly. 'I'll match my

rhythm to yours. That way you and Jackie may both come together.'

As he plunged deep inside Kristina she could have cried out with pleasure as the blissfully familiar sensation of fullness flooded through her. Now the ache that hadn't been assuaged since she had first become aroused that evening was at last stilled, and as he moved her gently up and down on him, his fingers manipulating her clitoris at the same time, she knew that she was going to have the most wonderful climax.

Jackie, unaware of precisely what was happening, could hear her friend's rapid breathing and she squirmed helplessly against the twin restraints of Laurence's grip and the ropes at her ankles.

Kristina continued to caress Jackie's tender tissue, taking care to spread oil over the sensitive area to make arousal easier. Just the same she could tell that Jackie was a long way from a climax, while her own was fast reaching the point of no return.

Suddenly Tarquin slowed his movements. 'Sorry, but you have to come together,' he reminded her, his voice muffled against her ear. 'Bring her on more quickly.'

'I can't!' said Kristina despairingly, but then she remembered something that always worked for her and she moved her fingers until they were very lightly touching the skin around the opening to Jackie's urethra.

The moment she began to press against it, Jackie's hips thrust upwards, and she started to gasp. 'No, please stop! It's too intense, and I'm exhausted, I can't come, I know I can't.'

'You can,' said Kristina firmly. 'I know how this feels; it makes you tight and hot, your stomach feels ready to burst and even your legs ache with the pressure. Isn't that true? Isn't that what's happening to you?' As she talked she continued to massage the area, but at the same time her other hand was working at the flesh above Jackie's pubic bone, pressing down firmly so that even more nerve endings from the same area were stimulated.

Now Jackie was lost. Her body took on a life of its own, twitching and leaping with mounting excitement that was beyond her control and even as she continued to protest, her body began its relentless ascent to a final climax.

'Good girl,' murmured Tarquin, and now his clever fingers continued their skilled movements' and he lifted Kristina up and down on his erection, faster and faster. Suddenly there was a flash of white light behind her eyes and she felt her whole body begin to spasm. With one final, almost cruel movement, her hand pressed hard above Jackie's pubic bone and all at once the room was shattered by the loud cries of both women as they tumbled into a simultaneous orgasm that was the most intense either of them had ever experienced.

When it was over Kristina leant back against Tarquin and he cradled her in his arms, but Laurence simply unfastened the exhausted Jackie and pulled her off the table. After a few minutes, when Tarquin had led Kristina back to the seat, Laurence brought Jackie, whose eyes were now open, over to them. 'Right, this is where we change, then. Jackie, I want you to go with Tarquin for the rest of the evening.'

'But I'm finished, I won't be any use to him,' protested Jackie.

'It's still what I want. Will you do it? Or do you wish to remove the bracelet?'

'No, I'll do it,' murmured Jackie, to Kristina's astonishment.

Then, to add to her shock, Tarquin turned to her. 'And I want you to let Laurence make love to you in any way he wishes. Do you agree? Or do you wish to remove the bracelet?'

Kristina felt as though he'd slapped her. During the past hour she'd been closer to him than ever before, had really thought that she meant something to him and yet here he was handing her over to Laurence as though she was nothing more than some kind of modern slave girl.

She looked at him with a mixture of pain and disbelief and then looked at Laurence. He was smiling, but the smile was cold, without any feeling at all and she knew then that despite his technical skill and undoubted sexual attraction, he was not a man she would trust to take control of her body while she was wearing the bracelet.

'Well, Kristina?' asked Tarquin calmly.

She stood up and looked down at him. 'I'm sorry, but that's something I can't do. I wish to remove the bracelet,' she said firmly, and under the startled gaze of Laurence and Jackie she removed it from her wrist and handed it back to Tarquin.

He took it from her and put it back in his pocket, his face betraying no emotion at all. 'You'd better get dressed then,' he said at last.

'Yes,' agreed Kristina, wishing that she didn't have such a lump in her throat or feel so desolate.

'Well, at least you've got Jackie,' said Laurence. 'I'm left with no one.'

'Thank you,' said Tarquin politely, 'but I don't think I want to take up your offer. I'm sure Jackie needs a rest, and I'd like to escort Kristina home.'

'But she's forfeited her relationship with you!' exclaimed Laurence. 'You don't ever have to see her again.'

'I've never *had* to do anything,' Tarquin pointed out in a mild voice. 'I only ever do what I choose to do, and it seems that Kristina is the same. I respect this, which is why I wish to escort her home. It's been a very interesting evening, Laurence. Thank you for the entertainment.'

As they left the room, Laurence turned to Jackie, his face tight with fury. 'I'm leaving too, as soon as I'm dressed,' he snapped. 'Why didn't you ever refuse anything I asked of you? Don't you see, you spoiled it all in the end?'

'Spoiled it?' asked Jackie incredulously. 'Surely that was the whole point of the society?'

Laurence shook his head. 'You became too involved on a personal level,' he said sadly. 'You changed. You adopted the persona of the bracelet all the time. You're no longer the kind of woman I want, but I have the feeling that Kristina is exactly what Tarquin wants, and I have to say that if he gets her I really envy him.'

Jackie was still screaming furiously at him when he finally left her house.

Chapter Eleven

A week later, Kristina arrived home late, tired, but for the first time in the six days that had passed since Tarquin had seen her home from Jackie's house, happy. Not that her happiness had anything to do with Tarquin. On the contrary, his continuing silence was a permanent ache that nothing could assuage; no, she was happy because she'd finally managed to make her peace with Lucretia.

It hadn't been easy, and she knew that Lucretia had every right to make it difficult, but after two lunches, countless telephone calls and then a highly successful meeting with the new editor, Martin Frost, Lucretia had agreed to stay on with the agency.

Kristina opened a bottle of her favourite wine and poured herself a glass. This was definitely a cause for celebration, and she wasn't going to let her unhappiness over Tarquin's silence spoil it. Her business was safe, and she knew now that this was more important than anything. She had to have her own life, play a leading role in the publishing world, because unless she did she would end up like Jackie.

At the exact moment that she thought of her friend the telephone rang, and she knew that it would be Jackie calling. She called around this time every evening, pouring out an endless stream of complaints and ending up in tears. Nothing Kristina said helped, but still Jackie kept calling.

'Hello,' she said briskly, hoping that this time the call might be shorter.

'You're late,' complained Jackie. 'I rang at my usual time and got no reply.'

'Late for what? I'm not accountable to anyone any more. I'm a big girl now. We both are, remember?' said Kristina lightly.

'I just meant later than usual,' muttered Jackie sulkily.

'I had a long day at work, but it was worth it. Lucretia isn't leaving the agency, so I live to fight another day! Have a glass of wine for me to celebrate.'

'Have you heard from Tarquin?' asked Jackie.

Kristina bit on her bottom lip, 'No, and as I told you yesterday, I don't expect to. I took off the bracelet and so, in effect, ended our relationship. He's no doubt replaced me by now.'

'Laurence thought Tarquin was in love with you,' said Jackie.

Kristina blinked hard. Briefly, when he'd taken her home and kissed her gently on the lips as they parted, she'd thought so too. But now, as the silence continued she realised that he had probably only been behaving in the way he thought correct. He was a good man, and a polite one, but he enjoyed the strange erotic excitement of the bracelet, and she could no longer provide that thrill for him. As for a regular girlfriend, she'd known all along that he had Estelle.

'Well, Laurence isn't exactly an expert on love is he?' she pointed out.

'I thought he loved me!' wailed Jackie, and Kristina's heart sank. 'I still can't understand why he never sends for me any more. I did everything he wanted. I wasn't like you. I never took the bracelet off, and yet he told me that's why I spoiled it. How can both of them be right? You spoiled it by taking the bracelet off and I spoiled it by leaving it on. That doesn't make sense!'

'It does,' said Kristina sadly. 'I've thought about it a lot, and I can see that although we're on our own it's for different reasons. You still don't seem to understand that men like Laurence and Tarquin only wanted self-sufficient women with lives of their own. That was the turn-on for them, to be able to take sexual control of women who were more usually dominant. Once you lost your job and concentrated solely on pleasing Laurence you stopped being the kind of woman he wanted.'

'Well, you didn't change. You stayed in control and took the bracelet off because you were asked to do something you didn't want to do. I often wanted to take the bracelet off. There were times when I longed to rebel but I didn't because I didn't want to have to lose

Laurence like you've lost Tarquin. There was no way to win, was there?'

'It wasn't a competition,' Kristina pointed out, settling down on the sofa and taking another sip of wine. 'No one was expected to win. The best thing to do was just enjoy the sexual pleasure and keep emotionally detached. We both made the mistake of getting involved with the men we met. I didn't want to go with Laurence because I felt that Tarquin and I had something special, so I refused. Now I realise that Tarquin couldn't have felt the same and I spoiled the night for him.

'You tried to become what Laurence wanted, but all the time, not just when wearing the bracelet, so there was no erotic thrill for him when you put it on, because nothing changed. We shouldn't have fallen for them, Jackie, but at least you've never removed the bracelet. You'll meet other men. You might even find someone more exciting than Laurence. I won't because I did remove it, and I have a feeling that kind of information goes on the computer. Sometimes I wonder how I'm going to manage without the release the society of the bracelet gave me, but I don't think I'll be sent for again by Tarquin or anyone else.'

'I don't want to see anyone else,' complained Jackie.

'Well, you've got to do something,' said Kristina sharply. 'You can't sit around at home wasting your brain and your sex appeal for the rest of your life.'

'When you see Laurence, does he ever mention me?' Jackie asked wistfully.

Kristina sighed. 'I haven't seen him since our last night together. I've spoken to him on the phone, but only about his book. He never mentions you or the society.'

'You wouldn't tell me if he did,' said Jackie, starting to cry again. 'I know he fancies you. You're probably already sleeping together. The fact that you weren't wearing the bracelet didn't stop you before.'

'I'm going to get myself something to eat,' said Kristina, exhausted by her friend's emotions. 'There's no point in ringing me every night. I can't change what's happened to either of us. We've got to get our own lives in order, and if you really want my advice I think you should get yourself a job and stop thinking about Laurence.'

She put the phone down and wrapped her arms round her knees. It was easy advice to give, but she knew that during the long hours of the night she often thought about Tarquin.

He'd become such a large part of her life that it still didn't seem possible he was no longer involved in it. When they'd parted he'd told her that she'd hear from him some time, but even then she'd suspected that she might not because he'd sounded so vague, as though it might be months rather than days in the future.

Time and again she'd replayed their sessions of love-making in her mind. She'd remembered the first time he'd sent for her, and the way he'd touched her then.

She would shiver with delight at the memory of their urgent love-making at the publishing party, and then tremble as she recalled the time he'd suspended her by her wrists in the room at the top of his house. Their times together had been filled with wonderful, dark eroticism that had allowed her to discover a new side to herself, and having discovered it she found it very difficult to subdue it simply because Tarquin was no longer there.

Today, one of the senior editors at Saunders Publishing House had asked her to a party the following Saturday, but although he was nice looking and witty she'd refused because she knew instinctively that he'd expect her to be the dominant partner when it came to sex. He possessed none of Tarquin's charisma, none of the quiet depths that concealed such sensuality, and she realised that she'd rather be alone than with that submissive kind of man again. She'd had too many years with men like that. Tarquin had changed her irrevocably, and now he was lost to her.

'You've still got the business,' she reminded herself fiercely as she put a meal for one in the microwave. 'You're successful, you enjoy your work and through the bracelet you learned a lot. Be grateful for that and move on.' It was sound advice, but like Jackie she knew it would be hard to follow.

Much later, after she'd listened to some Mozart and watched an old black and white film on TV, she was just about to go to bed when the phone rang again. 'If that's

Jackie with a midnight weep I'll scream,' she muttered, picking up the receiver.

'Yes?' she asked abruptly.

'Is that Kristina?' asked a deep, gloriously familiar voice.

'Yes,' she whispered, her knees suddenly turning to jelly.

'This is Tarquin. I'm sorry I haven't been in touch, I've been busy working on an outline for this book Roberta Mitchell's interested in.'

'How's it going?' asked Kristina brightly.

He laughed. 'Not too well. Writing's more difficult than I realised! But I didn't call to talk about work. I wondered if you'd care to come round for supper tomorrow night? About eight would suit me very well.'

'I think tomorrow's all right,' said Kristina, knowing perfectly well that she was free but not wanting to sound too eager. She waited a few seconds as though consulting her diary. 'Yes, that's fine.'

'Good. It will only be the two of us, but if you'd like to dress up please do. In my opinion dressing for dinner should be compulsory, it makes an evening so much more special.'

'Right, I'll remember that,' agreed Kristina. 'It will be lovely to see you again.'

'Yes,' he said softly. 'I've missed you. Goodnight, Kristina, sleep well.'

'Goodnight,' she murmured, but she didn't sleep

well. She hardly closed her eyes all night for excitement as she tried to work out what kind of a 'special' evening Tarquin had planned for them both.

The next day passed in something of a blur for Kristina. She spoke briefly to Laurence about his book, negotiated a good two-book deal for one of her new authors, lunched with an incredibly boring children's book editor and sent some emails, but all the time she was thinking about the evening that lay ahead of her.

She wondered whether or not it was going to turn into anything sexual, or if the invitation was simply intended as a polite way of terminating their relationship. She couldn't believe that was all it was, but on the other hand Tarquin was the kind of man who wouldn't want to leave any loose ends. If he thought that Kristina was harbouring hopes of continuing their affair but he wanted to end it then he'd certainly make sure she understood this. Her mood swung from one extreme to the other as the hours passed. Sometimes she was picturing them locked in a passionate embrace, at other times she envisaged them sitting in awkward silence at opposite ends of his dining table making stilted small talk.

When she finally got home she took a long bath then washed her hair in apricot shampoo, conditioned it and finally hung her head upside down, feeling rather like a fruit bat as she dried it with her diffuser. When she straightened up, though, she knew that it had been worth the discomfort. Her dark hair was full of bounce, the soft curls sexily disarranged providing the perfect frame for her face.

She took more care than usual over her make-up as well, emphasising her dark blue eyes and adding the faintest blush of colour to her naturally pale cheeks. At last, satisfied that she was looking as good as possible, she turned her attention to choosing a dress.

From what Tarquin had said she sensed that he wanted her to look her best, and she certainly wanted to look her best for him because when she looked her best she always felt sexier. He'd already seen a lot of her evening dresses, but there was one that she'd never worn anywhere yet and she took it out and looked at it carefully.

She'd bought it on a whim, attracted by the originality of the design, but later she'd lost her courage about wearing it. It wasn't that it was exceptionally revealing, but it was dramatically different and because it half-concealed most of her body it had a far sexier effect than her more daring numbers.

Finally she decided that if she was ever to wear it then tonight was the night. Tarquin would appreciate it more than any man she might meet in the future. Once she'd slipped it on, she studied herself carefully in the full-length mirror.

The dress was plum coloured, a fit-and-flare design with a double layered skirt that ended in jagged points. The narrow shoulder straps were attached to a cobweb-style lace top with a rounded neckline that covered the upper half of her body, was nipped in at the waist and then swept out again in fine lace points that rested just below her hips. The sleeves ended in inverted V-shapes at her wrists, leaving a tiny section of flesh exposed, but apart from that she was totally covered up, although the skin of her arms, upper chest and shoulders could be seen in tantalising glimpses through the cobweb-patterned lace.

Looking at herself, Kristina felt certain that she'd made the right choice. With a half-smile she clipped gold studs on to her ears and slid her legs into semi-opaque navy holdups before putting on her high-heeled strappy navy shoes. Finally she threw a white shawl over her arm and then went outside to her waiting taxi. Tonight was not a night for driving herself.

When Tarquin opened his front door to her and she saw the expression in his eyes, Kristina knew for certain that she'd been absolutely right. He gazed at her for so long that she wondered if she was ever going to be asked inside, and then he suddenly came to his senses and stepped back, but he still didn't stop devouring her with his eyes.

When he spoke his voice was as quiet and controlled as ever, but Kristina could see that his breathing was more rapid than normal. 'I see you took my advice and dressed for dinner,' he remarked.

'Yes. The taxi driver might have had a shock if I hadn't!'

He smiled. 'You might not have arrived here if you hadn't! It's a lovely dress, and you look wonderful in it.'

Kristina smiled back at him. 'Thank you. It's lucky I did take your advice. I didn't expect you to be in a dinner suit.'

He looked slightly uncomfortable. 'Would you prefer it if I changed?'

'Of course not! I think men look terrific in dinner suits.'

'Good, then even if the food doesn't come up to the mark we can sit and admire each other!'

'Yes.' Kristina handed him her shawl and as their fingers brushed she felt a tremor run up her arm. 'I'm sure the food will be excellent,' she continued, suddenly feeling terribly nervous.

'I hope so. I have a new chef and this is his first real test. Let's go into the study and have a drink. We won't be eating for another half hour yet.'

It was as though they were strangers, thought Kristina. This was the kind of ritual you went through when you were first being seduced by a man, but for some reason coming at this time after all the things they'd done to each other it was even more exciting and erotic than if they really were new to each other. Somehow, by creating this atmosphere, Tarquin had managed to re-erect the barriers that had originally existed between them and now Kristina was sexually on edge, her senses heightened by the clothes and the atmosphere, her body already aware of the pleasure he could give her but uncertain as to whether he was going to or not.

He didn't ask her what she wanted but handed her a glass of very dry martini with a twist of lemon and a lot of ice. 'I hope you like it,' he said as he raised his own glass. 'It's my speciality.'

Kristina was just about to take a sip when he put out a hand and stopped her. 'We must have a toast,' he said gently.

She stared at him. 'Did you have anything special in mind?'

He thought for a moment. 'To times past,' he said at last.

'To times past,' she echoed, her stomach plummeting with disappointment.

'And times to come,' he concluded.

She took a deep breath of relief. 'And times to come,' she agreed swiftly, and then she drank. As the ice-cold liquid ran down her throat she knew that Tarquin's eyes were on the tender skin of her exposed neck.

'When I called you, I wasn't sure you'd want to come this evening,' remarked Tarquin as they sat down.

'Why not?' asked Kristina in surprise.

'I'd asked you to do something you found distasteful. As a result you had to take off the bracelet and so may have felt you'd lost face in front of your friend. That was thoughtless of me and I have to admit I hadn't thought it through properly. I hadn't understood the implications for you personally, although naturally I had thought it through from my own viewpoint.'

Kristina watched him closely. 'You had?'

'I rarely act on impulse,' he said slowly.

Kristina smiled wryly. 'It's strange, but I imagined that you understood me. Perhaps the fact that you're a psychologist, and also very good at making a woman feel special, misled me.'

'I did understand you.'

Kristina frowned. 'What do you mean?'

He stared at her and his long lashes blinked rapidly as he tried to assemble his words correctly. Once again she was fascinated by his heavy dark eyelids and the almost imperious structure of his face. Her whole body was aching for him, but she knew what he had to say was important and that she must concentrate.

'I would have been very disappointed if you hadn't removed the bracelet,' he said at last.

Now it was Kristina's turn to blink in surprise. 'You mean, you never intended me to go with Laurence? You didn't want to watch him make love to me?'

'I certainly did not. Ever since I've joined the society I've known that each of the women I've met would remove the bracelet eventually. All the others have disappointed me by removing them far too soon, at a point where I'd hoped they'd still be excited by the adventure and lost in their own pleasure. With you, we'd reached the moment when it was time for you to remove the bracelet. It was no longer needed. Our game was at an end.'

Kristina's glass was empty and he refilled it for her. 'You still look bewildered,' he commented.

'I am. If our game was over, then that means you'd tired of me and wanted the relationship to end, so why am I here?'

'You misunderstand me. The game was the beginning for me, not the end.'

'The beginning of what?' she asked.

'A far better adventure. A journey of erotic discovery that might go on for a very long time, but only through the society of the bracelet could I meet the right kind of women, the kind who attracted me physically and mentally, as well as the kind who enjoyed our brand of sexuality.'

'But surely the women who wore the bracelet for you were just a hobby, a release of tension if you like? After all, you do have a girlfriend.'

Tarquin frowned. 'I do?'

'Estelle.'

He nodded. 'Yes, there is Estelle, but the journey that Estelle and I have shared began a long time ago and if it hadn't already been nearly over I don't think that I'd have joined the society, do you?'

Kristina shrugged. 'I've no idea. Men can separate sex from emotion more easily than women. I thought that Estelle met your emotional needs, and she certainly enjoyed watching me when I was wearing the bracelet. I think you make a good pair.'

He was watching her like a hawk now, his back very straight and his head erect as he listened to her words, carefully weighing each one. 'We made a good pair once,' he conceded. 'Our relationship has now come to an end.'

'By mutual agreement?' asked Kristina in surprise.

He sighed. 'Reasonably mutual. There's always one person who remains involved longer than the other, as your friend Jackie knows to her cost.'

'At least you've still got the society,' laughed Kristina. 'I'm sure you'll meet plenty of other women of the kind you mention. Women like me.'

'Why should I want them?'

'For the excitement, the variety and the lack of commitment that drew you to it in the first place I suppose.'

Tarquin stood up and moved over to sit beside her. 'You haven't been listening to me,' he said quietly, running his fingers over the back of her hand. 'As I said, the games you and I played were only the beginning. Now I want us to carry on, but this time on the journey I mentioned. The erotic journey that will, I'm sure, last a very long time.'

Kristina's heart was thumping against her ribs but she struggled to keep her voice calm. 'You're saying you want our affair to continue?'

His hand moved to the nape of her neck and then

lightly through her hair, caressing her scalp with incredible tenderness. 'Yes, that's what I'm saying. Of course, it may not be what you want, but it's certainly what I want.'

'But without the bracelet it will be different,' she murmured, beginning to wriggle beneath his caress.

'Different yes, because we'll come together as equals. That doesn't mean it won't be as good, in fact I imagine it will be even better. We still belong to the society, and I shall keep the bracelet. You can always wear it for our own pleasure if you choose to, but I don't think that will happen very often.'

His hands were massaging her shoulder blades now, easing away the tight knots of tension that had formed there and releasing trapped nerves so that her skin started to tingle as blood coursed freely through her veins.

'What about emotions?' she asked hesitantly.

'Do you have a problem with emotions?'

'Of course not, but surely you do? The last thing men from the society want is personal involvement, as Laurence demonstrated only too clearly.'

'I can't picture you as a clinging type of woman under any circumstances, and that's the only kind of woman I couldn't cope with. Of course I get emotionally involved with women I make love to regularly. That's why it's so wonderful to give them pleasure, and help them discover new things about themselves. I have to be involved, in my own way.'

'Yes, I suppose you do,' agreed Kristina, but she still wasn't certain what he meant by his own way. She doubted if he was as committed to her as she was to him, but for the moment that didn't matter. It was enough that he was telling her he wanted them to remain lovers and that he was talking about the long erotic journey that lay ahead. She could worry about the rest another time. Right now all she wanted was physical proof that what he was saying was true.

Suddenly he rose to his feet. 'Excuse me a moment, Kristina. I'll just have a word with the chef.'

While he was gone she sat sipping at her drink and thought about all he'd said. He wanted her, and he'd wanted her to take off the bracelet. That was what mattered, that her show of independence had been what he'd expected, which meant he wasn't the kind of man who'd feel threatened by her success. He wanted to make love to her as an equal, and she wanted it too. In fact, at this moment she wanted it far more than she wanted to eat dinner or make further conversation.

At that moment he returned, his face even more sombre than usual. 'There seems to have been a disaster in the kitchen. The meal won't be ready for some time yet. I wonder, would you like to come upstairs with me? There's something I'd like you to see.'

Kristina rose to her feet and looked into his eyes. The true question he was asking wasn't whether she wanted to go and see something upstairs, it was whether she wanted them to make love or not, but he was leaving the decision entirely to her. She didn't hesitate. 'That sounds like a good idea,' she said with a smile.

At last one of his rare smiles lit up his face. 'I hoped you'd say that. Here, let me show you the way,' and he held out his hand. She slipped her hand into it and let him lead her up the wide staircase and along the first floor landing until he opened a door and drew her into a vast bathroom.

'Much as I adore your dress,' he said huskily, 'I have to take it off now.'

The bathroom was already hot and humid, the sunken marble bath filled with perfumed water so hot that steam was rising from it. It was a beautiful room, with daffodil yellow walls and a deep green and yellow carpet. The high window had matching curtains tied back with yellow cords and on the various shelves and stands candles in the shape of oranges and lemons burned brightly, emitting the perfume of the fruits they represented.

Because it was so hot, Kristina was grateful when Tarquin carefully unzipped the back of her dress and then eased it off her shoulders and down the length of her body until she was able to step out of it.

When he saw that she was entirely naked beneath it, except for her stockings, Tarquin made a tiny sound of appreciation, before kneeling at her feet and rolling the holdups slowly down each of her legs in turn. Then, when she was totally naked, he stood up and slowly ran his right hand down her left side.

'You're even more gorgeous than I'd remembered,' he said huskily, and Kristina trembled with excitement. 'I'll make sure Lydia's got the temperature of the water right,' he added. 'Then, you can step in and after that I'll take care of everything.'

Kristina was glad. Despite the fact that she wasn't wearing the bracelet, at this moment she didn't want to be the one to take the lead. She needed to have Tarquin assume command, and her body was straining for his skilled attentions as memories of past pleasures flooded through her.

'It seems fine,' he murmured a moment later. 'Here, let me help you in.' Carefully he took her hand as she stepped down into the deep water. Then, as she lay back against one end of the bath, resting her head against a soft padded cushion that was fixed there, he began to remove his own clothes.

Through half-closed eyes she watched him closely, revelling in his well-muscled body and the soft, golden-brown skin. He was already becoming aroused, and she couldn't stop watching the slowly swelling penis as it rose up from its surrounding cluster of thick dark curls.

For the first time since she'd met him, Tarquin didn't bother to fold his clothes neatly. His dinner suit, shirt and tie were discarded carelessly and at speed, ending up in a crumpled heap in one corner of the bathroom.

With a brief smile at Kristina, Tarquin pulled a bathroom stool over to the side of the tub, sat down on it at the end where her feet were and then reached into the water and pulled up her left foot.

'I'm going to wash you all over,' he said softly. 'By the time I've finished you'll be cleaner than ever in your life before.'

With a sigh of contentment, Kristina gave herself over to him. She watched as he soaped his hands and then began working on her imprisoned foot, pulling on each toe in turn before sliding his fingers into the gaps, moving them rhythmically in and out in an imitation of love-making that made her whole body tremble.

As he moved slowly upwards, over her calves and thighs, she continued to shake beneath the water, but he left her genitals alone and instead took the stool to the opposite end of the bath where he proceeded to soap her neck, spine and shoulder-blades where they rose above the water as she sat upright.

As he washed her breasts he took extra time and care, working the soap into the swelling flesh for so long that she started to feel the first tiny tremors of an orgasm beginning. Sensing this he stopped, and instead got her to kneel up in the bath so that he could wash her belly, hips and buttocks, again touching her with teasing eroticism that aroused but never led to fulfilment.

Finally, when she was expecting him to start soaping her aching vulva, he turned away from her. 'Just a moment, there's something else I need,' he murmured and for a moment she was left alone, her body no longer relaxed because it was too sexually aroused.

When Tarquin returned a few moments later he was carrying an airbed which he laid on the carpet next to the bath. As Kristina watched curiously he picked up a bottle of body shampoo from the shelf over the basin and using water from the basin tap began to work the shampoo into masses of suds which he then spread over the surface of the airbed, teasing the bubbles into pointed peaks until the airbed vanished beneath the snow-white lather. Tarquin nodded to himself in appreciation of his own work and then held out his hand to Kristina. 'Time to step out now. This is the most exciting stage of the game.'

She climbed out carefully and then hesitated, unsure of what he expected of her. 'I want you to lie face down on the suds,' he explained. 'Then close your eyes and wait.' Kristina lowered herself into the foaming soap bubbles and felt them breaking under the weight of her body. They prickled and popped, teasing her already excited flesh, and the sensation was delicious, rather like sinking into a bowl of meringue, she thought with a smile.

Once she was face down, Tarquin proceeded to cover her back with an equal quantity of suds, heaping them high along her spine and across her back. For Kristina the sensation was one of utter bliss and she gave a sigh of delight at the gentle touch of the lather.

Once he was satisfied with the way she looked, Tarquin soaped the front of his own body and then he knelt at Kristina's left side before stretching himself over her, taking some of the weight on his elbows at the opposite side of the airbed.

Now, as Kristina whimpered with delight, he began to slide his body all over her, moving up and down the length of her spine with his body positioned like a cross beam over hers. Just as she was becoming used to that he altered the position of his elbows and slid diagonally up and down from her right buttock to her left shoulder. As her breathing grew increasingly ragged he pressed his abdomen to and fro over the softly curved cheeks of her bottom so that her belly and vulva were forced down on to the airbed and the sexual tension inside her grew and grew as a climax drew nearer.

He moved slowly at first, and then more quickly, changing rhythm regularly so that he never quite allowed her body enough time to reach an orgasm. Eventually Kristina became so desperate that she started to cry out, begging him to press harder, keep the rhythm going for longer, but in reply he merely turned her on to her back and then after staring into her beseeching dark blue eyes he procceded to cover every inch of her front in the same way.

She felt him easing the lather into the crevices at the join of her thighs, into her belly button and all over her straining abdomen before covering her upper thighs and then he added a few more suds to his own body before starting to tease her in earnest.

This time he lay straight along the length of her, although still taking some of his weight on his elbows, and as he slid up and down her body she could feel the tip of his penis brushing against the entrance to her vagina. Every time he did this she thrust her hips upwards, but he was always too quick for her and instead the swollen glans would brush against the soap-covered clitoris so that Kristina was squirming and wriggling like a creature in torment as her nerve endings grew tighter and tighter under his clever arousal.

'Please, I want you inside me, Tarquin,' she begged him at last, unable to keep silent any longer.

His black eyes stared down at her and he nodded, but when he moved his body on the next upstroke he merely let the tip of his penis enter her for a few brief seconds. She cried out with disappointment, but he smiled. 'Patience, it won't be long now.'

She didn't want to be patient, although her body was revelling in this long-drawn-out foreplay and she realised that now with every upward movement he was plunging a little deeper inside her, and then he started to rotate his hips as well so that the nerves just inside the entrance to her vagina were aroused and sharp tingles began to spread outwards through her entire vulva.

Finally, when her nipples were harder than she could ever remember them and her stomach felt as though it was swollen to twice its normal size as the sexual tension made the muscles of her belly ripple beneath the skin's surface, Tarquin took pity on her and on his upward movement he allowed himself to penetrate her totally.

Kristina gripped the length of him with her internal

muscles, her body frantic to feel every centimetre of his erection brushing against her vaginal walls. Tarquin struggled for control as she tried to hurry his climax along, and he lowered the whole weight of his body on to her and then slid one soapy hand between them so that he could push back the tiny hood of skin that was covering her retracted clitoris. He then manipulated the slippery nub by rolling the pad of one finger around the smooth sides.

Kristina's body jerked underneath him, and she started to pant with the almost unbearably intense sensations that were engulfing her. Her whole body was on fire, stimulated relentlessly by his body's movements for the past half hour, and now it was all coming together with such force that for a moment she was frightened by the power of the contractions that were beginning deep within her body.

Now Tarquin allowed a second finger to slide lower, below the clitoris itself so that while he continued to massage that he also slid the other finger up and down the damp channel beneath until he felt the slender body beneath him heave helplessly as her long-delayed orgasm was finally released.

Kristina heard herself scream aloud at the incredible hot flooding pleasure, centred deep behind her clitoris but spreading out to every particle of her body, and now her internal contractions were uncontrolled and Tarquin felt himself gripped by her convulsions so that he too climaxed with a shout of triumph and delight.

For a long time afterwards they lay silently together, side by side with their arms wrapped round each other's bodies, both of them unwilling to break the eroticism of the moment or admit that for now at least the sex game was over. Finally Tarquin stirred. 'We must get dressed,' he said with a laugh. 'What will the chef think?'

'Do you know, I don't think I care,' said Kristina lazily.

Tarquin smiled at her and wiped some remaining suds away from her breasts. 'Somehow I thought you might say that.'

As he brushed at the suds, Kristina realised that her nipple was hardening again and she quickly sat up. 'That's enough! As you say, we must think of the chef.'

'Then I'd better let you dry yourself off,' said Tarquin. 'If I do it, I won't be held responsible for the result.'

They ate sitting side by side at the dining table, with Tarquin frequently stopping to feed Kristina titbits from his own plate. Much later when they'd rested and talked, they undressed in the drawing room and lay naked on the soft rug, pouring wine into each other's mouths and then laughingly licking up the spills. Finally, in the early hours of the morning they went upstairs to Tarquin's bedroom and there, for the first time since she'd met him, Kristina spent the night in his arms.

When she woke in the morning she looked down at him as he lay sleeping and knew that whatever it took she was never going to let him go, and neither was she going to let her business slip again. She really was going to 'have it all', she thought to herself.

Six months later, Kristina arrived back at Tarquin's house at midnight, carrying an award from the Publisher's Association dinner she'd just attended. She still had her own house, but spent most of her time at Tarquin's. They were generally accepted as a couple on the social scene, and she'd taken particular delight in going with him to a publishing party that Roberta had organised to announce the fact that her publishing house had finally managed to sign him up. Roberta's face had been a picture, something Kristina would long remember. Much to her relief Jackie had at last regained control of her life. Realising what had gone wrong in her relationship with Laurence she'd found herself another job and had started going out with men like William again. But then when that had palled, as Kristina had guessed it would, Jackie had announced that she had landed herself a job in America with one of their top women's magazines.

'It probably won't be any different there,' she admitted to Kristina, 'but it will all be new, and American men are meant to like English women.'

'I'm sure they'll like you, as long as you don't try to make yourself something you're not!' laughed Kristina.

Jackie shook her head. 'I won't make that error again. Believe me, I've learned my lesson. I still envy you though; you really have got it all now.'

As Kristina turned her key in the lock she remembered those words and wondered with a sense of unease if it was true. She'd thought so, and Jackie had endorsed her feeling, but lately she'd sensed that things weren't the same between her and Tarquin.

He met her in the hall. 'Well?' he asked in his deep, soft voice that still had the power to make Kristina's knees go weak.

'I won!' she shouted, and held up the silver pen that was her award.

'I knew you would!' he laughed, and pulling her to him kissed her with such intense passion that for a moment she wondered if they might just sink down and make love there and then in the hall, but even as the thought passed through her mind he drew away. 'Let's have a drink to celebrate.'

As they drank the champagne Kristina finally found the courage to voice her fears. 'Are you happy, Tarquin?' she asked.

He raised his eyebrows. 'Of course I am. I told you, you deserved to win.'

Kristina shook her head. 'I didn't mean about this, I meant in general. Are you still happy with me?'

For the first time in many months he tilted his head to one side and looked at her thoughtfully. 'What do you mean exactly?'

'I mean what I say,' she said sharply, nerves making her sound more aggressive than she felt.

'Of course I'm happy with you. We have a wonderful

sex life and two interesting careers. You're witty, self-sufficient and incredibly sexy. What more could a man want?'

'I don't know. I could say the same about you, and ask the same question about a woman.'

He nodded. 'I see. So you feel it too?'

Terror dried her mouth but she managed to keep her voice softer this time. 'Yes, I probably do. Something's changed, but I don't know what it is.'

Tarquin sighed. 'I think I do. It's probably just human nature, but because we're the kind of people we are, I suspect we're both a tiny bit bored. Not with each other, not with our work, but with the predictability of it all.'

'What can we do?' asked Kristina. 'I want it to be like it was.'

'So do I.' Tarquin assured her. 'I'd be lost without you, but I sometimes think we need more than we've got.'

'You mean, something like the society of the bracelet?' asked Kristina softly.

His eyes glittered and she knew that she'd said the right thing. 'Yes, probably something very like that.'

'Well, we still belong, don't we?' asked Kristina.

'You know we do.'

'Then why not use our membership again, only this time we'll both take part? After all, lots of women get very turned on by the idea of a threesome with a man and a woman.'

'Are you sure you wouldn't mind?' asked Tarquin slowly. 'Have you really thought this through?'

'Yes,' said Kristina. 'I've thought about it a lot and the idea turns me on too, but it was something that happened today which convinced me.'

'What was that?' asked Tarquin with interest.

'I've got this new author. She's set up her own business from scratch, it's a mixture of aromatherapy, beauty products and some kind of oriental massage technique. The combination of the three is meant to have incredible results on how you look and feel. Her business is doing so well we got her signed up to do a book and DVD about it. Well, when we were talking she happened to mention that her long-term partner had left her because he couldn't cope with her success, and she said how difficult it was to find men who could.'

'And?'

'And I thought, since she's very attractive and sexy as well as clever, that she would enjoy wearing the bracelet.'

'Perhaps she would,' agreed Tarquin.

'And if she did, if I told her about it and got Jackie to put her name forward before she left for the States, then you could send for her.'

'But she's your client!' protested Tarquin.

'I know, that somehow makes it all the more exciting. I'd like to see you touching her, Tarquin. I'd love to see her being made to wait for an orgasm, to hear her begging for release with every fibre aching with desire.

You'd like her, I know you would and together we could have a brilliant time as well as giving her what she's looking for.'

'I'll think about it,' promised Tarquin. 'Right now, I want to make love to you.'

It was clear to Kristina that her words had rekindled the intense passion of their early days together because he made love to her for over two hours, giving her one mind-shattering climax after another before finally taking his own pleasure. When it was over he propped himself up on one elbow. 'What's the name of this new client of yours?' he asked softly.

'Marianne.'

Reaching into the bedside drawer, Tarquin drew out the familiar thin gold bracelet and held it up to the light. 'Let's hope the bracelet fits Marianne, then,' he said slowly.

Kristina shivered with keen anticipation and rubbed her naked breasts against his chest. 'Somehow I know it will,' she said with assurance, and when she fell asleep that night she was once again content.

At last, thanks to the bracelet, Kristina truly did have it all.

Also available from Black Lace:

The Accidental Call Girl
Portia Da Costa

It's the ultimate fantasy:

When Lizzie meets an attractive older man in the bar of a luxury hotel, she is mistaken for a high class call girl on the look-out for a wealthy client.

With a man she can't resist . . .

Lizzie finds herself following him to his hotel room for an unforgettable night where she learns the pleasures of submitting to the hands of a master. But what will happen when John discovers that Lizzie is far more than she seems . . . ?

A sexy, thrilling erotic romance for every woman who has ever had a *Pretty Woman* fantasy. Part 1 of the Accidental Trilogy.

Also available from Black Lace:

On Demand
Justine Elyot

I have always been drawn to hotels.
I love their anonymity. The hotel does not care
what you do, or with whom.

The Hotel Luxe Noir is a haven for hedonistic liaisons.
From brief encounters in the bar to ménages in the
elevator, young Sophie Martin has seen it all since she
started on reception. But as she witnesses the dark erotic
secrets of the staff and guests can she also master her own
desires...?

**Welcome to the Hotel Luxe Noir – discretion
assured, satisfaction guaranteed.**

Praise for On Demand

'Indulgent and titillating, On Demand is like a tonic
for your imagination. The writing is witty, the personal
and sexual quirks of the characters entertaining'
Lara Kairos

'Did I mention that every chapter is highly charged with
eroticism, BDSM, D/S, and almost every fantasy you
can imagine? If you don't get turned on by at least one
of these fantasies, there is no hope for you'
Manic Readers

Also available from Black Lace:

Pleasure's Edge
Eve Berlin

Alec Walker should come with a warning. A man who lives on the edge, he is famous for his love of dangerous sports, kinky sex and independent women.

Dylan Ivory has come to interview him for her latest book but instead he issues her with a challenge – and the perfect way to do her research.

Part 1 of *The Edge Trilogy*, a dark sensual romantic series, perfect for fans of E.L. James and Sylvia Day, from the acclaimed author of *The Dark Garden*

Desire's Edge
Eve Berlin

Give in to desire . . .

Kara Crawford doesn't expect to find anyone
who can fulfil her dark fantasies until she experiences
one of the most incredible nights of her life with a
man she's always admired from afar.

Dante De Matteo may be a master of control now,
but his troubled past means he won't let anyone
ever get too close . . .

**A dark sensual romantic novel perfect for fans of
E.L. James, from the acclaimed author of *Exotica***

Also available from Black Lace:

Temptation's Edge
Eve Berlin

When Mischa Kennon meets sexy Alpha-male Connor Galloway at the wedding of her best friend, she finds the green-eyed Irishman hard to resist.

But while she's happy to surrender to a brief affair with him, Mischa realises Connor could easily master her heart as well as her body.

If she gives in to desire, will it be too much to handle, or will it open her to a kind of love she never thought possible?

Part 3 of *The Edge Trilogy*, a dark sensual romantic series, perfect for fans of E.L. James and Sylvia Day, from the acclaimed author of *The Dark Garden*